"What do you want from me, John?"

He drew a careful breath. "Your friendship, Kamisha, and your caring and your needs."

Kamisha nodded her head doubtfully. "Why me?"

"Because I see something in you that is good and fine. Not your face or your body, although they're lovely. I mean inside."

She drew a quavering breath. This was difficult. Wonderful and exciting, but difficult too. "I'm a mess inside," she confessed. "My best friend keeps telling me that I can't love anyone because my parents never loved me. I'm terrified she's right."

He shook his head. "You're full of love, Kamisha."

"How do you know?"

"Trust me. I know. Now tell me, Kamisha. What do *you* want?"

"You, John. I just want you." She held her breath, afraid she'd been too bold, too direct. But then he leaned toward her, gathered her in his arms and kissed her. Gently at first, almost with reverence, and then with growing passion. And Kamisha knew everything was going to be all right.

ABOUT THE AUTHOR

The writing team of Lynn Erickson is back
with another romantic, spine-tingling story
set in Aspen, Colorado, New York City and
Costa Rica. "We especially loved writing
about Aspen," report Molly Swanton and
Carla Peltonen. "We both live there, and it
was lots of fun describing all our favorite
restaurants." Molly and Carla have been
writing together for fourteen years and have
as many Superromances novels to their credit.

Books by Lynn Erickson

HARLEQUIN SUPERROMANCE

Silver Lady

LYNN ERICKSON

Harlequin Books

TORONTO • NEW YORK • LONDON
AMSTERDAM • PARIS • SYDNEY • HAMBURG
STOCKHOLM • ATHENS • TOKYO • MILAN

Published January 1992

ISBN 0-373-70482-8

SILVER LADY

CHAPTER ONE

KAMISHA HAMMILL LOOKED the young man square in the eye. "So you're going to Hawaii, just like that." She snapped her fingers. "And I guess the commitment you made to the Ute City Club doesn't mean a thing to you. What about the party tonight? In a few hours this place is going to be packed with three hundred guests. You're my main bartender, Jeff. You can't just walk out on me like this."

"Look, Miss Hammill," he said, "I'm sorry. But this man I met offered me a ride in his Lear jet, and I can't just pass it up. He's going all the way to Maui."

Kamisha tried to keep the anger out of her voice. "Aspen is full of people with private jets. Get a ride next week. You *owe* the club, Jeff. Mr. Simons helped you with employee housing, your ski pass last winter, that bonus in April."

"But, Miss Hammill, I got this job offer in Maui."

In the end it was no use. Like so many of the youth who flocked to Aspen seeking the good life, Jeff could change jobs as often as his polo shirt—jobs, housing and girlfriends. Kamisha sighed, frustrated, and decided not to argue any longer. She'd had him in her employ at the Ute City Club for nine months, and Jeff had probably broken the club's length-of-employment record, anyway.

She stood gazing out onto the sun-splashed deck that overlooked the tennis courts and the crystal-clear Roaring Fork River below and figured that if worse came to worse, she'd tend bar herself. Maybe even Rick Simons, the club manager and her boss, could jump in if she got swamped. She guessed she'd better find him and tell him the score. He wasn't going to like it. Tonight was the midsummer charity fund-raiser, with over three hundred guests expected—tennis greats, movie stars, diplomats, politicians, business moguls and power brokers from all over the world. And now they'd be lucky to even get a glass of wine for their five-hundred-dollar donations! No, Rick wasn't going to be happy.

Kamisha informed some of the other employees about Jeff leaving and asked them the usual question: "If you know someone who could fill in tonight..." Then she headed into the sprawling depths of Aspen's largest tennis and sports fitness complex to find Rick.

She loved the club—the state-of-the-art exercise studios, the well-equipped weight rooms, the indoor-outdoor pools, Jacuzzis, pro shop, conference rooms, tennis courts, the brand-new sports medicine facility run by a National Football League orthopedic surgeon, the sedate rows of executive condos nestled in the aspen groves, the winding bicycle paths and summer gardens, the rugged mountains that jutted skyward directly behind the stone and wood and glass structures. She even liked its name—not something predictable such as "The Aspen Club," but "Ute City," Aspen's original name and the name of the Indian tribe who'd lived in the valley.

She loved Aspen, Colorado, too, her adopted home for the past eleven years, her refuge from a short marriage, her refuge from the media hype of her years as a ski racer on the Olympic team. They'd hung the Silver Medal for the downhill around her neck in 1980, and she figured it had been the highlight of her life. So much had been out of synch since then—her marriage to Josh Nichols, the Gold Medal winner in 1980, the divorce that had made headlines in every yellow press journal there was, her fight in divorce court to keep the little Aspen Victorian house they'd fixed up, her parents' comment: "Josh is such a nice boy."

For five years Kamisha had worked various jobs in Aspen—ski instructor, summer event coordinator for the prestigious Aspen Institute, the mountain retreat think tank for greats such as Henry Kissinger. But none of her jobs had been satisfying. She'd sensed her employers were using her as a figurehead and not giving her any real responsibility. Even as a ski instructor. She'd have gladly taken ordinary classes down the steep slopes of Aspen Mountain, but the ski school director of the Aspen Skiing Company had seen to it that she was assigned only private lessons for the celebrities that flocked to Aspen in the winter. They came for the fresh white powder snow, the azure-blue Colorado sky and the world-renowned nightlife.

But Rick Simons had given her a break. "Absolutely," he'd said when the club was still under construction, "you'll be running your own show as PR director. You'll put together all the events, all the exhibition tennis matches, hire your own staff, coordinate the food list with our chef, make up the guest lists. It'll be hard work, Miss...Kamisha, but there are a lot of perks in it, too."

"I'm not going to be a figurehead, Mr. Simons," she'd said. "I've been that route. I can handle any responsibility you give me."

"You have my word on it. And," he'd added, his white teeth sparkling in a narrow, darkly handsome face, "Mr. Leopardo, the owner, you understand, has given your employment his blessing. It's a go."

She'd worked hard. She'd worked her buns off to make sure the club ran smoothly. At thirty years old Kamisha felt she'd finally found her niche in life. Someday she'd find the right man, too, a man who'd understand her past, her insecurities, a man who'd father her children. And they'd raise them in Aspen, sharing the wonderfully satisfying life you could live here.

"Seen Mr. Simons?" she asked the tall blond woman at the front desk. Three hours...three hours till the guests arrived for the final evening of the charity event.

But the girl shook her head and resumed folding towels; they were shorthanded in the locker rooms, too.

"Say," Kamisha said, pausing, "have you got any friends who know how to tend bar? It's only for tonight. It pays sixty-five a shift and the tips are always great."

Nina Cassidy tilted her head. "Sixty-five *plus* tips?"

"Yep."

"I'm off at five. Would you give me a shot at it?"

"Ever slung gin before?"

"Once. I helped my boyfriend out at his bar."

"You're on. And, Nina, no shorts, no jeans. This is glitz city tonight. Look the part."

"I've got this shiny blue thing with straps..."

"Perfect. Be here at six-thirty to set up."

"You got it, Miss Hammill."

Well, saved in the nick of time, Kamisha thought. But she'd best let Rick know about Jeff just the same.

She headed down the carpeted corridor that led to the executive offices. She knew she looked disheveled, her long silver-blond hair falling out of its French braid, her white cotton slacks smudged from rummaging in the storeroom looking for a case of club matches. She stopped for a moment and tucked in the hot coral T-shirt she wore and tried to smooth her hair. It was rumored that the absentee owner of the club, the reclusive John Leopardo from New York City, was in town, and Rick might just be with him. It was odd, but she'd been working for Mr. Leopardo—albeit under Rick—for over four years now and had yet to lay eyes on the man. Of course, in Aspen, absentee ownership was hardly a rarity, but she'd have thought by now she would have met him at least once.

Indeed, Rick appeared to be in his office. At least the blinds were partially closed. And that meant he was busy and might not want to be disturbed.

Kamisha hesitated outside his door, her hand lingering uncertainly above the knob. He could very well be with Mr. Leopardo, and maybe she shouldn't interfere. On the other hand, she needed to tell Rick that she had to leave—to run some errands before the party—and, of course, she had to shower and change. She was curious, too, Kamisha admitted to herself. The rumor mill in Aspen had it that John Leopardo was connected to *the* Leopardos of New York. Big-time Mafia. She'd never been able to help herself, but when she pictured the club's owner she imagined a Robert De Niro type, or Al Pacino from *The Godfather*. Dark hair. Olive skin. Expressionless black eyes. An aura of danger...

A silly decision, childish—knock or leave. She felt awkward standing there. Rick wouldn't mind if she interrupted for a moment and, besides, for all she knew he was alone.

Then she heard voices, two men, speaking quietly, intimately, and it just seemed wrong somehow to disturb them. Besides, if John Leopardo really were in there, then she'd meet him tonight. Sure.

Kamisha backed away from the door silently, her tennis shoes soundless on the plush green carpeting. She began to move past the window, heading toward the back door that led to the parking lot and her car, and as she did she glanced momentarily through the thin cracks in the blinds. She could make out the shadows of the two men inside the private office, standing, their dark heads bowed together over the desk. And then, for a fleeting moment, she was certain one of the men glanced up and saw her, or at least registered her silhouette poised in the hallway. A faint, unaccountable chill brushed her neck before she pushed open the back door and strode into the bright mountain sun.

CITY MARKET WAS jam-packed with summer tourists buying hamburger meat and buns and chips for their campsites. And all Kamisha needed was a few lemons and limes that the Denver food supplier had left out of the shipment. She stood in the long checkout line and glanced at her watch. She had to be showered and dressed and back at the club in forty-five minutes.

She knew people noticed her as she waited in the line. "That's... you know," she heard a man whisper behind her. "Ah... the downhill skier... ah... she married that blond guy... Hammill!"

"Shh!" came a harsh reprimand, probably the man's wife.

In the summer the tourists in the mountain hideaway were of a different breed than the winter ones. They were young families and older retirees on fixed incomes, people who often came in campers or brought tents and stayed in the many Forest Service campgrounds that dotted the mountains. Of course, there were people there for the Aspen Music Festival or the internationally famous Design Conference. But, for the most part, the winter tourists were wealthier—people who could afford the high-season prices. These wealthy visitors studiously ignored the famous. But in the summer...

All her life Kamisha had been told that not only was she a terrific athlete, but beautiful, as well. She did have a well-toned, lean body. She carried herself gracefully, and she had long pale blond hair that contrasted strikingly with her very blue eyes—her father's eyes. In the summer her skin tanned a nice, rich golden color and her features were good, well-delineated, close to the bone, her mouth a bit wide, her nose straight and smallish. She was five foot six inches tall but looked taller. It was her long arms and legs, her leanness, that lent the impression of height.

Yet, inside, she didn't feel particularly pretty. Her best friend, Brigitte Stratford, was always telling her that she had been an abused child. But no one, least of all her socialite mother or her busy oil executive father, had physically "abused" her. Rather, she realized, they had ignored her. Still did, in fact. Before boarding school in Taos, New Mexico, where she'd met Brigitte, Kamisha had been raised in Los Angeles, the "Hammills' darling little daughter." They'd dressed her adorably and shown her off to their friends; they'd exclaimed over how pretty and sweet she was; they'd flown off together to Houston and London and Mexico City and told her to be a good girl for Lucinda, the housekeeper. Heck, Kamisha often thought, Lucinda had been a better parent than her mother and father combined.

They hadn't been at the Olympics, either, when Kamisha had won the Silver Medal. They'd been in Japan at an oil conference. They'd sent flowers, though, dozens and dozens of roses. Josh Nichols had asked her to marry him on the plane home, and she'd thought about how lonely she was, and she'd said yes.

Then, for ten months, it had been Josh's turn to manipulate and use her....

"That'll be $3.58," the checkout girl said.

"Oh," Kamisha replied, digging into her purse.

"How are you today?" the girl asked.

"Oh, fine. Busy. The MS fund-raiser. You know."

"Yeah. Summer'll be over soon, though, and the town will be ours for the off-season."

That was Aspen. Small, intimate, the checkout girls at the store treated as equals to the wealthier residents. It wasn't odd to have your dinner served by a PhD from Harvard who was taking a season off from the "real world."

Kamisha drove home in her bright red Saab convertible along the back streets of Aspen. She *did* love the town. Winter or summer it was glamorous. Oh, maybe the silver miners of the 1880s were long gone, but the townfolk still reaped plenty from the "white gold" that covered the ski slopes in the winter and the elegant classical music that echoed in the valley in the summer. Kamisha could not recall a week in Aspen going by when there wasn't an art show or jewelry fair or charity event. There were horse shows, white river fishing, tennis matches, kayaking races. There was hunting and hiking and Jeeping. Bicycling. A car could barely make it up the steep inclines of Independence Pass east of town in the summer due to the joggers, walkers and bicyclers. It was crazy. Health-crazy. Sometimes she thought it was the dry, warm, scintillating air that brought people; other times she knew it had to be the charm of the quaint city streets. But when it came right down to it, she couldn't put her finger on what precisely made Aspen so unique, what lured people from everywhere, a special kind of independent person who had pride in his mind and body—a whole town full of Renaissance men and women.

She pulled up to the curb and smiled. Eleven years ago she and Josh had bought the Victorian on Bleeker Street at a bargain-basement price. Of course, it had been a miner's shack, really, and practically falling down. You could see the blue sky through the cracks in the walls. But they'd worked their knuckles raw, invested a few dollars and created the quaint, gingerbread-style Victorian, painting it gray with plum and aqua trim. There were only two bedrooms and one bath. A tiny kitchen. But the living room was adorable, centered around a turn-of-the-century potbelly stove. Lots of plants. Lots of wood furniture. And now, Kamisha knew, she could sell it for five times what she'd paid for it. Josh had gotten the bank account, Kamisha the house.

She opened the wrought-iron gate and hurried up the two front steps, remembering to turn the sprinkler on the garden out front. The dry mountain air felt great, but not to her grass and flowers.

Fifteen minutes later Kamisha was ready. She wore little makeup in the summer and had simply put two rhinestone clasps in her hair to hold it back. Matching the clasps was a wide glittering belt that she wore over an emerald-green silk jumpsuit that was both understated and elegant, draped in loose folds over her bosom, leaving one shoulder bare. She needed no other jewelry. The hair clasps and belt said it all. And, essentially, Kamisha was an athlete, not a glamour girl. Rick always complimented her taste, anyway. And she guessed that was what counted.

She found her clutch purse, slipped into comfortable silver open-toed sandals and headed back out. Fifteen minutes to spare. A miracle.

Naturally the phone rang just then.

"Kamisha," came the familiar dispirited voice of her best friend, her lifelong friend.

Kamisha sighed. "Hi, Brigitte, what's up?"

"I'm not coming tonight."

Kamisha knew her friend so well, knew exactly what was behind the insecurity and anxiety in those words. Brigitte was having one of her low spots. "Come on, Brigitte, everyone's expecting you. You promised."

"I can't. I'm miserable. I'd drag everyone down with me."

"You won't. It'll do you good to get out. Get your hair and nails done and get all dolled up."

"I don't know. I just..."

"Brigitte. You know you want to go. Wear your pink dress, the one with the fringe. You'll look gorgeous." They'd been through this before—Brigitte needing support, Kamisha providing it. Even before Brigitte's divorce and the move from Los Angeles to Aspen, she'd called Kamisha at least once a week for propping up.

"Do you think I can still get a hair appointment?" Brigitte was asking.

"Sure, call around." Kamisha glanced at her watch, tried to squelch impatience. Brigitte had been having a bad time lately, mostly because of her boyfriend Bullet Adams.

"I guess I'll try." Brigitte sighed. "Thanks, Kamisha."

"You'll be fine. Everyone will love you."

"You think the pink dress?" Brigitte's voice sounded brighter.

"It's perfect. I'll see you there, okay?" She glanced at her watch nervously. Ten minutes to spare now.

"Well, all right."

"Bye, I've gotta run."

The drive through the West End streets down to the river where the club was situated always calmed Kamisha and reminded her just how very much the town meant to her. Stately cottonwood trees planted by miners a century before lined the streets in front of the homes. She basked in the feel of the late-day sun that filtered through their slender leaves onto her shoulders. There were the cars parked in driveways, Jeeps covered in mud proudly sitting next to Grand Wagoneers and BMWs. A few kids on bikes, dogs chasing sticks. Cats sat in bay windows of the Victorian homes, framed by lace curtains and ferns. This was the quiet time of early evening when the downtown malls began to empty out for a few hours, the tables in the many outdoor cafés awaiting the night crowds that were certain to fill the streets and nightclubs and brick-paved malls. People watching mimes and jugglers, listening to the music students who had set up music stands right on the sidewalks, shopping, eating popcorn or ice-cream cones, sitting on benches in front of the splashing fountains.

It struck her then, out of the blue, as she drove. She wondered, for no reason whatsoever, if John Leopardo, the club's owner, had ever left the grounds of his club to see Aspen as it really was. She knew he stayed in the executive condo high above the river. She knew he had been seen by the grounds' keepers walking the river path early in the morning on his rare visits. But did this man really know the first thing about Aspen? How odd, she thought, a man who owned one of the most beautifully situated clubs on earth and who chose to live in the rush and clamor and pollution of New York City.

Kamisha arrived at the club to find Rick already in high gear. As always, he was rushing around the flagstone terrace, straightening chairs beneath the colorful umbrellas, pulling linen tablecloths an inch this way and that, replacing silverware on napkins, snapping his fingers at the waiters and busboys.

"Bobby," he called, "get four fresh wineglasses for this table. Now!"

She wished he would let her do her job—just once—without stepping in. But in truth, Kamisha knew, Rick really had kept his promise to let her take responsibility. It was just that he was so hyper. Handsome, hyper Rick Simons, a man who made it his business to know all the "right" people. Evidently he'd worked for Mr. Leopardo before in one of the man's other clubs—Miami, Kamisha recalled. And getting control of operations at the Ute City Club in Aspen had been a reward. Darn nice reward, too, she thought, watching him. And it occurred to her: if John Leopardo really was Mafia-connected, could Rick be, too?

Kamisha shook her head to clear her thoughts. There was so much left to do, and the guests would begin to dribble in before she knew it.

"Ah, there you are," Rick said. "Where's that kid, Jeff? He should be setting up the bar, checking the ice machine."

"He quit." Kamisha put her hands on her hips. "But don't worry. I've got it covered."

"Damn kids. Right in the middle of everything they walk out."

"Look," she said, "go on home and change. I've got everything lined up. We're in good shape."

Rick looked down at his white tennis gear. "Guess I better get ready. What do you think? My gray slacks with a pink shirt? The white ones?"

"White," she said. "Pink shirt and that sweater I love, the deep violet color."

"What would I do without you?"

"You'd manage."

For Kamisha, as hostess, it was a bit dressier. But, a former city boy, Rick adored the casual Aspen style. The joke around town was Aspen Black Tie: shirt, tie, sport coat, blue jeans and cowboy boots.

Three trips to the storeroom to help Nina get stocked and Kamisha was ready. She wouldn't dare venture into the kitchen, Chef LaForte's domain. Rumor had it that he'd worked on President Reagan's staff but was canned when he waved a French knife in the face of the sous chef. Nevertheless, the man could cook up a storm, and Kamisha had never known him to fail.

Although it was still daylight, she had the waiters light the torchlights that lined the perimeter around the sweeping flagstone patio. The flowers still had drops of water clinging to their petals from the gardener's careful hand, and the pine forests on the slopes behind the club provided the scent for the final touch. Kamisha looked up. Not a cloud in sight. She never knew if one

of those frequent summer cloudbursts would strike. But
not tonight. It was glorious out. They'd wine and dine
outside and then, when it came time for Rick to present the check to the Denver MS representative, they'd
all move into the inside tennis courts, now covered with
a temporary floor, where there was another bar and a
band that was scheduled to play at ten.

The first guests began to arrive even before Rick was
back, but Kamisha enjoyed entertaining them and
showing off the club. There was the state representative
from Glenwood Springs and his wife, a stately white-
haired woman who was dressed to the nines. And the
tennis celebrities, most of whom were actually movie
stars who spent the summer doing fund-raising events
across the country. There was Martina Navratilova, who
lived in Aspen year-round, and Jimmy Connors, her
weekend houseguest. And then Kamisha noticed U.S.
Senator Luke Stern arrive. A popular man whom the
Washington Post had dubbed the Jewish Kennedy of the
nineties. And as debonair as they came, with his thick
salt-and-pepper hair, a perpetual tan and a physique
that belonged on a thirty-year-old. He went straight to
the bar, ordered a double Scotch from Nina, flirted with
her, then moved off into the growing crowd of the rich
and famous. At one point he gave Kamisha a wink from
across the patio, and she wondered if the next President hadn't just flirted with her, too.

The patio filled up. Rick arrived and set about
charming the throng. And then Brigitte Stratford came
breezing in, smiling, adorable, petite, teetering on spike
heels, wearing the pink dress whose fringe shimmered
and swayed in the torchlight. Kamisha's heart sank. She
could tell, knowing Brigitte so well, that her friend had
already been drinking—to fortify herself. Oh, God.

Brigitte came over, trailing a few enthralled men and the scent of expensive perfume. "Hi, Kamisha! Oh, wow, you look terrific, honey! Listen, I'm so glad you made me come. I feel better already. Is Bullet here yet?"

"No, not yet."

"Oh, well, I guess I'll just have to make do with this lonely guy," she said, flashing one of her admirers a smile. "Sweetie, could you get me a teensy-weensy drink?" And then she was gone, leading her captive away.

Nina ran out of glasses. Kamisha rushed to the basement. And then the ice ran out, too, and the machine hadn't recovered, so she sent a waiter scurrying downtown to the store, with *her* car. God, she hoped the kid could drive!

The last rays of sun struck the multimillion dollar homes on Red Mountain, reflecting off the picture windows and the copper roofs in dazzling bursts of burnished gold.

Torchlight flickered on the flowerpots and massed blooms. It grew cooler, but still warm enough to serve dinner outside. Some took tables. Some stood with plates of food in one hand, a drink in the other. Some just drank. But everyone was having a great time, rubbing shoulders with the celebrities who had come, talking tennis and golf, reminiscing about the great skiing they'd had in town last winter.

The cocktail napkins ran out. Kamisha quickly replenished them. And Rick took to mixing drinks with Nina, chatting all the while with the guests, a pro behind the bar. At forty-five he seemed to be experienced in almost everything, Kamisha noticed, thankful for his presence.

Senator Luke Stern buttonholed her once. "I'll never forget that downhill run of yours," he said, smiling, handsome, the consummate politician. "The Silver, wasn't it?"

"Yes. It seems another lifetime ago, though. Years and years."

"And here you are. In Aspen. You still ski much?"

"Not as much as I'd like. The club keeps me—"

"Kamisha!" It was Brigitte, now even drunker. "Where have you been all evening?"

"Working."

"And you're..." Luke Stern searched his mind. "I know. Brigitte Stratford. Soap operas. Let's see. *The Young and the...*"

"That *was* me," she slurred, "your former average all-American nice lady on TV. But you should get to know me better, Mr..."

"Brigitte," Kamisha said, "it's Senator. Senator Stern."

"No, no. I insist you call me Luke."

"Well, Luke," Brigitte began, and Kamisha ducked away unnoticed.

It was a crime, she thought while she ushered the busboys around, but Brigitte's drinking had only been getting worse since she'd moved to Aspen last year. Kamisha had hoped the beautiful clean mountain atmosphere would help. But obviously not. To make matters worse, her former boarding school roommate had taken up with Bullet Adams.

Bullet, Kamisha thought derisively. What a user. A former National Football League superstar quarterback who was now a sportscaster on cable TV, the thirty-seven-year-old stud continually rubbed Kamisha the wrong way. Currently he was living at Brigitte's

Castle Creek home when not out on assignment. And Tracy, Brigitte's daughter, didn't like him any better than Kamisha did.

Casually Kamisha glanced around to see if Bullet had made his famous "late" arrival. She spotted him over near a group of attractive women, charming their panty hose off. He did have charisma—with men and women alike. He was outgoing, attractive in a rather rugged way—big, big-boned, with snub-nosed boyish features, curling sandy blond hair and a wide, mobile mouth. Some of the things that came out of that mouth, however, drove Kamisha to distraction. He wasn't exactly stupid, but uninformed about most everything except sports. In the six months that Brigitte had been seeing him, Kamisha had arrived at the conclusion that he was one of those super high school athletes who had gotten a college scholarship despite his poor grades. Oddly Rick, well-educated and worldly, had taken to Bullet, too. They played a lot of golf and tennis together, anyway.

Oh, yes, Bullet was in his element tonight, the usual "groupies" hanging around him, fawning over him, giggling. A legend in his own mind, Brigitte's daughter Tracy called him, and she was right.

If Brigitte didn't have so damn much money, Kamisha was sure Bullet would have dumped her long ago. Right now her friend was back at the bar, spilling her drink on her pink Dior dress, looking cross-eyed into the crowd, grinning vacantly.

Night settled over the valley, and the stars dotted the black velvet sky in mountain brilliance. A few of the movie stars who had played in the charity tennis matches gave speeches for the cause. Luke Stern took the microphone for a quick "hello" to the group, Bullet told a few bad jokes to the entourage, and even Rick managed a minute to step up and thank everyone for their generous support.

"In a few minutes," he said over the din, "we'll go inside and present the check to Aspen's favorite charity."

The check! Oh, my Lord! Kamisha rushed inside, flew past the front desk and down the corridor to Rick's office. Her fingers fumbled on the combination lock of the wall safe. She had to respin the dial. How could she have forgotten the check? But then there it was. A one-hundred-thousand-dollar cashier's check made out to the MS Foundation of Colorado. Phew, she thought, gripping it.

She turned to leave, reaching for the light switch, when abruptly she paused and stared at the desk, wondering. John Leopardo. Today he'd been here. But why wasn't he here tonight? Surely he hadn't flown back to—

"Christ, Kamisha," Rick's voice came from the door, startling her. "We're ready to present the—I see you've got it. I couldn't find you. I thought maybe you'd taken that drunken friend of yours home and forgotten the check."

Kamisha felt heat rise up her neck. "Is Brigitte—?"

"Hell, yes. You better call her a cab." He took the check out of her hand. "I don't get it," he said, "a great-looking chick like her. She'll kill herself like this."

"I know," Kamisha said softly. "I know."

They began walking down the hall together, Rick eyeing the check proudly. Kamisha cleared her throat. "You know," she began, "I understand Mr. Leopardo was here, and I was wondering—"

"How did you know that?" Rick stopped abruptly.

"Well, one of the maids mentioned that he was in the condo, and I—"

"Mr. Leopardo," he said carefully, "is a very private man. You tell that maid that if she wants to keep her job, she should keep her mouth shut."

Kamisha could only nod.

The check was presented right on schedule, and the band began to play. A moment later, as the rock music spilled out onto the patio, Brigitte Stratford, small and cuddly, with soft brown eyes and honey-brown hair, virginal and innocent-looking, slipped off the bar stool and sagged to the flagstones.

"Hell," Bullet said, slamming his glass down on the bar.

But Kamisha was there. "Never mind," she said to Bullet as she helped Brigitte to her feet. "I'll call her a cab."

"Yeah," he said, giving Brigitte one last look before disappearing inside, "you do that."

"Some friend you are," Kamisha muttered to his back.

Nina ended up calling the taxi, and Kamisha began to steer her friend toward the entrance and the long paved path that wound down, crossed the river on a narrow wooden bridge and led up to the parking lot. Brigitte was teetering precariously all the way. She reeked of gin.

"Where's Bullet?" she mumbled.

"I guess he's staying."

"Screw him."

"Brigitte."

"Ah, so what? I think I'll dump the creep." She rocked on her high heels, and Kamisha had to take her arm more firmly.

"Is Tracy home?" she asked.

"Don't know. Maybe she's spending the night at a friend's. I'm okay."

"You are *not* okay, Brigitte. You're drunk."

"Jus' tired."

"Sure. Tomorrow we'll have lunch and we're going to have a talk about this. You can't keep—"

Brigitte stopped, swayed and tried to focus on Kamisha's face. "Mind your own business."

"Come on," Kamisha said, "the taxi's waiting. You have any money?"

"I'm loaded, you know that."

"In more ways than one," Kamisha said under her breath.

Rick was waiting for her when Kamisha arrived back on the patio. "Where have you been?" he snapped.

"I was getting a taxi for—"

"That lush?"

"Look," Kamisha said, her hackles rising, "I can take a minute to—"

"Senator Stern wants to talk to you. And that waiter Bobby spilled a cup of coffee on Mona Claymore's dress. She's in the locker room now, and you better get in there and offer to have it dry-cleaned."

"All right, Rick," she said, "but getting ticked off at me isn't solving a thing."

"Yeah, well, then see if you can find Stern. Okay? He wants to talk skiing."

"Fine." Kamisha headed off to the locker room, smarting. She liked Rick usually; at least she respected his business acumen. But sometimes he treated her—and other women, as well—more like lackeys than people. He was one of those men who had never quite accepted the coming of age of women's rights.

The throng danced and drank till one when the band finally packed it in. Kamisha dutifully called taxis, chatted with tired but happy guests, as, one by one, they made their way down the lighted river path. The busboys finished clearing drink glasses and coffee cups and lights were turned off, the torches extinguished. In five hours, Kamisha knew, Nina was scheduled to open the front doors again and man the desk for the early-rising health buffs.

"Go on home," she told Nina. "I'll finish up. The cleaning crew will be here at seven, anyway. And thanks. You were a lifesaver."

"Miss Hammill," Nina said, putting on a sweater, "I'll do it anytime. I got rich tonight!"

Rick was nowhere to be seen. Kamisha assumed he'd headed on up to his condo. It was just as well, she thought as she turned off the last lights. He'd been curt with her for most of the evening. Heck, the event had been a smashing success. He was going to give himself a heart attack over nothing.

Wearily Kamisha walked down the hall past the offices and pushed open the back door. She remembered that kid using her car to go and get the ice earlier and wondered if her car was still in one piece out there. It'd better be. She fumbled in her purse for the keys, her footfalls sounding too loud on the pavement in the still night. It *was* late.

And then she heard it. As if someone were sobbing. She stopped short, cocking her head, the car keys dangling from her fingers. Odd. She listened, peering into the night shadows, into the stands of pine and aspen. Finally she shrugged and began to walk toward her car in the empty lot.

And it came again. Definitely a sob.

Kamisha strode purposefully toward the dimly lit edge of the parking lot. She could make out a figure then, leaning against a boulder, half hidden in the trees.

"Hello," she called, "is everything all right?" Her first assumption was that this woman—or rather girl, she saw as she approached—must have had too much to drink, or had had a spat with a boyfriend at the party. Whatever. But it was the middle of the night, and the club was really quite isolated. The girl belonged at home.

"Hello," Kamisha said again. "Are you okay?"

The girl turned her face up into the light. She was hugging herself, shivering. Her eyes were red-rimmed and swollen. Still, Kamisha recognized her immediately. It was Carin, the sixteen-year-old daughter of the Pitkin County sheriff, Ed McNaught. What was she doing here? Could she have been at the party? But she was much too young.

"Carin?" she began, then froze. On second glance it was clear the young woman's dress was torn at the shoulder, and there appeared to be blood dried on the corner of her mouth. Kamisha's heart swelled in her breast. Had the girl been raped? "Carin," she whispered, "what happened?"

It took a while. Carin McNaught sobbed and hiccuped and made little sense. Kamisha held her, stroking the girl's head on her shoulder, sitting on the boulder next to her. The girl was plainly terrified. But the story finally emerged, coming out in pieces in between the racking sobs.

"Senator Stern's party. He tried to...but I wouldn't! He...he hit me!"

"*Where* was this party?" Kamisha urged, her stomach knotted sickeningly.

Carin nodded upward toward the lofty row of condos. Of course, Kamisha realized, Stern was one of the club's guests. He was staying in the VIP condo, kept open for certain visitors, free of charge naturally.

"How did you end up at his party?"

Carin sniffed. "Sometimes I go to them," she said in a whisper.

"Go to them? There have been other parties like this?"

A nod.

Oh, Lord, Kamisha thought. "Tell me more about these parties. Carin, you must."

Slowly the truth began to emerge, and the picture the girl painted wasn't pretty. It seemed that every few months, always when VIPs were in town, Carin and a few other local girls—all shockingly young—were invited to attend private parties at the same condo. Invited. And then paid. There were out-of-town girls, too. From California, Carin thought. She didn't know. She did know, however, that they all received hundred-dollar bills for being nice to these "older guys." Booze usually flowed and other substances, too.

"Carin," Kamisha said, trying to control her voice, "*who* calls you?"

"I can't . . . I promised. . . . ."

"*Who?*"

A long moment of silence stretched between them. Finally the girl looked at Kamisha with glassy eyes. "Mr. Simons," she whispered. "Rick Simons."

CHAPTER TWO

KAMISHA CLOSED the door of Rick Simon's office behind her. "Got a second, Rick?"

The club manager looked up at her, and she noticed he had circles under his eyes. As if he'd been up late ... partying. "Sure, what's up?"

She sat down in the chair across from him, then wished she hadn't. This wasn't going to be easy, and she would prefer to be standing. At least it would have given her a slight advantage. She crossed one leg over the other and smoothed her linen slacks with a hand. "Well, I guess I better be frank. I was told last night that you're arranging private parties in the VIP condo."

Rick looked at her sharply and answered too quickly. "Yeah, so?"

"With underage girls, Rick."

"Who told you that?"

"One of the girls."

He pushed his chair away from the desk and tapped his fingers on the arm of his chair.

"It's against the law, Rick."

"Don't give me that baloney." He made a cutting gesture with one hand.

"Are you telling me the girls aren't underage, Rick?"

"I'm telling you, Kamisha, that it's none of your business."

She drew back. She'd expected glib explanations, denials, anything but stonewalling. "It *is* my business."

"Not unless you make it so."

She got angry then. "I'm supposed to ignore it? I'm supposed to carry on as public relations director, knowing that the club's manager is a pimp and he's selling women to the highest bidder?"

Rick straightened, his expression as sharp as a hatchet. "Watch your step, honey."

"*You* watch your step. You're breaking the law."

"What are you going to do about it?"

"Go to the police. I expect they'll call in the FBI from Denver."

Rick leaned back, a smug smile on his face. "You won't do that. It'd smear your precious club's reputation all over the scandal sheets."

"You'd be fired, Rick. Out of here."

But he only shrugged. "Don't be so sure of that."

All night. She'd been up all night planning this confrontation, framing her lines in her head over and over in the dark of her bedroom. But she hadn't expected this—Rick's complacency.

She felt cornered. Even knowing she was in the right, she felt trapped. She didn't mind taking physical risks, fighting the elements, but this verbal sparring made her heart pound sickeningly. It made her sweat. She uncrossed her legs, recrossed them the other way. "I'll go to Mr. Leopardo. I don't think he'll like it."

Rick made that slicing gesture again. "Don't bother. He's the one who sent down orders to arrange the parties. They're a great draw."

"You're lying."

"Am I? Fine. Go to him. But I'm only following orders, honey. And Mr. Leopardo will be really ticked off if you bug him. You don't want to tick off John Leopardo," Rick sneered. "You might end up in cement shoes at the bottom of the East River."

She thought furiously. Was he bluffing? My God, all those stories about the Leopardos. Were they true? Was the Ute City Club owned by a Mafia don, a criminal?

Rick was watching her appraisingly. Maybe he had more to lose than he let on. Or maybe he was only the middleman following orders. What should she do?

"Look, honey, don't worry your head about these parties," Rick said ingratiatingly. "A little harmless fun. The girls have a ball and make a few bucks. Nobody's hurt. This isn't your concern. You were hired to look pretty, not to think too hard. Relax."

Kamisha felt herself go cold all over. There it was again, that awful rut she could never escape. As if she were a mannequin to dress up, a perfect size six, with limbs that someone could arrange to suit his desires. There *was* no Kamisha at all, only the doll, and inside she was a void. She stood and held herself stiffly. She felt as if she'd break in a second, as if the facade would spill out in a black ooze.

"Go take a Jacuzzi," Rick was saying. He'd picked up a paperweight and was weighing it in his hand absently. "Play some tennis. Chrissy was in earlier looking for a partner."

"I don't think I'm in the mood for tennis, Rick," Kamisha said bleakly.

He shrugged, still hefting the paperweight, and smiled a tight little smile that split his narrow, tanned face like a cut. She turned and walked out and shut the door softly behind her.

"I CAN'T STAND IT!" Kamisha said, pacing. "It's disgusting. Perverted!"

"Take it easy, Kamisha," Brigitte replied, wincing. "You're making my headache worse."

"I've got to do something. I can't let this go on. The club stands for something fine and wholesome. It's one of the best clubs in the country. Simons is using it as . . . as a front."

"But you said this Leopardo is really the one—"

"Maybe Rick just said that to shut me up. Maybe I should see John Leopardo. For God's sake, why would he do such a thing?"

"For money, honey," Brigitte said wanly, "what do you think?"

"But Leopardo's filthy rich already."

"How do you think he got that way?"

Kamisha stopped pacing. "What if Rick's only following orders? My God, Brigitte, I can't work there. I can't. I'd have to quit. Do you realize the girls at those parties aren't much older than your daughter, than Tracy?"

Brigitte sipped at a warm soft drink and made a face.

"What should I do, Brigitte? What would you do?"

Brigitte ran a slender hand across her forehead. "I don't know. I can't think this morning. But knowing me, I'd ignore it and keep my job. You love that gig, Kamisha. Why would you give it up?"

"For my principles."

"Ha. You know how far principles get you in this life?"

"I think we've had this discussion before," Kamisha said dryly.

"About a zillion times, from ninth grade on. I say, 'lighten up and have some fun.' And you say, 'I gotta stick to my principles.'"

Kamisha sat on a stool at Brigitte's kitchen counter. She sighed and played with some crumbs on the tiles. "It hasn't gotten me anywhere, has it?"

"Well, going with the flow hasn't gotten me anywhere, either. And just maybe you like yourself better than I do," Brigitte said slowly. Then she asked, "Was I awful last night?"

Kamisha looked straight at her friend. They had never lied to each other. "Pretty bad."

Brigitte put her face in her hands. "It's that Bullet, that son of a... He never came home last night, Kamisha."

"You're better off without him, Brigitte."

"No," she said, her voice muffled, then she raised her head. "No, then I'd be alone. Completely alone."

"You have Tracy."

"It's not the same."

"*I* live alone. Heck, I haven't dated anyone seriously in years. I survive."

"I wouldn't, Kamisha. I'm too scared. You're brave. You're tough. I'm weak and lonely. I need him."

"Tough, ha!"

"You are."

"I don't feel it. God, Brigitte, you've seen me down, you've seen me at my worst. How can you say I'm brave?"

"You pick up the pieces and go on."

Kamisha put her hand on her friend's arm. "For God's sake, Brigitte, so do you."

IT RAINED that June afternoon, a typical mountain cloudburst that washed the dust from the air and fled across the Continental Divide as quickly as it had come. Kamisha ran to her car and slammed the door behind her. The rain beat on the fabric roof and sluiced down the windshield. She was leaving the club early; she couldn't stay another second, avoiding Rick, jumping at every interruption and phone call. She had to think things out.

She had a powerful urge to call John Leopardo despite Rick's warning. Of course, Rick had said that Leopardo knew about the parties. But if indeed Rick was throwing the parties on his own, the last thing in the world he wanted was for the owner to find out. On the other hand, if Leopardo was behind the parties, Kamisha would be putting herself in danger. At the very least, in danger of losing her job. At the worst, in danger of . . . losing her life?

She sat there in her car, hearing the rain drum over her head, and weighed her decision. You heard about Mafia killings, but how true was it? She was a nobody. She'd get fired, warned off, but she couldn't stay at the club, anyway, not if Leopardo let Simons run a whorehouse in the VIP condo.

Kill her? Ridiculous. Simons was just trying to scare her off.

Yes, she'd do it. She had nothing to lose, really. Maybe John Leopardo was a reasonable man.

Her pulse quickened. She thought of confronting this faceless man who held so much power over her life.

It was going to be interesting, all right. But then suddenly she frowned. She had no idea how she was going to get in touch with him. Private. Rick had told her how private he was. But surely Rick had his number in the index file on his desk. She could go into Rick's office, get the number.

No. That wasn't the way. Phoning the man wasn't going to cut it. It was darn near two thousand miles to New York, though. But by air only a few hours. She had her savings account: she could afford the luxury of this confrontation. It was going to be worth every penny. Face-to-face, Kamisha thought. It was going to be more than interesting.

She turned the keys in the ignition of her car, heard the throaty roar that never failed to lift her spirits. It was a powerful car, a turbo model, much too fast for the around-town driving she did most of the time. But it had fine engineering under its hood, and she loved speed and perfection in anything.

So her trip to New York could be dangerous. But no more so than flying down an icy mountainside at seventy miles an hour. Or hang gliding or lots of the things Kamisha had done in her life. She loved thrills. She loved physical danger. She adored putting herself at risk.

She drove out the winding driveway of the club, splashing through puddles, smiling at a bicyclist peddling miserably through the rain to get back to the club.

What made her seek danger? What switch in her brain didn't open and close quite right? Was it her way of assuring herself she existed? Or was it yet another way she lived with her insecurities rather than confronting them?

She knew that this peculiar facet of her personality verged on the self-destructive and didn't help her achieve happiness or fulfillment, but it had become a habit, an addiction of sorts. It was the way she achieved highs in her life—perhaps, she often suspected, because her emotional life was otherwise so very sterile.

Yes, she'd go to New York and see John Leopardo in person. The Ute City Club was her baby. Its reputation must remain intact. Leopardo didn't need the money. Surely he could be made to understand that he was only ruining a good thing.

KAMISHA LOVED TO DRIVE. In the summer she could drive to Denver's Stapleton Airport in three hours flat. Easier than flying, she always said, especially when Independence Pass, a steep and winding shortcut, was open.

She turned into the remote parking lot at Denver airport at 8:30 a.m. sharp, pulled her bag out of the trunk, locked her car and took the shuttle van to the terminal. It was already hot in the city, and the sky held a bronze tinge of pollution. She carried her white jacket over one arm and her carryon bag over the other. This was going to be a quick trip, a day or two perhaps, that was all.

She'd told Rick she had some business to do in Denver. No sense stirring him up. She'd know very quickly where Rick stood in this business—and where she stood. But she'd told Brigitte exactly where she was going.

"Oh, Lord, Kamisha," Brigitte had said. "Causing trouble again. Can't you just relax?"

"No."

"Well, good luck then. I think you're nuts. Did I tell you Bullet came back? He was so sweet."

"That's nice," Kamisha had said. "Now, listen, I'm staying at the Sheraton on Fifty-ninth Street. In case anyone wants me. But don't tell Rick."

"I won't."

New York was hot and humid. She always forgot how wet the air was back East. It hit her like a suffocating blanket when she walked out of the terminal toward the taxi stand.

"It's a heat wave," the cabbie told her proudly. "Gonna hit ninety-seven today."

She telephoned John Leopardo's office just before closing time. She'd been afraid his number would be unlisted—in fact, she'd concocted several contingency plans just in case—but to her surprise she found it immediately in the Manhattan directory. Leopardo, John, and the address. Nothing more. She wasn't even sure if the number were his home or office. She supposed it didn't matter.

The air conditioner in her hotel room whirred monotonously while she waited for someone to answer. She felt her heart beating heavily against her ribs—in anticipation and pleasantly stimulating nervousness.

"John Leopardo's office," answered a woman's voice, crisp, efficient.

"This is Kamisha Hammill from Mr. Leopardo's club in Aspen. I'm here in New York, and I'd like to see him about something very important."

Kamisha was put on hold for a minute. What if he said no? What if he was leaving town? Maybe he wasn't even there. She leaned back against the pillows and let out a long breath. *Be there, Mr. Leopardo.*

The woman came back on the line. "Tomorrow, Miss Hammill. Say about eleven in the morning?"

"That's fine. Thank you," she said, and hung up. It had been too easy, far too easy. Almost as if he'd been expecting her. Maybe he had been. Maybe Rick had telephoned him. *Darn.*

The next morning at eight o'clock the radio announcer said it was already eighty-eight degrees. Kamisha looked down from her window onto Fifty-ninth Street and watched the crowds surge across intersections, heard the muted, faraway honk of cars. She loved New York in small doses, but it could be darn uncomfortable in the summer.

She let the sheer drapery liner drop into place and padded across the room. Three hours to kill. Her breakfast tray sat on the table, a pile of empty plates and crumbs. Her white pants suit hung, freshly pressed overnight, in the closet. It was too hot to shop or stroll in Central Park, and she was too impatient to go to a museum.

John Leopardo. The name conjured up fantastic images in her mind, a leopard, sleek and powerful, a creature of quick kills and utter ruthlessness. She knew he had dark hair, from her glimpse into Simons's office in the club; the rest of his appearance was a cipher.

Was he a jolly plump grandfatherly Italian? A grim, whipcord-slim one?

She sat on her bed and stared into the middle distance. She was crazy to be doing this, out of her mind. She should have listened to Brigitte and left well enough alone.

John Leopardo. Perhaps he'd been born in Italy and spoke broken English. But he'd done well in the States; the address of his office was impressive, the very heart of the financial district. And his business—what was it? Did he just tell people he was in the "importing" business?

Did he even know who Kamisha Hammill was? Did he have any real interest in the Ute City Club?

She rose and walked across the room, her emerald-green silk pajamas clinging, and turned on the TV set. News, weather, a talk show. There would be something to keep her occupied.

While she watched Kamisha did her exercises, a daily routine, a calming routine. Fifty sit-ups, fifty push-ups, bending, stretching.

A shower, the spray sliding off her head. The water in the East always felt silky to Kamisha. In Aspen it was hard, reluctant to lather.

She wore a red silk tank top and the white suit. No jewelry. Her hair was caught back in a silver clasp. Very little makeup.

John Leopardo. She took a deep breath, let it out in a quavering sigh. She felt like an errant student called to the headmistress's office, yet *she* had been the one to initiate this meeting. She rehearsed what she would say to him, then gave up. She would just tell him, straightforward, frankly. He'd listen, believe her, understand what had to be done. And even if he were involved, as Rick had said, she'd try to convince him to be reasonable. The club made plenty of money without having to throw those parties on the side.

God, it was important to her! If he didn't listen, she'd have to resign. She couldn't stay at the club, not unless the parties stopped. Then what would she do? Where would she go? Aspen was small, its opportunities limited. He *had* to listen.

She could have killed time and walked to his office, but the heat enervated her, and she'd look bedraggled when she arrived. She took a cab, paid the driver and looked up at the office building. On brass plaques by the doors were the names of the tenants. Yes, there it was, tenth floor. John Leopardo. That was all. Not "company" or "enterprises" or anything. Just "John Leopardo," as if you were supposed to know what he did, who he was. Of course, maybe everyone in New York *did* know who he was.

His office door had the same understated brass plaque on it. His name, nothing more. She went in, noticing sweat on her palm as she turned the doorknob. The waiting room was carefully done in tones of gray, a cool room, meant to calm. Behind a semicircular metal desk sat a middle-aged woman with severely cut hair.

"May I help you?" the woman inquired.

"I'm Kamisha Hammill."

"Yes, have a seat, please. Mr. Leopardo is on a conference call at the moment. He'll be right with you."

She sat down and leafed through a magazine. Her hands were still damp, clinging to the glossy pages.

The door to his office was just behind the receptionist's desk. What was he doing in there? Talking to his Mafia partners, rigging an athletic event, arranging a drug deal, starting another club where the manager could throw "parties" with underage girls?

She tapped her fingers on the arm of the chair she sat in and stared, unfocused, at the pages of the magazine. John Leopardo. Tiny, nervous tremors shot through the tips of her fingers.

The woman was pushing a button, saying something into an intercom. She looked up, directly at Kamisha, and said, "You can go in now, Miss Hammill."

Kamisha stood, smoothed her slacks over her thighs with her hands and followed the woman, who held the door open for her. She stepped inside and was aware of the door closing with a quiet snick behind her.

The room was large, elegant and sparsely furnished, slightly dim. A spare contemporary couch in black leather sat against one wall, a heavy, bare glass coffee table in front of it. But her eyes were drawn to the desk across the room—chrome and steel. Very neat, very spare, very large.

A man sat behind the desk. He didn't move or speak. The window behind him cast his features in shadow, but she had the impression of broad shoulders in a dark suit, dark hair. A chill crawled up her limbs despite the heat outside. There was something about this man, something about the stillness of him and the pitch of his head.

She stepped forward. "Mr. Leopardo..."

"Miss Hammill." His voice was low, a rough voice held in check by a strong will.

She walked closer, aware of his steady gaze on her. He gestured to one of the chrome-and-black-leather chairs in front of his desk. "Please."

"Thank you." She sat, crossed her legs, smoothed her slacks again nervously. "I appreciate you seeing me so quickly."

"What brings you to New York, Miss Hammill?"

She could see his face now, and she studied him as she spoke. His eyes were dark, heavy-lidded and secretive, his nose a slab, his dark hair combed back. There was a Continental flair to him, something old world and solid. His suit was impeccably tailored, double-breasted. One button was fastened, and the coat hung open a bit, lying in elegant folds against his broad chest. European, Italian, yes, olive skin, a shadow of a heavy beard and a surprisingly sensitive mouth.

"Mr. Leopardo," she began, "there's a problem at the Ute City Club. I . . . I think you should know about it."

"I should imagine Mr. Simons would take care of any problems there." He spoke dispassionately, his voice neutral, his expression impersonal.

She looked down at her folded hands. "Rick Simons is part of the problem."

"I guess you'd better tell me then, Miss Hammill."

She told him, leaving out only Rick's assertion that Leopardo had ordered the parties. When she finished, he sat so silently for so long that she was ready to burst with anticipation.

"Well," he finally said, "this is all very interesting."

He kept his eyes on her, pinning her with his dark regard but not judging, not yet. A wild notion buffeted her: he might be sitting there, not three feet from her, planning her demise. *My God.* She looked up from her hands. His gaze was penetrating her, probing, silent and utterly unreadable. She had to swallow to continue. "I'm very upset about this whole thing, Mr. Leopardo. It's breaking the law. I'm not a goody-two-shoes, but these parties, the young girls. . . It's wrong. I was tempted to go to the police, but I decided to speak to you first. The publicity wouldn't be good for the club," Kamisha added.

A faint smile teased the corners of his mouth. She noticed that there was a mole near its corner. "No, it certainly wouldn't. And Aspen has had its share of bad press lately." He leaned his elbows on the desk. His hands, she noticed, were strong and square, capable hands. He wore no rings, and she could see the dark curling hairs that covered the backs of his hands and retreated up under the white starched cuffs of his shirt. "Does Rick Simons know you're here?"

"No."

He played with a letter opener, turning it over and over, slowly, deliberately. She stared at his hands. Did he kill people with those hands? Her eyes flew up to meet his. The notion was both frightening and exhilarating.

"Miss Hammill, I appreciate you coming to me with this problem." He set down the letter opener and steepled his fingertips, eyes still on her. "I want to assure you that I had no knowledge of these parties and nothing to do with them. You must have suspected that I knew, at the very least."

"Well, I..."

He spoke so calmly. They were speaking of his reputation, his honor, not to mention an employee who was deceiving him, yet he could have been passing the time of day. "I'm quite aware," he went on, "of the rumors surrounding a connection with my family. My father, to be precise. They are unfounded. I have never had any connection to the family business." The faint smile tugged at his lips again. "Rest easy. I'll make sure the sordid activities at the club end."

"I'm relieved, Mr. Leopardo. I really couldn't have gone on working there if you condoned such things."

"Certainly not. I understand completely. You're very courageous to come to me like this."

He was dismissing her. Her appointment was over. She felt confused, as if the meeting were an anticlimax. She wanted to believe him, but she had no way of knowing what he really felt. He could be lying.

She stood. "Well, thank you, Mr. Leopardo." Her words died away. It couldn't be this easy! He was playing with her, mocking her, lying so smoothly that she'd never know for sure... It crossed her mind swiftly that he might press a buzzer somewhere on his desk and two men, clad in black suits, would be waiting for her outside. They'd follow her, wait for the right moment...

"You're quite welcome, Miss Hammill." He rose then, picked something up that leaned against his chair and began to come around his desk. "And by the way," he was saying, "I was wondering..."

Kamisha had a moment of utter shock. He walked with a cane and had a limp. No one had told her. But he was talking, asking her something, and she had to wrench her gaze from his legs and look him in the eye and answer his question.

"...be pleased to take you to dinner tonight, if you'd so honor me. You've come such a long way. If you leave the name of your hotel with Martha, my driver will pick you up at eight. That is, of course, if you're not otherwise engaged."

Surprised, she hesitated just a heartbeat too long. Dinner? With John Leopardo? Then came the heavy, expectant pulse in her veins—the challenge, the risk. She smiled. "I'd be delighted to have dinner with you, Mr. Leopardo. What a lovely idea."

He took her hand for a moment. His other rested on the knobbed head of the cane. His fingers were warm and alive, strong.

Breathless, unnerved from bearing up under the aura of silent force surrounding the owner of the Ute City Club, Kamisha made a graceful escape.

She added, "Well, thank you, Mr. Leopardo." Her words died away. It couldn't be this easy! He was play-

CHAPTER THREE

JOHN SAT SILENTLY, utterly unmoving, and stared at the door where she had been only moments before. Never could he recall such exquisite poise in a woman. He let his mind dwell on the image of her cat-sleek body and those hypnotic, tilted eyes that had lured photographers since her early days as a ski racer. Surely every man who had ever been in her presence had been enthralled.

You're a damn fool, he thought, unaccustomed to the strong feelings he was battling. It had been ten years since he'd allowed himself such feelings, and then they had only caused him pain and rejection and failure. He knew he should call and cancel the dinner engagement. He also knew that, as surely as the sun would set, he wouldn't make that call.

A faint throb began in his leg. He stood, walked slowly to the window and tried to work out the annoying twinge that could too quickly become pain. As he stood at the immense plate glass window, his gaze fell to the street far below. He wondered if she was going to hail a taxi, or if she was walking along the street, the suffocating heat and humidity clinging to her, pressing on her. Perhaps he should have had Inky drive her to her hotel.

The buzzer on his phone sounded. Grimacing—the twinge was becoming an ache now—he moved back to his desk.

"Yes, Martha?"

"Mr. Leopardo, it's San José, Costa Rica. The contractor, on line two."

John frowned. He needed to talk to the man about cost overruns on the new health spa there, but he also needed a clear head. "Tell him I'll be back to him later today."

"Yes, Mr. Leopardo."

Kamisha Hammill, he thought, leaning back in his chair, propping up his leg, she'd taken him totally by surprise. And so had her accusations.

John slowly tapped a finger on the cool desktop. His eyes narrowed and a deep crease slashed his brow. Could Rick be involved in some illegal activities, using the club as a front? It was possible, of course. Booze, parties, young women—there was a lot of money to be made there. Rick was paid damn well. But his tastes were expensive. Or, at least, John had made mental note of that when Rick had still been at the Miami club.

He found his teeth clenching tightly in his jaw. The whole affair smacked of everything John deplored. By God, if Rick was truly involved in this business, there would be hell to pay.

On the other hand, he only had Kamisha Hammill's word to go by. And why should he trust her? For all John knew she might have some personal vendetta to settle. Rick might have come on to her. Maybe Rick had chewed her out, bruised her ego.

On the surface she appeared to be a cool customer. But John had reviewed her file when Rick first interviewed her five years ago for the PR position at the

club, just as he reviewed every potential employee's file.
It was another way of staying in control, of not leaving
things to the vagaries of chance. Kamisha's file con-
tained two photos: a picture from her ski racing days
and a snapshot of her leaving the courthouse after her
divorce that had made the front page of a yellow press
newspaper. An unwelcome thought nudged him: none
of the pictures had done Kamisha justice. In person she
was even more spectacular.

He recalled, as well, mention of her family in Los
Angeles. Her father was a CEO for an oil company.
Kamisha's mother was a socialite who dabbled in art.
An only child, Kamisha had been sent to boarding
school where she'd taken up with Brigitte Stratford.
John could only surmise that Kamisha's reputation as
unattainable was a direct result of a sterile existence as
a child, her barrier against an uncaring world. Idly John
wondered if she allowed herself an occasional affair—
Rick had commented in her file that around Aspen she
was known as somewhat of a thrill junky, always seeking a challenge. Were men a challenge to her? Although, to give credit where it was due, Rick had since
then updated her file to include such comments as:
loyal, dependable, hardworking, private, capable.

A slight, ironic smile curved his lips for a moment.
His mother would approve of this "date" tonight,
though she'd ask if Kamisha were Catholic. His mother.
He spoke to her on the phone on holidays and her
birthday. She always cried. She begged him to make it
up with his father, Mafia kingpin Gio Leopardo. But to
do so would open a door that John preferred to keep
closed. His father was always going to refuse to understand why John had left the secure, structured Mafia

life that had awaited him when he returned from Vietnam.

Yes, John thought, he had made a decision to go it alone those many years ago, a tough, hard decision, and one that, to this day, he wasn't even certain he understood. It had come as a flashing insight, swift and sure. It had come in a moment when his life had become abruptly too short. On that battlefield, lying there, wondering if he were going to live. That had been in South Vietnam. Over twenty years ago. But suddenly it seemed like only yesterday. . . .

He'd been in Nam for forty weeks and his tour would end soon. A couple of months, that was all, and he could go home.

It hadn't been John's idea to come to Vietnam, although many of his fellow soldiers in the Special Forces had put in for duty there. In fact, last year, at twenty years old and almost finished with his military hitch, John had been surprised when his orders had come in for the tour of Southeast Asia.

He'd been drafted; a single semester off from college and the military had nabbed him. But, unlike so many others, he hadn't tried to shirk his duty. Instead, he'd gone into the lower ranks willingly, patriotically, taken an interest in the intelligence schools offered by the Special Forces and, after a year in the war zone, achieved the rank of sergeant.

"The family is proud of you," Gio Leopardo, his father, had said on John's only stateside leave. "We know our duty and we do it. We're Americans."

His family was proud of him, true, but would they be so pleased when he returned to Brooklyn and told his father that he'd decided to pursue business interests outside the close-knit structure of the Leopardo empire?

John finished a short leave in Saigon on a stinking hot Sunday and returned to his outpost base near Chau Doc on the Cambodian frontier. He'd been on leave six days and, other than drinking and whoring and aimlessly roaming the French provincial streets of the city he hadn't done anything. He hadn't even bothered to call home. What was there to say? A distance had grown between John and his family, a need to put space between himself and the puppetlike strings with which his father manipulated everyone. The rift felt to him like a wound, deep and unhealed, and yet somehow inevitable.

Even after R and R John wasn't rested. No one in Vietnam ever rested. There was always that question hanging like a tarnished chain around a man's neck: would he make it out alive?

Now the steaming jungle rose around John's patrol and formed a lush canopy overhead. He checked the map and handed it back to Inky, his right-hand man, a black "lifer," huge and muscular with a shaven, bowling-ball head, who was both deadly and sharp in the field. If Special Forces offered a new school, Inky was the first in line. After eight years in the service, he knew his stuff.

The seven-man patrol moved west along the bank of the sluggish brown river. Their objective was clear-cut— intelligence gathering. There was to be no search and destroy.

A light rain began to fall, misting the jungle, silencing the invisible, exotic birds. John raised a fist, the sinews in his arm tightening, and the file of men behind him halted noiselessly.

He turned to Inky. "What do you think?"

"I can smell 'em."

John nodded. His patrol was six kilometers out from where the chopper had dropped them, close to Charlie. Aerial surveillance had indicated a VC buildup near a delta in the river. He checked the map once more.

"Half a klick," he told Inky quietly. "Pass it along."

Charlie was there, all right, erecting a veritable stronghold near the delta. Well camouflaged and well fortified. Crisp new tiger suits, the latest Russian weaponry. John and his men lay along the murky riverbank in a line, and he drew a detailed sketch of the camp. It would take more than a platoon and attack choppers to knock this one out effectively. An air strike would have to be called.

His mission complete, John signaled the men. On their bellies, ignoring a stinging cloud of mosquitos, they inched their way back into the thick undergrowth and moved away from the river.

So far so good.

"It's too friggin' quiet," the massive black man said. "Don't like it."

They spread out, crouching, silently forcing their way through the thick foliage, seemingly making little progress.

Wiping sweat from his eyes, John checked his watch. Three hours to go. The chopper would be in the clearing at 1600 hours, looking for the yellow smoke that would signal the pickup. They'd better get a move on.

The first sniper shot caught Inky in the flesh of his left forearm. The second drilled a neat hole in PFC Lemont's temple. Lemont was dead before he hit the soft jungle floor. John pulled his tags, and they were forced to leave him.

He signaled to his men, who had dropped for cover, and they crawled off into the bush again on their bellies.

"I can get 'em," Inky breathed fiercely.

"No." John shook his head. "Our orders are to get this intelligence to headquarters."

"Hell."

There was the distinctive odor of fear permeating the jungle now. It was seeping from John's men, oozing in oily droplets from their hardened bodies, soaking their camouflage shirts. But John wasn't afraid. There wasn't time for the luxury of listening to his heart. In the breast pocket of his shirt Lemont's tags rattled. John couldn't afford to listen to that, either.

Without drawing another shot they finally made it to the perimeter of the clearing. Twenty minutes early.

"How's the arm?" John turned to Inky from where they lay hidden together.

"Don't feel a thing." The black man's eyes bore into John's. "They're out there, Sarge, right behind us. Three, maybe four of the little—"

"I know."

"You want I should do a little circling?"

"No. Stay put."

"But, Sarge, we'll be sitting ducks when the chopper comes. I can knock 'em out!" He grinned and pulled out his knife. "Real silent like."

"No. We're not engaging. Orders. So forget it."

Inky bared his teeth in disappointment.

"Now pass it along, no talking. No anything. Got that?"

"Sure, Sarge. But they're gonna come in, anyway." He shrugged and moved off silently to tell the men.

Ten minutes jerked by. John lay on his back, his M-16 rifle cradled across his stomach, and looked up at the sky. The rain had stopped for the moment. There was a white haze filtering through the trees above, a patch of blue to the east. Reluctantly he saw Lemont's face, the hole in the boy's temple. He closed his eyes tightly to blot out the picture. Now he could see New York, Brooklyn. And his father's house was there. He imagined that it was winter. Winter in the city, cold and crisp. Patches of wet snow sat on the brown lawn and the maple tree's branches were bare and dark.

There was movement in the bush next to him. He opened his eyes and saw Inky, sweat streaming down the man's face. John killed a mosquito on his neck, rubbing it, red streaking his flesh.

"Gonna be more blood than that," Inky said, grinning dangerously.

Closing his eyes again, listening for the distinctive thump of the helicopter's rotors, John conjured up the house in Brooklyn once more. There was still snow, cool and inviting. Outside the front door of the solid, imitation-Tudor structure lounged two bodyguards in heavy black overcoats. The door opened and several laughing children raced out—his sister's children—dragging a brand-new American Flyer sled. Gio was standing on the threshold watching his grandchildren, smiling his big smile, chatting with his bodyguards as they lit cigarettes and rubbed their hands together.

"Handsome kids," one of the men said to Gio, his voice gravelly, rolling softly in the ancient accent of Sicily.

Behind Gio was the foyer. Dim and mahogany-paneled. Beyond that the hushed living room with its heavy dark furnishings and lace doilies. Farther on the warm kitchen. His mother. Substantial and womanly and gray-haired. Loving. There was no other security on earth like her embrace. No voice gentler, no hand more comforting.

And in that house John remembered a quiet strength. He drew on it as he lay on the murky ground, motionless and silent. His father, Gio, was the godlike source of that strength and the power, the restrained authority that ran the empire. There was often, when called for, ruthlessness, but Gio had a sense of right and wrong, as well. Simple lessons. God and mass on Sunday, a huge, animated family feast. On Monday Gio in his office behind closed doors and a ceaseless file of visitors. John's mother quieting the children.

"Damn chopper," Inky grumbled. "Where in hell—?" And as if to punctuate his complaint, the distant sound of thumping vibrated in the air.

"Thank God," came the voice of one of the men.

"Shut up," Inky whispered harshly. Then, his body growing rigid, he said, "Over there! In the bush!"

John snapped taut. Inky was right. There was movement in the bush. Charlie. They hadn't lost the enemy at all.

John looked to the east, over the treetops. *Thump, thump.* Yes! There is was, the chopper. If he could somehow get his men between the helicopter and the VC . . . Quickly he signaled for the yellow smoke canister to be blown.

A shot split the air. Another. Blind firing in their direction. Then, missing John's signal to stay under cover, two of his soldiers broke from the undergrowth and rushed, crouched in the swirling yellow smoke toward the open door of the hovering machine.

"Damn!" John shouted. "Get down!"

From the opening of the chopper a soldier was spreading a burst of machine gunfire toward the perimeter of the clearing. The two men made it on, a couple more broke for the helicopter, one went down heavily.

"No choice now, man!" Inky yelled to John, and the rest of them left the cover of the jungle and headed, firing rounds into the bush, toward the center of the clearing. One of the men stopped long enough to drag his fallen comrade toward the door, another crouched and tossed a grenade. Inky was ahead of John, firing also, cursing, yelping like an Indian. John scanned his surroundings, turned, fired a burst blindly behind him and ran in zigzags toward the chopper.

Twenty yards. Fifteen. His men, save for Inky, were aboard. Hope sprang in his chest. They were going to make it!

Suddenly pain exploded in his leg. He stumbled, tried to get up, stumbled again. There was a strange feeling of regret in him as he saw the VC breaking from the brush, their short forms crouched, swimming before his eyes.

Falling, staggering, falling again, John tried to wave the chopper off but, goddamn it, Inky was swinging out of the door! Never could follow orders!

Debris blown up by the rotors blinded him and sweat stung his eyes and the yellow air smelled of acrid gunpowder and torn flesh and gasoline.

He was really going down this time. Hell, his knee was half ripped off! He wasn't going to make it. His head thudded again with the pain, and everything was growing dark and, damn that fool Inky, he was crawling through the gunfire toward him, his teeth white in a grinning black face. . . .

Again, the buzzer sounded. "I'm sorry, Mr. Leopardo, but it's San José again, your contractor. He insists—"

John frowned. "I'll take it, Martha."

The club, situated on the Pacific Coast on the Nicoya Peninsula of Costa Rica, was nearly completed now, but John had had a few reservations about his contractor and some of the cost overruns. They had to be dealt with, but he'd be damned if he was going to have checks cut until he reviewed every last invoice.

"Yes, Juan Luis, it's Mr. Leopardo here..."

CHAPTER FOUR

KAMISHA STEPPED out of the cab in front of the hotel. The heat smote her like a bludgeon, but she welcomed the physical discomfort. It was far easier to bear than the mental gyrations of her mind.

She felt confused and uncertain, unable to decide how she was going to deal with John Leopardo. All her life, well, since she'd been a teenager, men had always taken notice of her. She was used to their compliments and to their preening and posturing. And usually Kamisha performed for a man. She knew how to dazzle and tease and how to posture. It was a game. Man was attracted to woman. Woman made herself even more attractive, hard to get but alluring, desirable. And then, after all the courtship and circling, man took woman to his bed.

But with Kamisha the script ended differently. She knew just how to play the game, true enough, but when the time came for physical and emotional entanglement, she severed the relationship with the cool swiftness of a scalpel.

Brigitte, good old wise Brigitte, was forever telling her that it came from her upbringing, that Kamisha was afraid to risk her heart in case of disappointment. Her ex-husband, Josh . . . well, Kamisha had taken that risk with him and where had it gotten her? Josh had never been truly interested in what lay below the surface of her

attractiveness and physical ability. And when the new-
ness had worn off, and there was plain old Kamisha,
insecure, desperately needing him, the winter of their
marriage had begun.

They were all like that, Kamisha had come to believe. Not a single man in her experience gave a hoot
who she really was deep down inside. She often wondered if she knew that answer herself.

But then there was John Leopardo. He hadn't even
acknowledged her as a woman. She could have been
anyone sitting in his office; it had been all business, an
impersonal appointment. Of course, he'd asked her to
dinner. That must have meant something. But what?
That she was an out-of-towner, an employee, alone?
Why had he asked her out?

John. The man had such consummate self-control.
She'd never in her life met a human being who exuded
such power—power over himself and power over others. It was attractive, that authority, and frightening,
too.

She went over every moment of their meeting, every
word they'd spoken, every gesture and movement he'd
made. She searched for nuances of meaning in the
man's bearing, but he was a closed book, utterly unreadable.

Had he lied when he said he didn't know about the
parties? She knew no more now than before she'd been
ushered into his presence. Tonight. Perhaps tonight
she'd discover more about John Leopardo. More about
why he fascinated her so, why he'd set her mind to ask
such difficult questions, why she cared so much to know
if he'd really been telling the truth.

And his limp. She wanted to know why he limped.
Had he been born that way? Had he been injured? She

couldn't help imagining his leg under the perfectly creased trousers—twisted scar tissue, perhaps old surgical incisions. Somehow she knew that it wasn't a new injury that was healing, knew it from the way he'd held the cane, as if it were an intimate part of him.

Such a strong, virile-looking man, a man with no weakness, no vulnerability, a man in perfect control— except for one physical infirmity.

He'd touched her in some indefinable way. Touched the untouchable woman, and Kamisha had to respect that despite her misgivings.

So how to handle this enigmatic man? It was all very new to her, very disturbing. She walked into her hotel with a frown creasing her brow. If John was any other man on earth, she'd simply attempt to bewitch him. On the other hand, he *was* a man. Different. More tightly controlled. But a man nevertheless. Perhaps all this confusion was for nothing. What she should do, would do, was play the game, only with a little more caution.

That decided, Kamisha stood in the hotel lobby, surrounded by the eddying crowd, and wondered what to do with herself until eight o'clock. Eight hours. A lifetime. An entire long, hot summer day until she'd see John Leopardo again and begin the game.

Where would they go? Not someplace for the rich and famous. No, not John. His taste would be superb. He'd know of a small, intimate restaurant with discriminating service and a fabulous chef, and the maître d' would recognize him.

Kamisha wiped the tiny dots of perspiration off her upper lip with her forefinger and wondered suddenly what she would wear. She'd brought nothing for an evening out in New York, certainly nothing remotely acceptable for a dinner date with a man who presented the ultimate challenge.

She smiled at herself. Clothes. What else should a woman think of at a time like this?

There were several small, elegant boutiques along Fifty-ninth Street. Kamisha browsed, even going into a couple of art and antique shops, too, just out of curiosity. The saleswomen were cool, superior, Manhattan types, but they sized Kamisha up as a great advertisement for their wares.

"Madame would look fantastic in this," a saleswoman said, draping a sequined dress over her arm with a flourish.

"No, not a dress," Kamisha said. "Pants. A pantsuit, perhaps."

"I have just the thing. Size six, aren't you?"

But it wasn't "just the thing," and Kamisha went onward, out toward Fifth Avenue and the crowds and suffocating heat. She found it finally, a black knit jumpsuit, backless, with thin straps and a lovely way of draping off her shoulders. Very plain, very classic, very expensive. And shoes, naturally, silver sandals much like the ones sitting in her closet at home. How irritating. But tonight would be worth it, and John would notice. She was sure he'd notice every last detail about her.

At three she set her new purchases down on a chair in her blissfully cool room and ordered lunch from room service. She also made an appointment for a manicure and a pedicure in the beauty shop off the lobby. She would treat herself well today. Just this once.

John Leopardo. So very Italian in a way. Probably Catholic. With a big family, lots of brothers and sisters and a loving father and mother. A Mafia don father, but a loving one, nonetheless. Utterly unlike Kamisha's uncaring, law-abiding WASP parents.

She ate, then kept her appointment in the beauty shop. The manicurist was an eccentric-looking girl with a beehive of frizzy blond hair, an amusing conversationalist with magic hands.

"So you're from Aspen, huh? D'ja ever meet Donald Trump? I hear he hangs out there."

"I've seen him, but never met him personally."

The girl chewed gum energetically while she painted Kamisha's toes. "Is it true that people serve bowls of cocaine at parties out there?"

Kamisha laughed. "Not at any party I've ever been to. I think that's an exaggeration."

"I just heard it somewhere. Do you ski?"

"Sure, I ski." Kamisha smiled inwardly, both pleased and chagrined not to be recognized.

"Boy, it must be nice up there in the mountains. Not as hot as New York, huh?"

"No, not nearly as hot."

By seven-thirty she was ready. Her heart was beating too quickly, and even in the air-conditioned room she was afraid her makeup was going to run. A dozen times she told herself that this was merely an invitation to dinner, a kind gesture from her employer. Or perhaps his motives were deeper. He might be planning to offer her hush money, or to convince her to keep her mouth shut if she wished to keep her job. A part of Kamisha prayed it was going to be strictly business. Another part of her craved the challenge, the excitement, the magic, that small slice of time out of reality.

She paced, then lifted the drapes to look down at the street, as if she'd see John walking—limping, leaning on his cane—toward the door of the hotel. How silly.

She checked herself in the mirror for the tenth time,
tugged at the bodice of her black jumpsuit, pulled at a
wisp of hair so that it fell in front of her ear. Leaning
close to the mirror, she rubbed at a smudge of lipstick
at the corner of her mouth. She stopped in that position, held by the look in her own eyes—they were
bright, expectant, filled with points of light, alive.

She walked to the window yet again and peered down
into the street. She hated waiting. Ever since she'd been
a small child, Kamisha hated waiting for anyone. She
smiled ruefully. It was because of her parents, of course.
Either she'd been waiting for them to return from Europe or the Far East, or just waiting for them to dress
for a gala and come into her bedroom to say good-
night.

Kamisha sat on the side of the bed, slipped off her
shoes and wiggled her toes impatiently. There was one
time in particular she'd waited on her parents—waited
for the wonderful surprise they'd arranged. Oh, yes.
She'd imagined a ski trip perhaps or a vacation with
them in Europe.

"We'll tell you all about it at dinner tonight," her
mother had said that July morning so many years ago.
"Don't be impatient, dear." Grace Hammill's lips had
brushed Kamisha's cheek, cool, impersonal lips, and
Kamisha had left for her tennis lesson. How excited
she'd been all day, excited and expectant. Her parents
had planned something for her. Just for her.

Everything was splashed in Southern California sunlight when she got home just before noon. She found
her mother by the pool, the telephone cord stretched
across the neatly mowed lawn and through the rose
garden. Kamisha tossed down her tennis racket and
kicked off her shoes, stretched out on a cushioned

lounge next to her mother's and listened impatiently to
the phone conversation.

Grace's laughter tinkled. "Now, Larry," she was
saying, "I know five thousand is a considerable dona-
tion, but think of the tax benefit." Grace laughed lightly
again. "Oh, Larry, you are such a dear. I knew I could
count on you. Now remember, the fund-raiser dinner is
on the twenty-second."

When her mother was off the phone, Kamisha asked,
"The art museum fund-raiser?"

"Yes, dear." Grace ran a slim brown finger down a
typed list of names and numbers she had propped on
her knees.

"Mom?"

"Yes, dear."

"Do you think we could have Ned drive us to Bev-
erly Hills and have lunch together today?"

Grace began to dial the phone. "Lunch? Oh, Kamisha, darling, I simply can't."

Kamisha frowned and sighed. "Why not?"

Her mother cupped the receiver in her hand. "You
can see I'm busy. Don't act spoiled, dear."

"I only thought..."

"Eileen? It's Grace Hammill," her mother was saying, "yes, sweetie. I know, it's been ages and ages." The
bell-like laughter followed Kamisha inside and up to her
room. Her mom *was* busy, and tonight she'd hear all
about the surprise, anyway.

Dinner was served formally at the Hammill man-
sion. Not that the three family members ate together
regularly. More often than not, Marcus was abroad on
oil business, or Grace was entertaining or out to an
event herself. In fact, Kamisha usually dined in the
kitchen with the help. There she could laugh and joke

and listen to Lucinda's stories about her family. To-night, however, Marcus and Grace sat at opposite ends of the table, and Kamisha was in her place between them.

"Well, can you tell me now?" Kamisha asked.

Marcus exchanged a glance with Grace.

"Let me guess," Kamisha was saying, oblivious to her parents' unsmiling countenances, "I bet we're go-ing on a ski trip to New Zealand. Of course, it could be Chile."

"Your soup is getting cold, dear," Grace said, eye-ing Kamisha.

"Or maybe a trip to Europe." She looked at her fa-ther and cocked her head. "Last year you said we were all going on a bike trip someday through France. Re-member? I just bet—"

"Kamisha," Grace interrupted, "put your napkin in your lap. I can't imagine where you pick up such bad—"

"Grace." Marcus put up a hand. "I think it's time we tell her the good news. It's unfair to keep her guess-ing."

Kamisha would always recall that moment when ex-citement filled her, so much so that she failed to prop-erly read the look of guilt in her father's eyes, or the cool, impassive expression on her mother's face.

Marcus cleared his throat and steepled his fingers. "We've enrolled you at the boarding school in Taos, Kamisha. You recall the place? We visited it three years ago when we were on that ski trip in New Mexico."

Kamisha furrowed her brow, uncomprehending. "What?"

"Boarding school," Grace said, smiling, sipping on her soup.

The enormity of what they were doing hit her then, and she couldn't get her breath for a minute. She looked from one to the other, her stomach knotting up, wanting to expel the food she'd so innocently put in it moments before. Boarding school. They were sending her away. They really were. They didn't love her, they never had, and now they were getting rid of her.

"You'll be able to ski there," Marcus was saying. "They have their own coach and ski team. They—"

"I don't want to go," Kamisha said through clenched teeth. She wanted to scream and cry, to pound the table and throw things, but she couldn't, she couldn't. Something deep inside her kept warning: *Be good and they'll love you.*

"Oh, sweetie, everyone says that," Grace replied lightly. "You'll love it once you're there."

"Please," Kamisha blurted out.

"It's all settled," Marcus said.

"But..."

Grace's face stiffened. She looked at her daughter sharply. "We thought this would delight you."

For a long moment Kamisha met her mother's hard gaze. Finally she said, "I'm not hungry. May I be excused?"

"Of course," Grace said, taking her spoon back up. "Oh, Marcus, did I tell you that Larry is going to donate..."

Kamisha left the room quietly, but when she reached the stairs she took them by twos, flinging open her bedroom door, unable to stop herself from slamming it so hard that the dishes in the kitchen rattled.

Not another word had been spoken about the subject.

Now Kamisha rose from the bed in the New York hotel room and padded to the window, pulling aside the heavy drape. Still waiting. He was five minutes late, too. Once more she smoothed her hair and checked her appearance in the mirror. She really hated waiting. If she was going to be disappointed, better sooner than later.

The phone rang finally. "Miss Hammill?" a strange male voice asked.

"Yes."

"I'm John Leopardo's driver. I'm waiting in the lobby."

"I'll be right down. How will I know you?"

She heard a low, throaty chuckle. "You can't miss me. I'm big and black and bald."

Well. Kamisha smiled. She was looking forward to meeting this man. Big and black and bald. At least the driver had a sense of humor.

He was there, close to the bank of elevators, when she stepped out. A big-barreled black man, his head shaved and shiny with dampness. He wore a well-cut pair of white slacks and a pale blue polo shirt. She walked right up to him and held out her hand.

"Hello," she said. "I'm Kamisha Hammill. And you're Mr. Leopardo's driver." She gave him a conspiratorial smile. "Or am I mistaken?"

"No, ma'am. You got the right man here. I'm Inky." He grinned at her, his teeth white in his dark face. "Ready? John's in the car."

The car was a black stretch limo, its windows smoky so that she couldn't see inside. Inky held the door open for her, and she ducked in, sliding onto the soft leather seat.

John Leopardo sat in the shadows, his cane resting against the back seat next to him. "Hello again, Miss Hammill," he said quietly.

She smiled and nodded. He looked very much at home in the big car, unselfconscious, relaxed. He wore a tropical-weight double-breasted gray suit with fine white stripes and a pale blue dress shirt with white collar and cuffs. His tie was a subdued navy and gray and burgundy stripe. He'd shaved. He must have to shave twice a day, a man with a dark beard like his. He smelled very, very faintly of a pleasant after-shave lotion.

The long car pulled out into the traffic. It was quiet and dim and cool inside. The heat and hot asphalt smell, the traffic noises, honking horns and screeching tires, all receded to a discreet distance.

Kamisha noticed that John hadn't acknowledged her appearance the way a man would on a date. A woman expected those things even if dealing with a customer as cool as Mr. John Leopardo. Inky had given her a second glance, though, back in the hotel lobby. Polite but approving. For the life of her she couldn't figure John out.

"I hope you had a nice day," John was saying.

"Oh, it was fine. I did some shopping," Kamisha replied casually. "It was too hot to do much else."

"It must be much more pleasant in Aspen."

"It is." She hesitated. "But then you were just there, weren't you?"

"I got back to the city two days ago." He nodded. His hands rested on his knees, those strong hands. They were very still, very quiet, as if he carefully kept them in check, not wanting to waste them on insignificant gestures.

"I saw you in Rick's office, but you were busy so I didn't stop in. Funny, I haven't met you before now." She gave him her brightest smile.

"I'm not in Aspen very often. A day here, a day there. I make it a point not to interfere in the club's management. Rick is very efficient."

"He certainly is," Kamisha remarked dryly.

He finally looked right at her. "Do you have any complaints about Rick's handling of the club, Miss Hammill?"

"I hadn't until I found out about these parties. Rick *is* efficient. Fair, smart. A tough manager but fair. I didn't come to New York to bitch about my boss, if that's what you mean."

"I like to clear the air about such things."

"So do I."

"I admire honesty."

What an odd thing to say, Kamisha thought, as if he was trying to convince me of it. She didn't quite know how to answer him. She judged that he didn't want the "proper" response, the glib reply. He wanted the truth. He was waiting for her next move.

"Too much honesty can be painful," she said carefully. "It's strong medicine."

He smiled. "Yes, but it cures many ills."

The car was stopping. Inky opened Kamisha's door and helped her out. John got out on his side. Coming around the front of the limo to join her, he walked slowly, a little stiffly on one side but steadily enough. She wondered if he really needed the cane or if it was a prop, a habit like smoking a cigarette or holding a glass in your hand at a cocktail party. She wondered too much about John Leopardo.

He took her arm and guided her under the red awning that led to the door of the restaurant. They were somewhere uptown on the West Side. Kamisha wasn't sure exactly where. She hadn't even seen the name of the place, but it exuded taste and style in a carefully unpretentious manner. The gleaming heavy glass door, the fern in a polished brass pot, the red carpet, the dark wainscoting and damask-covered chairs, all spoke of distinction.

"I hope you like Italian food," John said.

"I like almost anything," she replied, "if it's good."

"Oh, this is good."

The interior was small and hushed. Cool and intimate. The tables were filled, waiters in white jackets moved unobtrusively, and the place smelled tantalizingly of wine and garlic and the ever-so-faint aroma of the fresh roses that graced each table. It was definitely a big-city restaurant, different from the more casual ones in Aspen.

As she'd expected, the maître d' knew John. He even called him by his first name.

"Franco," John said, "meet Kamisha Hammill from my Aspen club."

Franco bent over her hand. "Absolutely charmed, Miss Hammill. Welcome to our humble establishment."

Their table was in a private corner. Their waiter was middle-aged and solemn, a professional. He also called John by his first name, and Kamisha wondered if they were all related to John somehow—family. Yet they weren't too familiar; they treated John with utmost respect.

"This is a beautiful restaurant," she said. "Do you come here often?"

"Yes. My cousin owns it. But the reason I come here a lot is the food." He folded his hands on the white tablecloth. "Would you like a drink?"

"A glass of wine, that's all."

A bottle, frosted and perspiring, appeared on cue, a slightly effervescent white Italian wine.

The waiter poured their glasses full and stepped back. John raised his in a toast. "To the Ute City Club, Miss Hammill."

Her eyes had never left his during the ritual. She touched his glass with hers and sipped. "Will you please call me Kamisha? I'm not used to being so formal."

"All right, Kamisha. And you're to call me John."

They were supplied with menus. She read the delectable-sounding dishes but didn't register what she was reading. She kept glancing up surreptitiously, expecting to find his gaze on her. But he seemed truly engrossed in the menu. It irritated her. She was used to male attention. She knew it would sound disgustingly vain if she tried to explain it, but Brigitte understood why Kamisha craved attention. Too bad she wasn't there to explain.

Kamisha sighed inwardly. Why couldn't she get a handle on him? Finally she cocked her head and cleared her throat. She lowered the menu. "I'm curious," she began.

"About what?"

"I hope you don't think I'm being presumptuous, but I'm very curious about Inky, your driver. He isn't the usual sort..."

John gave a short laugh, the first time she'd seen him do more than smile faintly. "Inky. He's more than a driver, as you probably noticed. He's a friend. He also saved my life in the war. So he feels he's responsible for me for the rest of my life.''

''The war?''

''Vietnam.''

''Oh, you were in Vietnam. Somehow I didn't think—''

''I took a semester off college and got drafted. My timing was lousy.''

Things began to fall into place in Kamisha's head. No wonder she got that feeling that there was something between the two men, some closeness that went far beyond employer-employee.

Their waiter hovered expectantly.

''I really can't decide. Please order something for me,'' Kamisha said. ''Something with seafood and a big salad. I trust your judgment.'' He hadn't brought up the subject of the club or Rick, the subject that lay between them like a shared secret. She wouldn't, either; the ball was in John's court.

He ordered. Caesar salad, pasta with seafood sauce for her, some kind of veal for him.

She played with the stem of her glass, twirling it. ''The war. I'm still curious.''

''It was a long time ago.''

''Your leg . . . ?''

''Yes, in Nam. My knee got shot up pretty badly. But they patched me up.''

''Um.'' He seemed completely unselfconscious about it. An interesting man. It occurred to Kamisha that she'd like to see him laugh, really laugh, in free, unconstrained mirth. She wondered if he ever did. She sipped her wine and studied his face, his strong neck, the way his hair was graying slightly at the temples.

She assessed him with the eye of a trained athlete. He was solid, his muscles well toned. You could always tell, even when a person was dressed. It was in the way he carried himself, in the way he moved. He must take care of his body. She wondered if he worked out at the Ute City Club when he was in Aspen. But she was sure she'd have seen him there if he did. She pictured him in shorts and a weight-lifting singlet, pumping iron, sweat-slicked, groaning with effort as the men did at the club. Yes, she could see him....

"Was your flight on time?" he was asking. "I know the Aspen airport gets backed up at times."

"Oh, I drove to Denver. I always do. I like driving, and in the summer it's almost as quick as flying. I have a car I really enjoy, too."

"A fast one?" he asked, smiling.

"Of course. A red Saab convertible. It's my one indulgence."

He watched her gravely for a moment, as if weighing her remark. "Your skiing," he said then. "I remember reading about you. The downhill, wasn't it?"

"Yes."

"Do you still ski?"

"Oh, yes, I love it. I think I enjoy it more now than when I was in training."

"I used to ski. A little. Before my leg."

She listened carefully. There wasn't one iota of self-pity or even wistfulness in his voice. He was merely stating a fact. She was determined to draw him out, to put him in a category with which she could deal. "Did you ever ski in Aspen?"

"No, here in the East. I wasn't very good." He looked at her. "I've seen downhillers on TV. You must like speed."

She grinned at him. "I'm crazy about speed. Cars, horses, skiing—whatever."

And then she waited for him to show curiosity about her remarks, the "whatever." Surely he got it, the mild reference to her fast approach to life, to relationships. But her meaning seemed lost on him.

"So," he was saying, "were you ever afraid when you were skiing?"

Kamisha felt a sigh of disappointment settle in her stomach. She shrugged. "Your body is ready when you're competing. You're nervous, but that's only the pressure of how well you'll do. You can't be afraid, not really, or you won't ski well enough."

"Did your parents like you racing? Weren't they worried about you?" he asked.

She shut down the quick, bitter remark that flew to her lips. "They were proud of me. I suppose they were worried," she said, lying and realizing that it was John who was drawing *her* out.

"How fortunate for you that they gave you the freedom to do what you wanted."

Freedom. That's the one thing the Hammills had given their daughter, but freedom without guidance or love became as much of a prison as overprotection. "Yes, I was lucky," she said.

"You must have worked at it."

"Oh, I worked, all right." She hesitated for a moment. "I deserved that Silver Medal, you know."

"I never had a moment's doubt about that." He regarded her for a moment, then asked, "I'm interested in your name. It's unusual."

She gave him a quick, wry smile. "Oh, it was one of my mother's fads—Indian art. She had the house full of it. One of her favorite potters was named Kamisha. So she named me after her."

"I see, Indian."

"Navaho, to be exact."

"It's a very lovely name."

"Thank you." If she were younger, less practiced, she'd be squirming in her seat, blushing. She wondered how he'd elicited such a girlish response in her. Odd. "John," she finally said, and realized it was the first time she'd said his name aloud. It rolled off her tongue with ease. "We're talking about me too much. Tell me about yourself. Are you from New York originally?"

"Brooklyn," he said shortly.

The food came. It was marvelous. She ate with relish. They talked, drank the alluring, effervescent wine of Italy. He smiled more often, and it changed his appearance so completely that she couldn't believe he was the same man. It was as if he wore the ancient Greek masks—first the mask of comedy, then switched to the mask of tragedy.

He'd been born in Brooklyn. His parents were still there. Yes, he had family in the area, one married sister, cousins, aunts, uncles. Whether or not he was single was never mentioned, but somehow she guessed he was. And still he never spoke of the club or Rick or why Kamisha was in New York.

"That was wonderful," Kamisha said, laying her fork down.

"Dessert?"

"God, no."

"Espresso?"

"I'd love some."

The meal was wending its way to a conclusion. He'd see her into his limo soon, drop her off at her hotel and that would be that. She'd fly to Colorado tomorrow and know little more than she'd known about John before coming to New York. She hadn't an inkling whether or not he'd lied to her about Rick. She hadn't any idea who he really was or what he was thinking. She felt awash with disappointment, left hanging in midair. She didn't even know what he thought about *her*.

There was the matter of her job, too. She needed that job. She loved her work. Her small trust fund from her grandparents certainly couldn't support her. What would she do if suddenly she was out on the street? He'd said he'd take care of things. But how? And when?

She'd ask him straight out. Not right now. Later, in the limo. She'd just ask him what he was going to do.

"I'll give you a choice," he said over the espresso. "I need to provide my leg with a little exercise after dinner. It gets stiff. I was going to go for a walk. It should be cooler out now. If you'd care to walk with me . . . Or I can drop you at your hotel."

Her spirits seemed to lift miraculously. She wanted the evening to go on and on. She wanted to discover more about the mystery that was John Leopardo. She wanted to know why he drew her and challenged her. "I'd love to go for a walk."

Inky followed them, above on the street, slowly inching the big car along as they walked a path down along the East River. It was a sultry evening, slightly overcast. Trees grew out of the concrete, and occasional birds chirped in the greenery. A few people jogged, slick with sweat, or walked their dogs along the pavement.

John moved slowly, stiffly at first. Then his leg must have loosened up, because his pace increased. Kamisha could feel the hot, damp air on her bare shoulders and the whisper of the fabric against her skin. Her hair clung damply to her neck, and she raised a hand to lift its heaviness for a moment.

The river moved slowly below them, brown and turgid, and lights reflected from it like thousands of eyes.

"Um, this feels good," she said.

"I come here often."

"Do you walk a lot?" she asked.

"It's good for me, the doctors say. One of the things I can do."

"You know, we have the best sports medicine clinic in the country right in the Ute City Club," she began.

He cut her off. "You're a walking advertisement, Kamisha. Believe me, I've been there. I've been everywhere. What you see before you is the best you're going to see."

"I didn't mean to—"

"You should get together with my mother. I'm sure the two of you could come up with a list of doctors for me to see," he said. But he wasn't angry, not at all. Obviously he found her suggestion, like his mother's, amusing, perhaps even a bit endearing.

He took off his suit coat then, shrugged out of it, and carried it over his shoulder, hooked on a finger. He loosened his collar button and tie. Dark curling hairs showed at the open V at his neck. Kamisha could see the tiny peaks of his nipples where the fine cotton of his blue shirt clung to his skin.

She felt utterly content walking with this man along the river in the heart of the hot, throbbing city. Utterly safe and at peace. Beside the very river that Rick had threatened John Leopardo would toss her into, attached to cement shoes. It was an ironic concept.

"Something funny?" he asked.

"Oh, no, just having a nice time," she replied.

Was John capable of killing her if she thwarted his plans? Was he showing her a preview of her own fate? She closed her eyes and let the warm, heavy air slide across her skin. She didn't care.

She was going to ask him what he planned on doing about Simons, but the time wasn't right. The spell was too powerful, too pleasant, to be broken.

He left her at the hotel late. Getting out of the long black car, he walked her to the lobby, stood in the too-bright light with her and touched her hand gently. "I enjoyed this evening, Kamisha. Very much."

"So did I. I'm glad you asked me."

He leaned on his cane, shifting his weight. "And don't worry about the club. I'll take care of it."

He'd brought it up himself, his timing perfect, relieving her of the responsibility. *I'll take care of it.* He would, too. She believed that. Just then she'd believe anything he told her.

"Thank you" was all she said.

"What time is your flight tomorrow?" he asked her then.

"Noon."

"Good. You have time for breakfast. Will you be my guest?"

"If I'm not interrupting your work."

"Not at all. I'll expect you at my apartment then. Eight o'clock. Is that all right?"

"Fine." At his apartment?

"Inky will pick you up. Say a quarter of eight."

It was happening too fast, and yet she knew she had to follow through on this new adventure, this new risk, this unique thrill. "I'm looking forward to it," she said.

"Good night."

"Good night, and thank you again."

It was as if neither of them wanted to end it, to finish the play. The curtain was about to fall, but the players were still on stage, following a script of their own.

"I'd better get this elevator," she said, gesturing.

"Yes. Sleep well."

She smiled as she stepped inside. The doors whispered shut on his face, and she thought it had looked a little sad, a little lonely.

But that, of course, was only her imagination.

CHAPTER FIVE

"MISS HAMMILL," the doorman said, "yes, you're expected."

For the first time that Kamisha could remember she felt out of her element. In Aspen everything was studiously casual. There were no doormen, few lobbies, fewer elevators. She absolutely never went to a man's home for breakfast. If she had an early appointment, they'd meet somewhere for breakfast—usually at the club. While she waited for the elevator doors to open, she glanced around the lobby, cool air from the central system washing over her.

There were two wingback chairs covered in gold lamé tapestry against a wall that was done in textured paper. Between them was a carved Chinese table and a large, ornate mirror. The floor was dark-veined marble, and a single potted plant stood beside one of the chairs. An old building, small and exclusive. She wondered if John Leopardo's apartment mirrored the lobby—impersonal, dim and hushed.

He opened the door himself. She hadn't quite known what to expect. A maid? A butler?

"Good morning," he said.

"Hello." Kamisha stepped inside past him. Her initial impression of John's apartment was one of spaciousness and light, with plenty of open floor space. Instantly she noted that there wasn't a plant to be seen or a thing out of place. Everything was lines and angles and spareness. The creature comforts were all present, but there was a distinct impersonal feel to the room.

Her discomfort increased. It was a mistake to have come here. Yet John seemed unaffected by her presence. Like the large area she stood in, the inanimate furnishings that greeted her eye, he gave off no feelings whatsoever. Unaccountably his self-control made Kamisha want to break his perfect shell to see what lay inside. And another thought made her heart knock against her ribs: she couldn't have been the first woman he'd invited there. John Leopardo surely had something in mind other than breakfast.

She put her purse on a chair, took a breath and felt as if she were in the starting gate, ready for a race, an important one. A sense of exhilaration filled her, quickly replacing her discomfort. Last night had been foreplay. This morning he'd proposition her. She wondered what he'd do when she turned him down cold.

"Orange juice, coffee?" he asked, nodding toward the kitchen.

"Juice, please." Idly she moved around the corner apartment. It was indeed sweeping, though that impression came more from the sparseness of furnishings rather than the square footage. The living room was ultramodern, a few pieces upholstered in shades of gray. There were carefully placed pillows on a steel-gray sectional. There was a cushioned chair on a stainless-steel frame, a pale blue-gray carpet on the floor. The walls were hung with architects' renderings of his holdings. She spotted the Ute City Club.

On the other side of the room was a long glass-topped table, four modern stainless-steel chairs around it—the dining area. But the table was covered with blueprints of some sort.

She wondered for a moment where they would eat, but then she noticed a patio beyond open sliding glass doors. There was a table set for two on it.

"They tell me it's freshly squeezed," John said, returning, "but I wonder."

"It looks fine, thank you."

He glanced at his watch, and she studied him over the rim of her glass. Yes, it was as if any emotion in John were like light from a black hole in space—it couldn't escape its source.

"The cook was due ten minutes ago," John stated with annoyance. "But I'm sure you have plenty of time to catch your flight."

"Lots of time." Kamisha followed him across the room toward the patio. He walked slowly—the cane. "You have a cook all the time?"

"No. She cleans twice a week and leaves a few things in the refrigerator. I'm a poor hand in the kitchen."

"Don't you eat out often?"

"I did last night."

"What about business luncheons and dinners?"

"I avoid them."

The patio, though narrow, ran the length of the apartment. From the rail Kamisha was afforded a spectacular view of both Central Park and the jumble of tall buildings that climbed skyward in Uptown Manhattan. Car horns blasting and an occasional siren could be heard below on the busy streets.

"Exciting," she said, aware of his nearness at her side. Maybe now he'd take the glass out of her hand, set it down and turn to her. She felt a tight knot form in her stomach. Perhaps she'd let his lips brush hers for a moment before she moved away. Perhaps . . .

"Ah," he was saying, "there's Gwen now. Would an omelet be all right? If you don't like eggs . . ."

"No. It sounds fine."

"I'll be back in a minute. Make yourself at home."

Kamisha smiled at the skyline. Yes, he'd have made his move if "Gwen" hadn't arrived. She was certain of it.

She turned and leaned her back against the rail. It was already warm out. Hot compared to the mountain climate she was used to. She could feel a thin layer of perspiration form on her upper lip, and her white linen suit felt damp and clinging next to her skin. John was standing inside, speaking to the maid—another woman pushing sixty, she noted. Kamisha watched him carefully, tilting her head slightly. He was wearing pearl-gray summer-weight slacks and a pink dress shirt rolled up once at the cuffs. His skin seemed pale next to the pink. City pale. His black hair, graying at the temples, was combed back, as if still damp from a shower. He smiled then, evidently at something Gwen had said, and Kamisha decided he was really quite handsome. A strong Mediterranean profile, strong jawline and teeth. Hooded black eyes. Eyes that told a person nothing.

She wondered again if he was really a member of the Mob. Oh, he denied it. But he would. She wondered if he was amused by her accusations or planning to have her silenced. Maybe he'd offer her hush money. Her thoughts were titillating, stirring her blood. She felt a single bead of perspiration roll down slowly between her breasts.

"I imagine," he said, stepping back outside, his cane in his right hand, "this is probably too hot out here for you. I could clear the table inside."

Kamisha smiled, pushing her hair behind her ears. "It *is* hot. And I'll help you with the table."

The blueprints spread out on the glass were of his latest venture. He began to roll them up. "Costa Rica," he told her. "The club is on the Pacific Coast. It opened a month ago, but the west wing still isn't completed." He was leaning over the table, reaching to point out the incomplete wing, his shoulders pressing against the pink fabric of his shirt. He had a good body, Kamisha thought once again, strong-looking despite the wounded leg. Her eyes traveled to his slacks, the nicely rounded buttocks, the firm thighs.

"It's one of the few peaceful countries in Central America," he was saying. "It's called little Switzerland. Has a neutral standing at the United Nations."

"I've never been there," Kamisha said, looking away, "but I hear it's lovely."

"You'd like it," he said as if he, alone, knew what she liked. "It's all mountains. Your kind of country."

"But no skiing."

"Definitely no skiing."

"Nice beaches?"

"Beautiful. Miles and miles of them in spectacular coves."

"Um, sounds lovely."

"It is."

Gwen served breakfast, then disappeared into the bedroom, probably changing sheets, gathering towels. Kamisha wondered if John had forgotten about the maid being there. She felt certain he'd invited her up for reasons other than breakfast. He must have. But why, then, hadn't he planned better?

He was nodding toward one of the preliminary sketches of a club on the wall behind them. "That one's in Amalfi, Italy."

"I've skied Italy, raced there. But I've never been to that coast."

"Ah, then you've missed a unique part of the country."

Kamisha put down her fork and dabbed at her mouth with the napkin. "You're very proud of your clubs."

"Yes, I am." His penetrating gaze held hers for a long moment over the rim of his coffee cup. The knot in her stomach grew to the size of a fist.

"How many clubs are there?" she asked, looking away, watching as the maid took a bundle of laundry and, keys in hand, left the apartment.

"Four," he replied. "The first one I built is in Miami. Coral Gables, actually. Then there's Amalfi and, of course, the club in Aspen."

"And now Costa Rica."

"Yes."

She wondered, while the conversation lingered on his accomplishments, if he was trying to convince her of his legitimacy despite his family's reputation. Perhaps. Or maybe he was simply making polite conversation. And she wondered, too, if he'd been married and divorced. Did he have children? There were no photographs anywhere that she could see. Perhaps by his bedside.

There was a lot about John, she realized, that stirred her curiosity. Too much.

"And you're from Los Angeles," he was saying, sitting back in his chair now, his fingers steepled beneath his chin as his eyes pinioned her.

"Yes. My parents still live there, in fact."

"You see much of them?"

Casually Kamisha shook her head. "We're all so busy. You know how it is."

"Um," he said.

She realized then that they'd been talking steadily since her arrival, but neither one of them had actually given a thing away. The conversation had stayed purposely on the surface of their lives. Remarkable. And she wondered just what had made John Leopardo as closed and wary as she was.

"Would you like more coffee?"

Kamisha shook her head again. He'd make his move now, she thought. The maid was off doing the laundry. Kamisha had to leave for the airport soon. He'd *have* to make his play now, or there would be no time. She felt smug with the knowledge.

She *wanted* him to lean across the table, to take her golden-brown hand in his strong, pale one. She wanted him to try to lead her through that half-closed bedroom door. This man might be the one she'd respond to. It was an intimidating realization.

"Are you sure you wouldn't like some more . . . ?"

"No, no, I'm fine," Kamisha said, breathless. And abruptly she was on her feet. "It's hot, isn't it? Maybe some air."

"Of course."

But the air outside seemed too filled with smoke and car exhaust, too hot, too close. She took a white stretch band from her pocket and pulled her hair back, fastening it with the elastic. All the while she was acutely aware of John's eyes on her, black and expressionless. Her skin felt supersensitive, tingly, too warm.

"Do you like the city?" he was asking.

"Yes. It's exciting. The shopping, all the people, the theater."

"But you chose the mountains."

"Yes, or rather the mountains chose me. Actually, I was born in Texas, but my parents took me all over skiing. And then we moved to L.A."

"I know."

Kamisha raised a dark brow.

A thin smile split his lips for a moment. "All of my employees," he said, matter-of-factly, "have a file, Kamisha. I like to know who's working for me."

"And what's in *my* file, John?" she asked coolly, challenging him.

He studied her for a time. "I'm afraid that's confidential."

"Oh, really?"

"Yes."

"I'd say it's more like secretive."

"What do you mean?"

"Like in the movies," she dared. "You know."

"No, I don't."

"The way big organizations ... big *families* handle their affairs."

An ironic grin twisted his mouth. "I see," he said.

Casually her heart racing, she said, "Yes."

And abruptly the amusement left his face. "I told you, that's my father, Kamisha, not me."

"Then why the file?"

"I'm a careful man."

"Oh, really," she ventured. "How about Rick Simons, then?"

"I'm human. I'm capable of mistakes. It has yet to be proven, though."

"But I told you ..."

"Yes, you did. I'm sure you believe that young girl, too."

"But you don't."

"Kamisha," he said, taking a step toward her, "I'll handle it. It's my affair."

"Of course." She could feel the rail against her back. There was nowhere to go.

"You'll have to trust me in this," he began, but then she could hear the front door open and close. Through the glass she could see Inky inside. An immense sigh of relief welled in her breast.

John, too, must have been aware of the interruption, but for an agonizingly long minute he stood his ground, too close, an emotion in his eyes now, but she couldn't read it. Finally he smiled and said, "Inky will drive you to the airport."

"I can get a cab."

"I insist." He reached out and took her elbow tentatively, as if he knew she was poised for flight. He steered her inside. "You're to mail me your tickets, too, and your hotel bill. This trip shouldn't have been at your expense."

"You don't have to..."

"But I do." And his tone left no room for argument.

Inky was checking his watch when Kamisha picked up her purse. "We better get rolling, Miss Hammill," he said. "Traffic's bad."

"Well," Kamisha said, turning to John and placing a smile on her lips, "I want to thank you for all the hospitality. You've been very kind."

"My pleasure," he said. He was standing in the center of the room, one hand in his trouser pocket, the other gripping his cane. She was struck by the aura of silent command in him, his strength and self-confidence. And then she saw Inky exchange a glance with him, a rather amused glance. She wondered about that as John opened the apartment door and they walked to the elevator. She wondered if Inky thought more had gone on back there than breakfast.

Kamisha was still tense, surrounded by two very compelling men. Men whose experiences together, whose obvious closeness, set her apart. There was too much understood between them, too much silence that seemed filled to bursting. She wasn't used to this, and she was wary of it.

John walked her to the car, giving the doorman a friendly nod. No, she wasn't used to any of this, to being acutely on guard, to being taken care of so lavishly. She wasn't certain she liked it.

John opened the car door for her and helped her in. "Have a safe trip. And, as I promised, don't worry about the club. I'll see to it."

"All right," Kamisha replied, wanting to believe him, needing to. "And thank you again."

The door closed with a solid chunk. She realized abruptly that she was feeling cut off, a tie was being severed. The notion left her at a loss and, as Inky pulled away from the curb, she automatically turned in her seat and watched John through the smoked glass. He was still standing there, favoring his leg, unmoving, his eyes following the limo until it rounded the corner and disappeared into the heavy flow of Manhattan traffic.

Kamisha sighed and turned back to face the front. What did John Leopardo really want from her? Why all the gentle treatment if he didn't expect something in return?

"Inky," she said, leaning forward, the leather cool beneath her, "you've known John for a long time, haven't you?"

"Yes, Miss Hammill, I sure have."

"Tell me, what's he really like? I mean, has he ever been married? Does he have children?"

But all she got in return was: "You better be asking him that yourself, ma'am." His coal-black eyes met hers in the mirror for a moment, then switched back to the street.

GETTING ON A PLANE for the return flight to Denver was like stepping out of Alice's Wonderland back into dreary reality. Colors faded, sounds became irritating, people were strident and ugly. Kamisha felt claustrophobic on the plane with its stale air and monotonous droning, closed in and unable to think.

Images kept flashing through her mind's eye: inescapable, pervasive thoughts chased one another through her head.

John, of course. Darkly handsome, a man of presence. There was a superb power to him, not to be denied or ignored, a carriage that defied any other authority. And yet he'd used her gently, with old-world courtesy, and not asked a thing of her.

What did he want? In Kamisha's experience people exploited her. Her parents had used her as an extension of their pride, a prop to their egos, another valuable belonging. Her ski coach had used her for his ego, too. Rick Simons used her, as he'd so bluntly pointed out, to look good and not think too much. Everyone had repeated this pattern all her life, taken advantage of her appearance, which was only an accident of genetics, and her athletic prowess, which was due also to her inheritance and her own hard work.

No one had ever looked beyond those attributes. Not her ex-husband Josh, not anybody, ever.

Except maybe John Leopardo. What did he want of her? She'd thought he was going to try to buy her off, but he hadn't even attempted to. She'd thought he was interested sexually. She hadn't been mistaken, either. Or had she? He'd made no move, spoken no word, ventured no suggestive touch. And yet . . . what other relationship could a woman have with a man? What did he want—mere friendship? Inconceivable.

The question puzzled her, bothered her, kept her restless and on edge. She couldn't read John, still didn't know if he was lying outright to her about the club. Maybe all his solemn courtesy was a sham, an act to put her off guard. Maybe he'd put out a contract on her as Rick had intimated. Cement shoes. How ludicrous. No doubt he'd just fire her, and that would be that.

She leaned back in her seat and closed her eyes. She could see John's face, the dark shadow of his beard, the mole near the corner of his mouth. She could see his strong neck and shoulders and hands—his hand on the cane. John used his cane as a courtesan used her fan, to beguile, to hide, to reveal. To warn. She had a sudden uncontrollable desire to see his bad knee, to touch the puckered scars, to knead it. A hot flush rose up her neck at the thought.

She wondered who had come off best in her meetings with John. Dinner last night—she'd say they'd been even. Breakfast. Well, perhaps she'd shown her hand a touch too much. Maybe he'd seen something she preferred to keep hidden.

No, no one except Brigitte réally knew Kamisha.
Others used her, and she'd learned to protect herself by
using them back. Only Brigitte knew her down to her
guts—and even Brigitte used her as a rudder, an an-
chor, a life preserver in the storm of existence. Kamisha loved her friend like a sister, but she recognized
Brigitte's needs and knew she was one of them. And
Brigitte was one of her needs, too, the only human being in the world with whom she never had to pretend.

She sat there in the droning airplane, thinking, remembering, recalling all those years ago when she first
met Brigitte Stratford. They'd both been fourteen years
old, freshmen at the exclusive Taos School in the
mountains of New Mexico.

She'd begun high school with a chip on her shoulder. The girls came in from everywhere in the country,
laughing, renewing friendships, moaning over Mom-
my's new husband or Daddy's chapter eleven, the drugs
they'd tried, the beaches they'd been to, the boys they'd
devastated. Kamisha had viewed them with disdain;
their problems seemed utterly inconsequential, their
experiences trite. She'd moved in a day early and waited
for the other bed in her room to be taken. The headmistress's list said that her roommate was Brigitte
Stratford, a new girl. Kamisha hoped Brigitte would be
quiet and pimply and leave her alone.

Brigitte wasn't quiet or pimply.

She waltzed in a minute after curfew the night before
classes started. A small, brown-haired, innocent-
looking girl, slight and pretty, wearing a man's sweatshirt that read Harvard, jeans with holes in the knees
and lugging an enormous suitcase.

"Goddamn!" she announced instantly, dragging her
case in. "I had to hitch a ride. Missed the last bus."

Then she grinned, and her face lit up with an inner glow of devilry and mischief and unholy glee. "But it was more fun that way." Then the girl held out her small hand, laughing, her head cocked prettily to one side like a bird. "I'm Brigitte and I'm going to be an actress. Who're you?"

Within three days they were inseparable. It was a revelation to Kamisha, who'd never had a really close friend. For the first time she felt accepted for herself. Brigitte was her alter ego, lonely too, abandoned by her rich society mother and her ambitious father in Hollywood, achingly insecure. Their dissimilarities were vast but unimportant. They were like differently shaped magnets with cores that cleaved one to the other.

One Saturday night in November Kamisha and Brigitte managed double dates. The four of them ate fiery Mexican food, drank a six-pack Brigitte's date Pete had stolen from home and got giggly together. At a quarter to eleven Kamisha reminded them all the curfew was in fifteen minutes.

Pete raised his head from the front seat where he was necking with Brigitte. "Bobby, take Kamisha back. Here are the keys. Brigitte and I are gonna sneak into my basement."

"God, Brigitte, are you nuts?" Kamisha asked.

"No, just in lust," came her friend's muffled voice from the front seat.

At four in the morning Kamisha was awakened by a windowpane smashing into the room. Groggily she got up to see Brigitte standing below the second-floor window, ready to throw another fist-size rock. "Oops," she giggled, weaving in the darkness. "I threw it too hard. Toss down a sheet or something, roomie."

"Shh!"

Brigitte snickered again, staggered and put her hand over her mouth. "Come on," she whispered loudly. "I gotta get in!"

Kamisha never understood how Brigitte managed to climb up the sheet. She was so drunk that she radiated waves of alcohol. She collapsed, panting and chortling, onto her bed. Then she sat up and tried to make her expression serious. "I have an announcement to make. I am no longer a virgin."

"Pete?" Kamisha gasped.

"I'm in love," Brigitte sighed dramatically, then sagged back and passed out.

Kamisha sank down onto the edge of her bed and put her head into her hands. Someone had to sign Brigitte in. *Everyone* had to sign in. It wasn't unheard of for an upperclassman to sneak in after curfew and sign herself in, but it was a risky undertaking.

Kamisha took a deep breath. She would have to do it. She put her bathrobe and slippers on and slipped out into the dark corridor. There was always the chance of the dorm mother prowling around at night, checking on the girls. What if she got caught? It meant grounding or expulsion or whatever the headmistress decided. Damn Brigitte!

Sneaking through the halls to the stairs, her heart pounding in her ears, stopping at every corner to listen. Silence. Blackness and silence.

The sign-in book was on a stand in the lobby. Quickly she scribbled Brigitte's name. If it didn't resemble her signature, Brigitte could say she was sick or something. Better sick than late.

So far so good. She glided away from the lobby. If she was caught now, it wasn't so bad. But what would she say? She was sleepwalking. That was it. She was a terrible sleepwalker. It happened, didn't it? She'd pretend to wake up and be confused.

Damn Brigitte!

Almost there. On her own corridor, passing the bathroom.

A flashlight beam caught her in midstride. "Miss Hammill? What's going on here?"

Uh-oh! It was Miss Donnelly, the dried-up old maid. "Oh, Miss Donnelly, I just had to go to the john."

"Very well, Miss Hammill. Next time please turn on the light."

"Yes, Miss Donnelly."

Brigitte finally appeared the next day at lunch, pale green and bleary-eyed. Kamisha was cold to her, torn between her anger and curiosity as to what it had been like for Brigitte to lose her virginity.

"Come on, roomie, what's the matter? I feel like a truck ran over me."

"Next time you pull that kind of stunt leave me out of it," Kamisha said. "I had to sign in for you."

Brigitte turned even paler. "Oh, God, oh, no! I'm sorry! I deserve it! You shouldn't have done it!"

"Well, I did it and saved your butt," Kamisha said, mollified. "But don't ever put me in that position again. I mean it, Brigitte. I hate being used. I hate it."

"I *thought* I went down there and did it myself. Or was that a dream? I swear, I was lying there in bed thinking I had to get up and go down there . . . I must have dreamed it."

"Now tell me, what was Pete like?"

Brigitte put her head in her hands. "I can barely remember. Did we do anything?"

"I wasn't there," Kamisha said dryly, "but last night you said you lost your virginity."

"I did? Oh, wow, I guess I did."

"What was it *like?*"

"Damned if I can remember," Brigitte groaned, holding her head.

Kamisha hadn't changed much since those days, not really. Neither had Brigitte. Despite their marriages, Brigitte's daughter, their divorces, their careers and fame, despite it all, they were both the same insecure teenagers inside—alone, except for each other. Kamisha was still trying to save Brigitte from herself, and Brigitte was as reckless as ever. But Kamisha needed her friend, because Brigitte was the only haven Kamisha had where she could just be herself.

The plane circled and descended over Denver. The mountains lined the horizon, dark and jagged, beckoning. Kamisha stared out the window at the familiar peaks and thought over and over again: everyone of any consequence in her life had wanted something from her. So, then, what was it that John Leopardo was after?

CHAPTER SIX

KAMISHA TURNED the key and the Saab roared to life. Two rows over in the outlying parking of Denver's Stapleton Airport, a man was getting a jump start from a service station truck. Boy, the Saab had been a good investment; it had yet to fail her.

She drove with the top down, her hair in a ponytail, sunglasses in place. There weren't too many warm months in the Rocky Mountains, months in which she could feel the wind in her hair and, whenever possible, Kamisha took advantage of the ideal weather.

It was a glorious summer day. As soon as she cleared the city on Interstate 70, the sky opened up, a spectacular pellucid blue bowl overhead, and the foothills of the Rockies jutted up out of the plains before her. It had been a great snow year, too, and the fourteen-thousand-foot peaks that formed the Continental Divide to the west of Denver were still splashed in white. The day was so perfect, so cloudless, that the thin Colorado air caused an illusion of nearness and the sharp delineation of sky and towering rock and pine forest. Kamisha downshifted, breathing in the thinning air as she climbed, and the red Saab responded with the perfection of a finely crafted machine, leaping to life, pulling out ahead of the line of interstate traffic on her right.

Georgetown, Idaho Springs, the quaint Victorian mining towns of the last century, flew by as Kamisha

ascended into the heart of the Rockies, up, up, passing
the slower cars and trucks as they pulled up the steep
hills, up toward the Divide, the ski area of Loveland
that stayed open often until June, up to the Eisen-
hower Tunnel that bored through the solid rock of the
Divide. The Saab whipped into the tunnel, and she
slowed to fifty miles per hour. No point getting a ticket.
As always, the exhaust trapped in the two-mile-long
tunnel smote her, but she could see the pinhole of daylight ahead. She breathed shallowly.

When Kamisha drove or skied or bicycled, she
thought of little else save perfection of movement. She
was a good driver, although Brigitte always hated to get
into the car with her. "Death Wish Three," Brigitte had
dubbed Kamisha's driving. But what did Brigitte know,
anyway? Kamisha smiled, her fingers light on the
leather-covered steering wheel.

The sunlight on the western slope of the Divide struck
her eyes, momentarily blinding Kamisha until she pulled
her sunglasses back down. She passed two flatbed
trucks crawling on her right, both hauling mammoth
pipes—probably for snowmaking equipment at a ski
area. All the trucks stopped at the far side of the tunnel
because the downhill grade was one of the steepest in
the country. There were two well-placed runaway ramps
on the descent, and it wasn't unusual to smell hot
rubber from the brakes of a descending behemoth or to
see a truck sitting halfway up one of those ramps, askew
in the deep, soft sand, brakes still smoking. It made a
body shiver.

The trucks were one matter, cars another. Generally
automobiles flew down the western slope, the driver
unused to the steep grade, not realizing his speed. In

front of Kamisha she could see a few cars in the outside lane, brake lights blinking on and off sporadically.

No, she usually never thought about much of anything except her driving, but that afternoon she found
herself wondering if she was going to get back to Aspen and find herself without a job. It was possible. Especially if she'd misjudged John Leopardo. And even
if she hadn't, Rick was eventually going to find out
about her trip to New York, and if John didn't fire him,
then working with Rick was going to be quite impossible. She guessed she couldn't complain too much
around Brigitte, though, because Brigitte had warned
her, hadn't she?

Darn that man ahead of her in the van! He wouldn't
move out of the passing lane. Kamisha tapped her
brakes while simultaneously touching the horn to let
him know she wanted to get past.

She put her foot on the brake again, pumping it
slightly, because the van hadn't gotten fully out of the
way yet. She had to pump the brakes yet again, and she
registered that they seemed low. She downshifted,
wondering about that as she sped past the van and gave
the driver a thank-you wave. She'd just had the car
serviced, for Pete's sake, and in the Rockies you always
had your brakes checked.

Two trucks on the right in a line, going as slow as
snails in very low gear, but there was another car out in
the left lane in Kamisha's path. Didn't he see her coming up fast?

She put on the brakes again. This time her foot was
halfway to the floor before they held. A surge of
adrenaline shot through her heart as she quickly downshifted and had to pump the brakes hard and fast.

The car ahead made it past the two trucks and, thank God, hurried into the right lane. By then Kamisha had put the Saab into third but was still flying. She tried the brakes and then swore. They were gone.

Oh, God. The last runaway ramp. Was it around this curve? Oh, God!

Kamisha's eyes flew to the dashboard. Sixty miles per hour. If she put the Saab in second gear, it would never hold at this speed. As if the brakes would magically work, she tried them again. Nothing. A loose pedal. Her eyes flew back to the road. Yes! There it was! The ramp! A cold sweat popped out on her back, and her hands gripped the steering wheel. Trucks and cars alike could easily flip when they hit that loose sand, especially at the speed she was going.

"Oh, God," Kamisha whispered, fighting for control. It was like seeing a new rut ahead on a downhilll race course and knowing you were just barely on the edge of control. Your blood pounded and you worked on adrenaline alone, that and every skill you could muster.

But this...

The Saab had gained speed. Sixty-five, sixty-seven. She had only one shot at that steep ramp and it better be good! Kamisha lined the car up, thanking the Lord that no one was blocking her path in the right lane. Carefully, skillfully, she let her car ease across the center line until she was heading straight for the ramp on a perfect line—one tug of the wheel when she hit that deep sand would be the end of her. The front tires crossed the asphalt shoulder, the back tires. She was doing seventy-two miles per hour. And then suddenly the two front tires hit the sand. The car seemed to lurch forward sickeningly while sinking at the same time. It pulled abruptly to the left, settled back down, lurched again while still climbing the steep, sandy track. And then slowly, slowly, it stopped. For an instant all was utterly, deathly still. Then the car slipped backward, one foot, two, and finally came to a reluctant rest. It was a full minute before Kamisha let out the breath she was holding.

"WHAT DO YOU MEAN, *no* fluid?" she asked the man at the service station in the resort of Dillon. She peeked up underneath the Saab where it sat on the hydraulic lift. "I just had the fluid—"

"Well," the mechanic said, "I'm just telling you how it is, lady. Whoever serviced this car really loused you up."

Kamisha frowned. Gary had serviced it at Auto Trek. Gary had been working on her cars since she'd first come to Aspen. He was the best in town, absolutely reliable.

The mechanic was scratching his head, wiping his brow with a grimy bandanna. "I tell you, though," he said, "can't see how your line got cut. It's a puzzlement, all right, lady."

But Kamisha knew. The sudden insight was like a light bulb being switched on in her head. John Leopardo. She felt her heart thump heavily once, then settle back down. "How long will it take to fix my car?" she asked calmly.

"Tomorrow afternoon. Maybe late morning."

"Then where can I rent one?"

He gestured with the dirty bandanna still in his hand. "Two blocks down is a Holiday Inn. I think they got a National Car Rental there. Maybe it's Hertz."

"And where's the police station?"

THE CHEVY AUTOMATIC had as much pep as a tortoise, Kamisha thought as she floored it, trying to hit forty miles an hour climbing Independence Pass on the way home. She clenched her jaw.

Yep. John had wined and dined her—a Last Supper, she thought bitterly. She even remembered a casual question he'd asked: "Do you always drive to Denver?"

Of course, she'd boasted to him then about her car, given him the description—how eagerly she'd fallen into his trap.

And how many cars fitting the description of hers—with Aspen's famous ZG license plates—were parked at Stapleton?

"Ha!" she said aloud, pulling out around a camper on a steep, narrow curve near the twelve-thousand-foot-plus summit.

Oh, yes, John Leopardo had tried to have her killed. There was no other possible explanation except for a crazy series of coincidences that simply couldn't have occurred in a trillion years.

"Oh, man, are *you* stupid," she muttered. "And blind." God, how he must have been laughing. That was why she hadn't been able to get a handle on him. Of course! That was why he'd behaved so differently from other men. How many other men had she dated who'd been planning to kill her? What a stupid, blind, naive idiot she was!

She drove down the inclines of Independence Pass, pushing the six cylinders of the Chevy to the limit through the series of straightaways and S curves that stretched along the lovely wide alpine meadows and the rushing Roaring Fork River. Then there was Aspen. It was late, but she headed directly to Brigitte's, bursting to tell her friend everything, to talk it all out. Despite Kamisha's self-reproach and anger, she knew she better come up with a plan—and quick. An SOB like Leopardo wasn't going to be stopped so easily.

"No, way" was Brigitte's initial reaction. "You've been watching too much TV."

Tiredly Kamisha propped her feet on the bar stool next to the one she was sitting on in Brigitte's kitchen. "I'm telling you what the mechanic said. And I saw it myself."

"God." Brigitte was wearing a bright red kimono, and she pulled the sash tighter around her small waist. She went to the fridge and began to poke around. "Want a white wine? I think I need one. Where's the darn bottle?"

"Are you listening to me?"

"Of course, I'm listening to you. I'd just like to talk this out over a drink, if that's okay with you."

It wasn't okay. But Kamisha knew Brigitte was going to search the refrigerator all night until she found the wine. "Listen," Kamisha said, rising, pulling the bottle of Chablis out from between a loaf of bread and a mayonnnaise jar, handing it to Brigitte, "I came over to sort this out in my head. But if you're going to get sloshed . . ."

"I am not going to get 'sloshed,' Kamisha. It's only a glass of wine, for God's sake. Cool it."

"Where's Tracy?" Kamisha asked, glancing into the darkened living room.

"Spent the night with a friend. They're going to a horse show early tomorrow, and you know how I hate all that banging around before noon."

"Still up at the crack of noon, are you?"

"You bet. Especially when Bullet's off on assignment. Here, you want a glass?"

"Okay, sure, why not?"

Finally Brigitte plumped herself down on a stool next to Kamisha. It was a huge two-story glass-and-stone house on Castle Creek, west of Aspen, but the gathering spot was still in the kitchen.

"You want my advice?" Brigitte asked, sipping, pushing her sleep-tousled brown hair behind an ear.

"That's why I'm here."

"Forget the whole thing. Tell Rick you made a mistake. Better yet, tell John Leopardo you were wrong. Apologize. That's what I'd do."

"Are you nuts?" Kamisha stared at her friend over the rim of her own glass.

"Look," Brigitte said, "you're the one who comes rushing in here at midnight to tell me someone tried to kill you. What do you want me to say? Tell you to confront this Leopardo again? You want I should hire you a bodyguard? You think I want to see you get yourself hurt?" Her voice had risen, growing shrill.

"Of course I don't. But when have I ever backed down from a challenge?"

"Oh, Lord."

"Come on, Brigitte, when?"

"Never, I guess."

"So forget the apologies. There must be a way to get that Mafia creep off my back."

"Sure," Brigitte sighed, draining her glass, pouring another as she dropped a new ice cube into the liquid, "I'm sure he'll back right down, shaking in his three-hundred-dollar shoes."

"I could go to the police."

Brigitte's eyes snapped up. "No," she said quickly. "God, he'll find out and really be after your hide. These kind of men aren't scared of the police. And what do you have on him, anyway?"

"Well...the parties, for one thing. I know I can't *prove* Leopardo had my brakes tampered with, but I could go after him through the parties, you know, get Carin McNaught to..."

"Forget it." Brigitte rose and paced the flagstone floor. Back and forth, one hand clutching her glass, the other on her hip. "No one's going to open up to the cops, Kamisha. No one. This is Mafia we're talking, kiddo, not a Sunday booster club gathering." She gestured in the air with her glass.

"You're some help."

"You bet I am! I'm telling you, apologize! Talk to them. Tell them you're sorry. I couldn't stand it if something happened to you." Her eyes, glassy now, bored into Kamisha's.

"Nothing's going to happen to me."

"Oh, right! You're tougher than the Sicilians. Great. Great thinking!"

"Will you settle down?"

"You've got me crazy, Kamisha. Isn't it enough that Bullet's gone half the time, and my daughter, God, my daughter's on my case about everything under the sun."

"What's wrong with Tracy?"

Brigitte put her hand on her forehead as if staving off a migraine. "Hormones."

"Is that all?"

"Of course it is."

"I think, maybe," Kamisha said tentatively, "she's worried about her mom."

Brigitte's reaction was to let out a string of oaths that would have impressed a sailor.

"Whoa," Kamisha said, shaking her head, "that was ladylike."

Another choice word from Brigitte. "Why am *I* always the problem around here?"

"You aren't," Kamisha said, walking on eggshells now. "It's just that we all love you so darn much and sometimes you—"

"Don't you start on me."

"Okay, I won't."

Finally Brigitte sagged against the counter across the room. "Hell. I need some sleep. I feel awful. But I won't sleep if I'm worried you're going to do something incredibly stupid."

"I'm not about to. The stupid thing was to trust that thug in New York."

Brigitte sighed. "That *was* odd of you."

"Yeah, well, I thought he was special. Different. He never even came on to me."

"That's a new twist."

"Isn't it? I was really on cloud nine there, too. He's something, all right."

"He's dangerous. You keep that in mind. Now let's hit the sack. You stay in the guest room, and in the morning—"

But Kamisha raised a hand. "No one's going to run my life for me, Brigitte. Especially not Mr. John Leopardo."

"Kami—"

"I mean it. I sleep in my own bed in my own home. Period."

"Swell."

"Yes, it is. I'll think of something. I'm tired now and not looking at this straight."

"Tired and mad."

"You bet I am."

"You won't go off half-cocked, will you? I mean, think about what I said, about talking to Rick and—"

"Okay, okay. I'll think it all out."

"Promise? And you won't let your temper make you do something dumb?"

"I promise. I'll cool off. I'll handle it."

"Good," Brigitte sighed, obviously relieved.

But it didn't quite work that way.

It was past one in the morning when Kamisha sat bolt upright in her bed and began to mumble to herself. "Oh, don't worry, Miss Hammill, I'll take care of everything. Right away." She frowned, punching a fist into her pillow. "Yeah, he took care of everything, didn't he? I wonder who he called in Denver to have my car worked on? I wonder how much it cost him? And some airport security! No wonder everyone complains!"

She tried a warm glass of milk, an aspirin. She tried watching an old Fred Astaire flick on a cable TV channel. But all she could do was pace and twist up her face and mutter to herself. What really rankled, too, was the fact that he'd totally taken her in. Oh, sure, she'd considered that he might have been lying to her in New York, but she really hadn't believed it.

What a slick character. Smooth as silk, so, so Continental, so suave, and that leg, the cane, the old war wound story! And what a prop Inky was! No wonder she'd let herself slip! He'd been too good to be true, hadn't he?

She dropped into the soft cushioned chair by her open bedroom window and rested her chin on her hands. A faint summer breeze stirred the lace curtains as she stared, unfocused, up at the night sky. A million brilliant pinpoints of light glittered above—a Rocky Mountain wonder. Tears of anger and frustration filled her eyes, blurring the spectacle. It wasn't fair. She didn't even care anymore that he'd tried to have her killed. Not really. It hurt too much to think that she'd actually liked him, been spellbound. If only she could break that hard, reserved shell of his and twist a knife into his guts just as he'd done to her.

Before Kamisha could rationalize her actions, she found herself reaching for the trimline phone by her bed. She dialed New York information. "Manhattan," she said, "Mr. John Leopardo on West Sixty-third Street."

Amazingly the operator had a listing. And then Kamisha sat there for a moment in the dark, the dial on the phone the only illumination in the room as she hesitated, holding the receiver in her hand. It was what time back East? Three-thirty in the morning? So what. He deserved everything she could throw at him. She began to dial: 1-212... Her fingers were shaky, her stomach knotted in anger.

The phone rang on the other end once, twice, three times. It occurred to Kamisha that she might be signing her death warrant, but her anger overcame all reason. She took a deep breath just as she would have in the starting gate at the beginning of a race. *Think.* If he answered, she'd better be darn clever.

"Hello?" Groggily, his voice deep and sleep-filled, hoarse. "Hello?"

Kamisha swallowed. She could see him lying in bed in her mind's eye—black silk pajama bottoms, no top—too hot. He'd be rubbing his eyes, his bristly jaw, coming to a sitting position...

"Mr. Leopardo," she said, careful not to use his given name, "this is Kamisha Hammill. Remember me?" It took all her effort to control her voice. It would never do to let the anger and the fear come through.

"Kamisha?"

"That's right. Are you surprised to hear from me?"

"Well, yes, to be honest. It's...ah, almost four in the morning here." His voice was losing its gravely pitch.

"That isn't what I meant," she said, then rose, pacing, the phone cord dragging behind her. "Didn't you think I was...dead?" Oh, God, she thought, what was she doing? Brigitte was right. She was playing a dangerous game with a lethal opponent.

"Kamisha," he said slowly, "I don't know what you're talking about."

"Oh, come on, John," she snapped, "we both know you tried to have me killed. I don't feel like playing this game with you."

There was a long pause on the line. "Let me get this straight. You think someone tried to kill you?"

Kamisha laughed bitterly. "I think *you* tried to have me killed."

He swore softly. She could almost hear his mattress creak as he came to his feet. She could see him switching on lights, rubbing that heavy growth on his jaw. "I want you to tell me what happened, *exactly*," he demanded.

"You already—"

"No. I don't. You've got to believe that. Now tell me."

She played along, amazed by his calm, by the fact that he thought her so gullible. "Now you tell *me*," she finished, "why I should think it was anyone *but* you."

"Damn," he said, temporarily losing that rigid control, "you should at least know that much about me,

Kamisha. I'm not a killer. I'm not dishonest. But you, lady, are in serious trouble.''

"No fooling."

"Listen, I'll try to forget this accusation. What I want you to do is this. I—"

"Come off it, John," she said, her anger welling up inside her again. "Brigitte knows what happened, and so does my lawyer," she said, lying. "If you pull another stunt like that, you'll never see the light of day again except through bars."

There was pulsing silence on the phone.

"You think I'm a dumb female, don't you? You're just like all the rest, *Mr.* Leopardo. But you've got my number all wrong. I know someone tampered with my brakes. It was no accident."

"Look," he said finally, his tone reasonable, though exasperation showed through, "I want you to go and stay with friends. You're not to be alone, Kamisha. I'm going to find out who's behind this. I swear it to you. But, meanwhile, don't do anything foolish."

"The foolish thing I did," she said, "was going to you in the first place."

"Kamisha, I—"

"Skip it, John. Just get off my back. I can play hardball, too."

Abruptly Kamisha slammed the receiver down. She dropped into the chair, let out a whistling breath between her teeth and then smiled shakily. Kamisha Hammill, a nobody, had just stuck it to Mafia king John Leopardo. An enormous feeling of satisfaction swept her. It was as if she'd just crossed the finish line a tenth of a second ahead of everyone.

CHAPTER SEVEN

KAMISHA ROLLED OVER, kicked the sheet off and promptly fell back into a deep sleep. And there it was again, the big, heavy black sedan, the kind you saw in thirties gangster movies. There was a faceless driver, and even as he steered with one hand, he leaned out the window and began blasting away at her with a Tommy gun. She was on foot. Running, running...

"Kamisha. Kamisha, wake up. You're having a bad dream."

Kamisha jerked awake, gasping, trying to run. But it was only Brigitte in her bedroom, shaking her. "My God," Brigitte was saying, "you're soaked with sweat. Are you okay?"

"Oh, Brigitte," Kamisha said, half gasping, "that dream. Oh, my Lord."

"Nightmare, huh?"

"Oh, a whopper. Oh, brother." She felt her head. It was drenched. And her pajamas, too. She looked down at herself as if someone else were in her body.

"I knocked and knocked," Brigitte was explaining, "so I used the spare key out front. God, I was worried."

"*You* were worried."

"Yeah, well, it isn't every day my friend tells me someone's trying to kill her." Brigitte got up off the side of the bed and straightened her skirt. "I'll go make

some coffee and you get showered. We'll go to breakfast. Okay?''

"Yeah, sure, okay." She came to her feet a little un-
steadily. "What time is it?"

"You'll kill me," Brigitte called over her shoulder,
"but it's seven-thirty. I couldn't sleep so well after you
left."

Kamisha sat back down. Brigitte, up at this hour?
Something must really be bothering her. Then, as if to
punctuate the early-morning hour, a persistent bird, a
flicker, was calling from one of the tall cottonwood trees
in the front yard, a raucous call, repeated over and over
until, with a rustle of leaves and a flutter of feathers, it
flew away.

It was Sunday. Sunday morning, Kamisha thought.
A glorious-looking day. Cool out. Absolutely clear. She
could smell newly mown grass somewhere, and more
birds were calling from trees across the street. Well, she
wasn't going to waste such a precious day worrying
about John Leopardo and what he might or might not
do. The summers were too short at eight thousand feet,
rare and doubly priceless because of their brevity. Winter was brilliant and starkly beautiful, spring was a long
time in making up its mind to behave decently, autumn
was lovely and golden, but summer was perfection.

There were a dozen things she could do that day. She
could play tennis or hike to Crater Lake. She could
drive down the valley and ride a horse at a friend's
ranch, or go to the music tent and listen to the Aspen
Festival Orchestra dress rehearsal for its Sunday con-
cert. Aspen was full of things to do.

But Kamisha lingered on the side of her bed, thinking. Maybe it wasn't such a great idea to go off by her-

self. Maybe John Leopardo had new plans for her now
that the old ones had failed.

"Are you in the shower yet?"

Kamisha shook herself. "Just climbing in!" Yes, he
might well be formulating something at this very minute. On the other hand, she thought as she slid out of
her damp pajamas and tossed them into the wicker
hamper, he might have been telling her the truth last
night. She hadn't considered that. She'd been too strung
out, too angry. But what if he hadn't been responsible
for her accident? What if he was really checking into the
incident, truly concerned about her? He'd sounded
worried. Or had she just been hearing what she wanted
to hear?

When she was dressed, Brigitte shoved a coffee mug
into her hand. "You've got circles under your eyes, my
dear."

"Yeah? So do you."

"Um."

"Where do you want to eat? I'm famished."

"Oh, I don't know. The Wienerstube or the Main
Street Café or something." Brigitte draped herself on a
kitchen chair. "Say, what were you dreaming about up
there? You were a mess."

Kamisha took a swallow of her coffee. "A Mafia hit.
On *me*."

Brigitte paled. "Don't say that. Seriously."

"And that's not all." Kamisha hesitated. But what
the heck. She'd end up telling Brigitte eventually, anyway. "I called John in New York last night."

"No way...you didn't."

"I did. I had to. I couldn't help it, Brigitte." She began to pace back and forth in her small kitchen. "He

had to know, darn it. I wasn't about to let him think
he'd gotten away with trying to kill me!''

"Kamisha." Brigitte ran a hand over her face. She
was really upset. "Do you realize what you're doing?
You're flying off half-cocked, accusing a man of murder. This is serious. This is no game."

"I know that."

"Look, you don't even know for sure it wasn't an
accident. You don't know who did it if it *was* deliberate. You're guessing. You haven't a thing to go on."

"It was no accident, Brigitte."

"You can't prove that. You can't even prove somebody meant to hurt you. Maybe they tampered with the
wrong car. You don't *know* anything!"

Kamisha stopped and stared at her friend. "You
sound like you're trying to defend Leopardo, for God's
sake, Brigitte."

"I'm not!" she cried, agitated. "I've never laid eyes
on the guy. I'm just trying to convince you how crazy
you sound. You're paranoid!"

"Oh, no, I'm not. I upset the applecart, and somebody wants me out of the way. I told you what Simons
said. Cement shoes in the East River!"

Brigitte put her head in her hands. "You're blowing
this up into something it isn't. Leave it alone. If John
Leopardo is involved in these parties, he'll fire you,
that's all. Stop being so dramatic. God! You're ad-
dicted to trouble. You love it."

"*I* didn't hold those parties, Brigitte. *I* didn't start
this whole mess," Kamisha said angrily.

"No, but you sure made it a lot worse."

"Was I just supposed to stand by and watch Rick Simons be a dirty old man and keep my mouth shut about
it?"

"Yes, damn it. That would have been a whole lot better!"

"I don't believe it. I don't believe you said that. They could invite your daughter to one of those parties in a couple of years, and you think I should have let it drop?"

"What does Tracy have to do with it? You think these are the only parties with young girls in the world? Are you going to go around stopping all of them? My friend, the crusader!"

Kamisha couldn't believe Brigitte's attitude. Sure, her friend was a little lax at times, but this was too much. "You don't believe what you're saying. I know you don't."

"I believe it, Kamisha. I think you're a trouble-maker."

"And I think you're totally unable to face reality because you and Bullet have been drinking together too much."

Frozen silence filled the room. Brigitte's face was pallid with anger. She took a deep breath and drew herself up to her full height. "And I think," Brigitte said quietly, venomously, "that you're jealous of me, and I think you're a workaholic so you don't ever have to face the fact that you don't have a man." Brigitte grabbed her purse and turned to leave. "And never mind breakfast. I'd rather eat alone," she said icily.

Kamisha stood in the still-paralyzing silence of her house after Brigitte left. She stayed there, unmoving, for a long time until she started trembling, and then she sank down into a chair and put her face in her hands.

"Oh, God," she whispered through her fingers. It was always the same, the wrenching sense of abandon-

ment and betrayal. How could she surround herself with
people who continually hurt her?

She sat there and cried and felt all that tearing emptiness again, and it occurred to her that maybe there was
nothing wrong with the people around her. Maybe *she*
was the one who was flawed. Maybe she brought out the
worst in people. Maybe it was all her fault.

SHE WAS STILL UPSET on Monday, but she was awfully
good at hiding her feelings. She'd had years of practice, and she knew no one at the club would come close
to guessing what was going on inside her.

She avoided Rick like the plague. He was one person
she wasn't up to dealing with today. She'd played tennis early that morning, her usual Monday morning
mixed doubles match, with the usual club members.
She'd had only one crisis, luckily—the aerobics instructor for the ten o'clock class had called in sick, and
Kamisha had taken it over for twenty minutes until the
replacement had arrived. The members enjoyed having
Kamisha up there on the platform sweating along with
them; they thought she was a good sport. Or so Rick
Simons had told her. He'd said it was good for business. He'd even joked—in the past—that he'd take on
an aerobics class once in a while if he looked better in
tights. That had been when he and Kamisha had gotten
along, back before she knew what kind of man Rick
really was.

She stayed in open areas where there were people
around constantly. Just as she'd done on Sunday. She
wondered if she was going to have to spend the rest of
her life in safe, crowded places. Maybe Brigitte was
right, she thought once. Maybe she never should have

opened her mouth in the first place. But then how could she have lived with herself?

Kamisha returned to her office to answer her mail, to set up a schedule for free visiting days for potential new members, to attend to a dozen other details.

Usually she spoke to Rick about now, just to check on everything, but she wouldn't today. She sat over her desk, still in a damp leotard, and leafed through the mail.

There were the usual brochures from other clubs across the country, trade magazines, invitations to club openings . . . A photograph on the front of one such invitation caught her eye. Yes, it was John's new club in Costa Rica, announcing its grand opening. There was mention of a Panamerican Trade Conference to be held there in honor of the new facility, and Kamisha frowned.

He hadn't mentioned the Panamerican Trade Conference. How nice for John and his new club. Did he have some kind of undue influence in Latin America, too? Did his underlings down there, drug lords and thugs, coerce men in high places to plan their meeting at John's club?

She tapped the pen she was holding against her chin. John. She had to admit the truth to herself—she'd wanted him to turn out differently from all the rest. When he didn't try to persuade her into his bedroom, she'd been at a loss, beside herself with a wild, crazy new sense of pleasure—happiness more pure than anything in her experience. No wonder she'd been confused.

But it had all been an illusion. A clever sleight of hand.

She glanced up to see Rick passing by her door. His eyes were straight ahead. Good, she thought. She didn't know how long she could continue this way, though, pretending around the guests and the other employees, smiling, acting as if everything was okay. She'd have to quit, Kamisha thought; they'd force her to—John and Rick. A formidable pair. And maybe it was for the best. She didn't know what she could do about the parties, but she'd figure something out. Whether she quit or stayed.

Suddenly she laughed. Maybe she'd go to the FBI, and they'd put her in the Witness Protection Program: a new identity, new home, sometimes a new face. Who would miss her, anyway?

Kamisha's grim amusement was interrupted by a call from Joel, the head maintenance man. "Miss Hammill, the showers in the men's locker room are leaking down into the conference room. You've got a luncheon set up there for the hospital staff. What do you want me to do?"

Oh, Lord. "Let me think. Darn it, Joel, I thought you had those pipes fixed."

"So did I, Miss Hammill."

"Well, have the crew move everything to the covered terrace in back. Just close the terrace off for lunch customers today. Put up a sign."

"Okay, Miss Hammill."

"And pray that it doesn't rain this afternoon."

Kamisha showered in the locker room and changed into tan slacks and a dark green camp shirt. She pulled her hair back into a big vertical clasp that kept it out of her way and put on lipstick.

She grabbed a sandwich at the coffee bar, then stopped in at the hospital staff luncheon. It was going

well, the slightly dotty but lovable chief of staff telling
his usual jokes. No one there had any idea their lunch
had been scheduled for the conference room up until
11:30 a.m. Another calamity averted.

All afternoon Kamisha sat at her desk clearing up
details, working on the benefit for the substance abuse
conference that was coming up in September. She was
getting responses from some celebrities already. Substance abuse was a popular cause these days. Maybe she
could even get Betty Ford to come; yes, the former First
Lady did interviews. Mrs. Ford could dash over just for
the evening from her place at Vail, only a hundred miles
away. She'd write her a letter.

What Kamisha really wanted to do was to call Brigitte and apologize. This couldn't be the end of their
friendship. It just couldn't. They'd weathered many
storms together, bad ones, but they'd always held their
friendship above their disagreements. Surely they could
do that this time, too. She wished Brigitte would call
her. Probably Brigitte felt equally as bad and was eyeing the phone just as she was. But Brigitte could be
stubborn, and Kamisha, well, she wasn't sure what to
say or how to say it this time. If Brigitte wasn't on her
side in this mess, she didn't know what she was going to
do.

The substance abuse benefit. She should get a big-
name athlete—Michael Jordon of basketball or John
Elway of the Denver Broncos football team, somebody
like that. Most of them were willing to speak at bene-
fits. She made a note to herself, then stared, unfocused, into the distance. Here she was planning a
substance abuse benefit when the manager of the club
was breaking the law using minors as prostitutes. Dear
Lord. That was child abuse.

How could Rick do it? How could John do it? What did they see when they looked at themselves in their mirrors?

Maybe John didn't approve, though. Maybe it was Rick all alone who had had her brakes "adjusted." It was possible. He knew her car. He might have found out about her jaunt to New York. Sure. And maybe John was confronting Rick right now, calling from his New York office, from behind that stark, neat desk. Or he could be checking up on her story, phoning some of the guests who had attended Rick's parties, asking what really went on.

Perhaps Rick *was* throwing the parties all alone. It would be easy for him as manager of the club, really simple. No one would question his use of the VIP condo. Kamisha finding out was a problem, though. He'd tried to shut her up by threatening her with John, but when that didn't work, maybe he'd decided to get rid of her.

A shadow, a flitting movement outside Kamisha's window caught her eye. She held her breath. Dear God, she was alone in her office!

Kamisha could barely move. But there had been someone, something, lurking outside her window. She'd seen it.

Abruptly it reappeared. Her heart nearly burst out of her chest. But it was a kid, twelve, maybe thirteen years old. He saw her in the window and grinned, holding up a tennis ball to explain his presence behind the building.

Immediately Kamisha was on her feet, cranking open the glass. "Are you kids slamming balls over the roof again?" she demanded.

"Not us, Miss Hammill," he said with all the innocence of Jack the Ripper before he scooted off and disappeared.

Kamisha sank back into her chair. She was losing it. And just when she needed a buddy the most, Brigitte had gone all crazy on her, too. What the heck was happening?

It wasn't a minute later that the phone rang on her desk. She jumped a little, then pursed her lips. *Get a grip, woman.* She picked up the receiver.

"Miss Hammill, this is Jody at the front desk. There's someone here to see you."

"Okay, I'll be there in a minute. Hey, it's not the plumber, is it? He should see Joel."

"No, it's definitely not the plumber."

She walked down the corridor toward the lobby, covering a yawn with her hand; she hadn't been sleeping well, too many bad dreams. She'd like to go home and curl up with a good book. Or go to a nice, funny movie with Brigitte. No, not now, not with Brigitte. Oh, damn.

A man stood by the reception desk. She recognized him instantly and with utter shock.

"Hello, Miss Hammill," he said. "You're looking fine."

"Inky?"

"Yeah, it's me." He grinned at her.

She tried to fit her mind around the fact of his presence there. "What...?"

"John sent me. He wants to see you."

"In New York? But I..."

Inky chuckled. "Naw, he's here. We flew in this morning."

"John. *Here?*"

"Yeah. Seems there was a little problem he had to take care of."

Kamisha cleared her throat. "Where . . . ah . . . where is he?"

"In his condo, the VIP condo."

"Oh, right."

"So, Miss Hammill, can you come right now, or did I get you in the middle of something?"

"No, no, I mean, I'm not doing anything special. I can come now." But suddenly she paused. Was she truly nuts? Ambling along with Inky like a lamb to slaughter. She'd be alone with the two of them and—

But Inky seemed to be reading her mind. "It's okay, Miss Hammill," he said, nodding toward the door. "Mr. Leopardo told me to tell you that."

"Oh," she said, "he did, did he?"

"Yes, ma'am."

"So I can go along with you. Just like that?"

"Yes, ma'am," he repeated. Then, quietly, he said, "John's not what you think. You got my word on that."

"And I should trust you?"

He smiled. "Absolutely."

Kamisha cocked her head, studying this impressive man. She believed him. At least she believed that John Leopardo wasn't going to try anything on the club's premises. He was dangerous, true, but certainly not a fool.

She turned to the girl at the desk and said, very deliberately, "Jody, I'll be in Mr. Leopardo's condo if anyone wants me, okay? Let's go," she said to Inky decisively, feeling just that little spurt of familiar excitement, the kick.

They walked out of the lobby through the double front doors, down the steps to the winding path that led to the parking lot and the condominium buildings. Kamisha saw nothing—not the neatly white-clad tennis players or the girl weeding flower beds or the young man on crutches headed toward the therapy clinic. She was marveling at the thoughts that crowded her brain.

John, here. John wanted to see her. Why? What for? Was he truly worried about her, or was he planning a showdown with her—firing her? Had he come to charm her, to learn about her, to convince or to—

"You had a little trouble with your car, I hear," Inky said.

"Does he tell you everything?" she asked, striding alongside his big frame.

"Everything that matters," the man said. "He told me someone tampered with your brakes."

"Yes, someone did."

"Have you told the police?"

"Only the ones in Dillon, where it happened. I filled out a routine report."

"That'll do a lot of good."

"I know."

The sun filtered through the trees and dappled the walk. John, here. She'd see him in a few minutes. Would he act the same here? Would he still carry that aura of absolute control? Maybe he'd be diminished somehow here in Aspen, away from the accoutrements of his power. Maybe he'd look like a city slicker, too formal, ill at ease in the deliberate casualness of this resort town.

Maybe he was here to gauge her reactions, to figure out another way to get rid of her. Yes, he'd need to see her in person, to judge whether she would go running to the police, or if she already had. Sure, he'd told Inky to ask her that question. *Be careful,* she reminded herself. *John Leopardo is a dangerous man. You can't trust him.*

"Sure is nice and cool here after the city," Inky remarked.

"You still have that heat wave?" she asked, forcing the conversation.

"Yeah. Hot as Hades in New York."

The worst part was that she actually wanted to see John, ached to look into those black, hooded eyes, to discover what secrets they held. She wanted to watch him move with restrained dignity, using his cane. Why did he fascinate her so?

Be careful, she thought again.

Abruptly she recognized the way her heart beat too heavily, the way her mouth had dried up. She felt exactly the same as if she were racing down a ski run in a blizzard, half blind, exhilarated, tempting fate. She glanced upward to the condo. The sun had set behind the mountain, and the building looked dark and somehow sinister, its curtains drawn, its windows blank, unseeing eyes, its bulk suddenly, unnervingly, unfamiliar.

CHAPTER EIGHT

JOHN HADN'T REMEMBERED how intensely Kamisha struck him. It hit him again, as it had the first time he'd seen her, like a blow in the solar plexus. Her strength, her carriage, the brilliance of her coloring, the flash in her eye. There was so much more to her, he thought, so much to learn, to know, beyond what she allowed a person to see. Just like him. They were kindred spirits.

And she believed someone had tried to kill her.

"Kamisha, good to see you," he said, taking her hand.

"Is it, John?" She withdrew her hand a little too quickly. She gave nothing away, but he sensed she was nervous. Nervous and wary.

"Please, sit down. A drink?"

She shook her head and seated herself on a white couch. Yes, she was edgy, but then she thought he'd tried to have her killed. He turned away to give her a moment to gather herself, made his way to the bar and poured himself a fresh-squeezed orange juice.

"So, John, what brings you here so soon again?" she asked.

He turned slowly and looked at her. "Kamisha, I told you I admire honesty. Let's have no games between us. Your call brings me, what else?"

She sat with one knee up, her hands locked around it. She jiggled her foot and stared at him. "Sorry," she said. "I guess that was a dumb question."

His leg was stiff from the flight out to Aspen, and he was walking badly. He was acutely aware of her eyes on him as he limped toward her, then lowered himself into a chair, leaning his cane against the seat. "Okay, let's start over. Tell me how you are. No more accidents, I take it?"

"No. But maybe it's only lack of opportunity."

"You've been staying with friends, I hope? I should have thought to offer you this condo. The security is very good here."

She smiled. "Here? You must be kidding."

"Oh, I forgot. Naturally, if I'd tried to kill you, this would be the perfect place to try again," he said reasonably.

Studiously she refused him a reply.

"Where are you staying then?"

"At home."

"Alone?"

"Yes, I—"

"Kamisha, that's really not in your best interests, if you'll allow me to say so."

"You can say it." She shrugged. "But no one makes me leave my own house."

Oh, she was stubborn. Gloriously stubborn. There was that strength, that daring, the attribute that made her so very, very fine and special.

How to handle her? He sipped his juice and studied her and wondered. It occurred to him that he couldn't handle her. No one could. She couldn't be handled, only convinced by love and understanding and trust.

"You don't trust me," he said.

"I don't know you."

"You accused me of trying to murder you. You were pretty explicit about not trusting me."

She looked away. "I was upset."

"Understandably. I've been under fire myself. It makes you act rashly." He turned the glass in his fingers and stared at it, frowning. "Ever since you called I've been trying to figure out how to prove to you that I had nothing to do with your accident. It's a very awkward position to be in as your employer. I'm not enjoying it."

"I'm not enjoying myself much, either," she said coldly.

"I appreciate your frankness," he said with a tinge of irony in his voice. "Be that as it may, I've come up with an idea. It had to be done, anyway, and I thought it might clear the air. Help our little impasse."

"Oh?" She eyed him with suspicion, and he got the distinct impression that she was poised to flee, on guard, judging his every move.

"Kamisha," he said, leaning toward her, "you're safe here. I won't hurt you." He put a hand on her knee and felt her flinch. "I have never harmed a human being except in war, and then I viewed it as my sworn duty." He held her gaze for a long moment. "Do you believe me?"

She returned his look, her dark brows drawn together. "You want the truth?"

"Always."

"I don't know. I'd like to believe you."

"I'm guessing that my family is a problem. I can only tell you again that I have no contact with my father and nothing to do with his business." He wondered if he was wasting his breath; his past was so pervasive in his life that he had to fight it every day, every hour. He had to fight the battle for his beliefs and reputation again and again. And how many people really believed him? He clenched his teeth, feeling the familiar frustration wash through him. This time it mattered so very much that he convince her of the truth.

"I've asked Rick to join us," he said abruptly, tired of the struggle, tired of the way she was looking at him with accusation in those lovely eyes.

"Rick?"

"Why not? I'm going to ask him straight out about the parties. It's time to get to the bottom of this."

She'd straightened, her expression puzzled. "Do you want me to leave?"

"No. Why would I want you to leave? I think you should be here." He made his voice deliberately hard, testing her.

"Will you stand behind me on this?" she asked. "You believe me?"

"I'll stand behind the truth, yes."

"He'll lie," she said.

"I'll judge that."

"He'll fire me on the spot," she said. "He'll have to. My job's on the line."

John gave a short laugh. He got up, took his cane, walked across to the bar to set his glass down and turned to face her. "In case you've forgotten, Kamisha, Rick Simons works for me. I own the Ute City Club. Either you want this matter brought out into the open and taken care of or you don't. Which is it?"

She eyed him steadily. "Yes, I want it taken care of. It's just that your methods are a little . . . well, I guess unorthodox."

"I abhor games. You came to New York to tell me about this problem. I assumed you wanted me to do something about it. I told you I would. I keep my word."

"It's a beautiful club," she said, "and I've worked very hard to make it successful. Nothing should spoil its reputation. I appreciate your concern." She spoke stiffly and fiddled with the collar of her blouse, a deep forest-green against her tanned neck. Her fingers were slim, with short nails and no polish. He wondered inadvertently how those fingers would feel on his skin. His gaze rose to her neck again, to the long silver-blond tendrils of hair that had escaped their clasp and curled, clinging to her skin. He felt suddenly tongue-tied. There were words churning around in his head, but he couldn't get hold of them. He was aware of Kamisha studying his face, and he wondered if his expression was as implacable as he hoped. He spoke often of the truth, to Kamisha he had, anyway. Perhaps he owed her yet another truth. Perhaps he should tell her of his innermost—

There was a knock on the door. Kamisha's head swiveled sharply. She looked at him. He nodded and went to the door and opened it.

"Mr. Leopardo, you wanted to see me?" Rick said. He had his normal breezy way about him—the easy smile, the casual clothes, the predator-sharp look in his eye.

He noticed Kamisha the minute he was inside the door. John saw him stiffen and saw the color drain from his skin, saw the rictus of muscles that turned instantly into a broad smile.

"Well, well, Kamisha. I didn't know you knew Mr. Leopardo," Rick said.

"We met very recently," John answered for her. "She visited me in New York."

Rick looked from one to the other, assessing, knowing, planning his escape like a wild creature caught in the fatal glare of a spotlight. John knew then. Rick was behind the parties, using the club as his private brothel, pocketing dirty money from the likes of Senator Stern and his cronies. Providing entertainment, young girls, the club's food and liquor in a classy, private, exclusive setting. Perfect. Lucrative. Discreet.

Rick was a pimp, pure and simple. John wasn't sure he could keep the man in his employ under any circumstances.

Rick put his hands in his pockets and stood in the center of the room, legs straddled. "Was there something you wanted?" he asked. "I'm pretty busy this afternoon."

"I'm sure you are, Rick, but this'll only take a minute." John shifted his cane to the other hand. "I've heard an unpleasant story about some parties you've had here in this condo, Rick. Parties with underage girls. Is this true?"

Rick blanched. "Who said that?" he blustered. "What son of a— "

"Kamisha told me," John said curtly. "She said she'd taken it up with you, and when you wouldn't listen, she came to New York to tell me. Are you denying her accusations?"

"Yes, of course I am. How dare she say that? What's she talking about?" Rick mouthed the words, but John suspected he was only saying what was expected.

"Another thing, Rick. She told me you said I was the one behind these parties, that I condoned them. I take real exception to that."

"She's lying," Rick muttered.

"I don't think so," John said quietly. "Why should she lie about it?"

"It's pretty obvious. She's a tough lady. She's ambitious. She wants my job, Mr. Leopardo. She's been scheming to get it from the minute I hired her. She's trying to get rid of me, the—"

"That's enough, Rick. Let's not have any name calling around here."

"You don't believe her, do you? God, she went behind my back and . . ." Rick was moving around in agitation, shooting scathing looks at Kamisha. But she only sat there, upright, lovely, her face washed clean of any feelings, her eyes taking everything in.

"I'm afraid I do believe her, Rick. She's given me the name of one of the local girls who was at the last party. I'll reserve final judgment until I consider all the facts, but I think, Rick, that I'm really going to have to reconsider your fitness for your position. I will not abide dishonesty in my management."

"You have no proof at all, not one bit. I didn't do it, Mr. Leopardo. You've got to believe me."

"I'll take it under consideration," John said.

"Mr. Leopardo, it isn't true. I wouldn't do a thing like that. You can't believe her."

"You know, Rick, I could go to the police with this. I have several reasons not to at this point. The reputation of the club, the lack of absolute proof. Let's leave it at that for now, why don't we."

"Kamisha." Rick turned to her, his hands out in a theatrical gesture. "Come on, enough of this. It's gone far enough. Tell him you made it up. For God's sake, Kamisha, I always treated you well, didn't I?"

"Yes, you did, Rick. But I told John the truth, and I can't change that. I'm sorry," she said.

Rick looked from one to the other, and his mouth twitched in a bitter smile. "Okay, I got the picture now. I can't fight what you've got going for you, Kamisha. Hey, I can't compete with that. Fine. You want your girlfriend in the top spot, Mr. Leopardo. I can't argue. Just don't make up stories about me to put her there."

"You're disgusting, Rick," Kamisha said hotly, half rising.

He held a hand up. "Far be it from me to come between true love. I'll leave without a fuss."

"Don't push me, Rick," John said, his voice as cold as death. "I'm a fair man, but I will not be pushed."

"Nah, you don't need to do the pushing, do you? You got men you can call. Okay, I'm going. I'm going nice and quiet. But you're making a big mistake."

"Are you threatening me, Rick?" John asked quietly. He could feel his temper boiling, bubbling under his tightly controlled surface. The temper he'd fought so long to restrain. It was always references to his family that ignited it, his family and their Mob connections.

Rick took a step back. "No, Mr. Leopardo, hell, no."

"You can leave now," John said tightly, grasping the knob of his cane with both hands, holding on to it hard.

Rick was pale. He gave Kamisha a look, then John. He backed to the door, felt for the doorknob, turned it and let himself out. The door shut with finality behind him.

John let out a breath he'd been holding for too long and willed his fingers to relax their grip. He wanted to swear and throw his cane across the room. But, no, control, that was the only thing he had to hang on to.

Keep under control. Don't let anyone see that you're human, that you feel. Don't risk it.

He turned to Kamisha. She was watching him speculatively, probably trying to figure out if he'd arranged this little farce to convince her of his innocence.

"I'm sorry you had to be part of that," he said to her. "Maybe you were right. I should have done it alone."

"His pride was hurt. I feel sorry for him," she said.

"Have you considered," John said slowly, "that Rick may have had your brakes tampered with?"

"Yes," she said. "I considered it. I suppose it's possible. He had the motivation. I'm not sure how he knew I was going to see you in New York, though."

"Did you tell anyone at the club?"

"No, only my friend Brigitte. And I told her not to let Rick know."

John paced, leaning on his cane. "I see. But it's possible he found out."

"I suppose so," she said doubtfully.

"I'd like to solve this problem. If Rick was responsible, you're still in danger. Even more danger."

"So are you," she said.

"I have Inky."

"Ah, yes, Inky."

John went to the bar again. He felt restless, not quite sure how to proceed from here. He should let Kamisha go, warn her about staying alone again, follow up on Rick to find out who had fixed the brakes on Kamisha's car. He should be thinking about who was going to manage the Ute City Club if he had to fire Rick. And there was the Montaña y Mar in Costa Rica. Business matters, vital concerns. There was no time in John's life for anything but business; he'd carefully structured it that way.

He found himself asking, "Would you like a drink now, Kamisha? I think I'll have one."

"Maybe a glass of wine."

They were being so careful with each other, both of them so terribly inhibited. Rick's insinuations had made them too aware of each other as male and female, too aware of what happened normally between men and women. If Rick only knew how very far he was from the truth.

He handed her the glass and wine and sat down, nursing his own drink. He wondered fleetingly if Kamisha believed him innocent, but then he couldn't know that, not yet. Her presence was enough, and he suspected that she'd stay if only because she was tempted by a challenge. "This isn't over yet," he finally said. "I have to find out more about the parties. Rick may not be working alone." He hesitated, swirling the ice in his drink. "You could leave, you know, take a vacation, get out of the way for a while."

"I don't run, John."

"It's a suggestion." He shrugged. He was pleased with her reaction, proud of her. Absurd of him. God, she upset his orderly life, made him feel things he didn't want to feel, had locked away for years. Youthful, futile dreams of a girlfriend, a wife, a family. But he'd decided long ago that he could never ask a wife and children to put up with his Mafia family, to put up with the bloodthirsty press that, to this day, found him guilty without a trial.

He held her eye. She was smiling slightly, covering up whatever uneasiness she felt. She was very cool, very poised, too damn beautiful.

"Come to dinner with me tonight," he said. "I don't know Aspen very well. You pick the place."

Their eyes met in acknowledgment of the challenge. She lifted the wineglass and sipped before she answered. "Are you sure it's advisable?" she finally asked.

"Yes, I'm sure."

She lifted her shoulders, then let them drop. As if it was unimportant to her, a thing of no consequence. Yet he didn't believe that for a moment. "All right, then. But I've got to change." She gestured at her casual attire.

"Inky will drive you home. Is that acceptable?"

"Sure, why not."

"May I ask where we're going?" he inquired.

"No," she said, giving him a smile, "I haven't decided yet."

When she was gone, John showered and changed. Aspen formal, they called it. Even an infrequent visitor like John knew enough not to wear a suit and tie out to dinner in Aspen. He wore white summer slacks, a white polo shirt and a beige slubbed-silk sport coat. He was ready too soon, far too soon. He wandered out onto the deck of the apartment, sat in a wrought-iron chair, leaned back and drank in the champagne-dry summer air, the warmth of the evening sun.

This woman excited him. He hadn't realized how isolated he'd become, how cut off from the reality of most human beings. Other men had wives or lovers. They fought and made love and nagged each other. It was messy, untidy, all uncontrolled feelings and emotional highs and lows. But it was life. What John was living was an artificial, insulated existence. Safe but empty. Now he'd met a woman he wanted, but he wasn't sure just what he wanted from her.

Did he want sex? Did he want companionship,
friendship, love? Or was it merely a temporary flirta-
tion, a passing lust?

He caressed the knob of his cane, felt its familiar
smooth hardness and wondered whether he dared exchange its sterile support for that of a woman's warm,
responsive flesh.

And yet... He felt instinctively that he could have
something special with Kamisha. She needed someone
to love and understand her, to calm her fears and earn
her trust. Her vulnerability melted that frozen spot in
him where his feelings lived. And like any frostbitten
flesh, as it thawed out, it demonstrated that it was still
alive by hurting like the very devil.

He hadn't learned to hurt yet when he was fourteen
years old. He remembered those days with longing and
guilt; longing for the security and happiness, guilt because John hadn't yet realized what business his father
was in and still loved him unreservedly.

He gazed out at the mountainside, its lower part
bathed in evening shadow, and let himself remember. It
was the dinners, he guessed, that he recalled with such
affection. His mother, Lucille, used any excuse for a
feast. Birthdays, first communions, holidays—any cel-
ebration would do. It was one way of getting Gio to stop
thinking about business and a way to lure his sister
Camille and her family to the old house in Brooklyn.
Camille was ten years older than John. She'd married
Henry young and had twins already, spoiled little ter-
rors, who called John "Unca Johnny."

Then there was Aunt Jessie, Lucille's spinster sister,
who always came to any family gathering, a few as-
sorted cousins, business pals of Gio, and—always—
Mario. Glum-faced Mario with his Italian accent, heavy

features and curly black hair. He was always there when
Gio was home, and he went wherever Gio went. His
chauffeur. In those days John had never thought to
question Mario's presence or the omnipresent bulge
beneath the breast of his dark suit. Back then the man
was as familiar and comfortable as an old piece of furniture.

It must have been Thanksgiving, John thought, the
one when the twins were three and Camille was pregnant again. He remembered that holiday in particular
because everyone made fun of how his voice was
changing.

"He's growing, so what can I say?" his father said
proudly, the chewed cigar butt stuck firmly in his teeth.
"He'll be tall, a real American, a regular John Wayne."

"Remember, Lucille," Aunt Jessie put in, "Uncle
Louie was tall. That's where Johnny gets it from."

"Sure, I remember Uncle Louie. We thought he was
a giant," John's mother replied.

"No, Lucille," Gio said, "you forget my grandfa-
ther from Palermo on my father's side. He was a big
man. Johnny has his nose, too. No doubt about it."

Everyone had an opinion. Family or as close as family. They all talked about him while they ate the turkey,
the pasta, the American pumpkin pie, the Italian gel-
ati. And they *cared* about him. Every time anyone got
up from the long table to walk by, he'd tousle John's
hair, chuck the twins under their fat, dirty chins, clap
an old friend on the shoulder, lean down to kiss a lady's
cheek. There was always touching, kissing, embracing.
Love. Love all around, fierce, protective love. Sometimes stifling but always there, unquestioning, utterly
dependable.

Sure, he squirmed when they teased him about his voice and the fuzz on his upper lip, but he didn't mind, not really. It wasn't mean-spirited teasing.

His mother sat at one end of the table, beaming, the lady bountiful, the living cornucopia of all this largesse, the reason why all of them were together at this feast.

"Very good, Lucille," Gio would invariably say. "You outdid yourself."

"I'm bursting, Ma," Camille groaned. "There's no room inside me anymore."

"Eat, darling. It's good for the baby. Eat," Lucille said, beaming.

"How's football?" Henry always asked John. "You catching those passes?" Henry had played football in high school, but now he was getting chubby. John swore he'd never let himself get that way.

"Pretty good. I made a touchdown last game."

"Good boy," Henry said.

"He'll get hurt, Lucille," Jessie said, shaking her head. "Football."

"Ah, it's good for him," Gio replied proudly. "Toughen him up."

Lucille shared a look with her sister: *men, what can you do?*

They talked at one another, all at the same time, across one another, spilling the deep red wine on the white tablecloth, dribbling gravy and tomato sauce, arguing, gesturing widely in one another's faces, the women yak-yak-yakking, gossip, stories, children, sales in department stores. The men in a lower key—sports, cars, the new hippie generation. Everyone talking knowledgeably, self-importantly.

The twins got bored and slipped under the table to play among the heavy fluted table legs that were like standing elephants, crawling over everyone's feet, trying to tie shoelaces together.

John had done that when he was small, but now he was nearly grown, and the men included him in their conversation.

He could see them as if he were there, the big bellies of the men, their suspenders. He could smell the reeking cigar smoke and garlic and roast turkey, feel his full stomach and sense of belonging, of being beloved.

But that was a long time ago.

IINKY RETURNED to fetch John at seven. "She's got this cute little house over in the West End, boss. Real cozy. It surprised me."

John sat in the back of the sedan and listened to Inky's opinions, something he did often. "Why were you surprised?" he asked.

"Well, she's so cool and sophisticated. I figured her for something more in character." Inky turned onto Main Street, heading west into the setting sun. "You know, more like your place."

Interesting. Kamisha chose to surround herself with cuteness and coziness. That said something about her.

"Right up here," Inky was saying, turning left off Main Street onto a side street that led toward the base of Aspen Mountain. "She's something, boss. If I wasn't married . . ." And Inky chuckled, putting John on the way he always did.

"Keep your nose out of my affairs," John said lightly. "This is a business date."

"Oh, sure." Inky rolled his eyes in the rearview mirror. "You shaved three times today for a business dinner. Right, boss."

"Goddamn it, Inky—"

"We're here, boss. You want to cuss me out in front of the lady, fine."

She was waiting before her house, dressed in a bright pink silk tunic and matching pants. The evening breeze tugged at the fabric, molding it against her breasts and thighs, then letting it drape into lines that touched shoulder, hip, knee. Inky opened the door for her, and she slid in, bringing with her the aroma of fresh air and shampoo and intoxicating femininity.

"Hello, Kamisha."

"Hello, John."

She sat near the door, as far from him as possible. She was still vigilant, alert for any move he might make. But she was there, with him, and he was confident that he could win her over and prove his innocence. "So, where are we going?" he asked.

"The Pine Creek Cookhouse," she replied. "It's up at Ashcroft, a ghost town about twenty miles away. I made a reservation. Do you mind the distance?"

"No, it gives me a chance to see more of this area. I've never been past the airport. Do you need directions, Inky?"

"Naw, I looked at a map. Ashcroft's on Castle Creek Road, right? Turn at the light out of town and past the hospital?"

"That's it."

Her hair was twisted up in a silver clasp, and tendrils lay on her neck. She wore no earrings, no jewelry of any sort.

"I hope you like this place. It's a bit different. It's an old log cabin, and the food and setting are very special. The ghost town is nearby. It used to be as big as Aspen."

"Sounds delightful."

She was relaxing a little, he thought. Enjoying herself. If she'd spend time with him, he was sure he could learn what made her tick, make her believe in him. But did he have that time?

They drove up a long, narrow valley. On the highest peaks snow still lingered. The mountainsides were deep, dark green, covered with spruce. Alpine meadows sloped up from the road. The sun had disappeared behind the mountains, but the sky overhead was deep and endless and blue shading to purple.

John saw it all with a sense of wonder, with new eyes. *To live surrounded by such beauty,* he thought.

"You're very fortunate," he said aloud. "Living here, surrounded by this."

"I know," she said softly.

"I can understand why people come here."

"They're really just visitors, though. They don't understand the real Aspen."

"It's a good thing. Picture this valley overrun with the crowds of Manhattan."

She laughed. "Sometimes us locals feel like they *are* here. But the Castle Creek valley is so peaceful, isn't it?"

The Pine Creek Cookhouse was a perverse blend of primitive log cabin and elegant dining. There was a large stone fireplace with a fire going; it was cool at this altitude on summer evenings. Casually well-dressed people filled the tables. Silver clinked and crystal gleamed. The conversation was muted and informed.

"Mr. Leopardo, two for dinner. Yes, right this way, sir," said one of the waiters, who was manning the door.

Kamisha followed the waiter, waved to an acquaintance across the room and stopped for a moment to smile and say hello to an older woman at a nearby table. John was unaccountably jealous that she lived here, fitted in perfectly, jealous of the Aspenites who saw her every day.

"Sorry," she said, "but Mrs. Wexner is a member of the club."

"No problem."

"You have to have the cold cherry soup," Kamisha said, not even looking at the menu. "It's their speciality."

The dishes were mostly vegetarian, with some fish, some chicken. Pilafs and vegetable soufflés and potato pancakes were featured.

John watched Kamisha study her menu. Her brow creased and she bit her lip. She was so beautiful. "You order for me," he said. "It's your turn."

"Oh, really, I'd rather not."

"Please. I'm not fussy. I'd love anything on this menu."

Their eyes met and locked and a jolt went through John. He wondered if she felt it, too. She must. And once again he had to ask himself: what did he want from her?

"Would you care to see the wine list?" their waiter was asking.

John took it, never removing his gaze from Kamisha's. She was flushing, a delicate pink staining her cheeks, her eyes bright and expectant. He put the wine list down and dared to take her fingertips in his. "I hope you're not afraid of me any longer," he said. "I want you to enjoy the evening."

She didn't pull her hand away, but she took her time answering. "I'm not afraid of you. I don't know. Maybe I should be. I told myself you were dangerous, but when I'm with you, I can't... I don't feel in danger."

"You're not, Kamisha, not from me."

"When you say that, I believe it, but when I'm alone, I think things. Does it bother you when I'm frank like this?"

He shook his head. "I want only the truth between us. On a business level and on a personal level."

She bent her head, and he had to strain to hear her. "But sometimes it's so hard to know what the truth is."

"Trust your instincts."

She looked up then and gave him a rueful smile. "My instincts are for self-preservation, for running away. Even from myself."

"You didn't run from me. You could have."

"Yes," she said slowly, "I could have."

He turned her hand over in his and ran his thumb across her palm. "You have calluses on your hand."

"Tennis," she replied. "First it's blisters, then calluses. Very unfeminine."

"Maybe to some."

He had a powerful urge to bring her hand up, to bury his face in her sweet-smelling skin, to rub her fingers over his lips. He let her hand go. He had to be careful with her, as careful as he was with himself.

"Wine?" he asked.

"Yes," she said, "a little."

They ate trout amandine, a grain pilaf, potato pancakes, perfectly cooked vegetables, sweet and crispy.

Coffee and dessert. A pecan pie for him, raspberries over coffee ice cream for her. He watched her sip, watched her chew and swallow, watched her flick a bit of ice cream off her lip with her tongue.

She told him a lot about the silver mining history of Aspen, about the present-day problems—too many extravagant second homes, no affordable housing for employees, the narrow, dangerous highway that led down the valley to the bedroom communities where employees lived. The changing character of Aspen—from close-knit, free-living Shangri-la to ritzy jet-set resort whose inhabitants were all rich tourists and celebrities.

"I remember when they first paved Main Street," Kamisha said. "I was a kid, of course. Here with my folks. We stayed in the old Hotel Jerome. Now all the streets are paved, all the lawns sodded and all the houses protected by security systems. Well, the tourists' houses at least."

"Not yours?" he asked.

"No, there's not much to steal."

"Do you lock your door at night?" he asked.

"Lately I do," she replied soberly.

He considered asking her if she'd like Inky to stay with her, but decided not to. She'd object. But he might have Inky keep an eye on her without telling her. Yes, that wasn't a bad idea.

"Good," he said. "And my offer still stands. Use the VIP condo if you want."

"With you in it, John?" she asked softly.

He shrugged. "There's plenty of room."

She smiled secretly. "No, I don't think so."

"I can't force you."

"No, you can't."

The candlelight flickered on the ruby-red wine in
Kamisha's glass, threw shadows on her bare neck, reflected points of light in her eyes. To sit across from this
silver-haired woman he desired was so very unique; he
would never have believed it if anyone had told him
these passions would rise once more in him. Life was
opening up before him, a cornucopia of possibilities.

"I'm afraid I'm going to have to get up. My knee is
stiffening," he finally said.

"Oh, I'm sorry. You should have said so sooner,
John."

"I'm fine. I just know by now when it's time." He
raised himself and took his cane, studiously wiping any
trace of a grimace from his face. He wouldn't be able to
bear her pity, not Kamisha with her athlete's body and
her skiing and her tennis.

A thought stirred in his head for an instant before
retreating: perhaps Kamisha found him distasteful. His
infirmity. A woman like her, so accustomed to living a
life in which she could bike or jog or play nine holes of
golf in the morning. In the afternoon it was tennis or an
aerobics class. A swim, if she liked. She could hike the
snowcapped mountains, ski . . .

"John," she was saying, "are we going?"

"Yes, yes, sorry, I was thinking."

She led, wending her way through the tables, a vi-
sion in shimmery silk, as bright as a flame. He could
feast his eyes on her proud, straight back, on her slim
neck, on the blond hair that was twisted on her head, on
the hips that swayed ever so slightly under the loose tunic.

Inky drove them back down the valley toward town.
The rented sedan was hushed, its ride smooth. They
whispered past the ghost town, its gaunt gray skeleton

buildings standing like sentinels in the dark valley, an echo of the past. A lopsided moon hung over a snow-silvered peak. Beauty walked in the night air.

"I had a very nice time," she said. "Thank you."

"I'm glad."

She sat closer to him than she had, he noticed.

"Are you leaving soon?" she asked. "I mean, to go back to New York?"

"Not immediately. But I do have a business engagement soon. I'd like to get this thing cleared up with Rick first. And you."

"I see," Kamisha replied. "So you'll be here for a day or two."

"I can stay."

"But you shouldn't."

"Kamisha," he said, "I believe this business in Aspen is more important than meetings elsewhere."

"Um," she murmured, and then looked at him, her features shadowed, then gilded by the lights of a passing car. "Listen," she began, "you really don't have to stay because of me, you know."

"It's my responsibility. It's my club."

"Well, I have to admit, I'm not looking forward to dealing with Rick." She made a face. "He's plenty miffed with me."

"I'll take care of Rick."

Inky pulled up at the curb in front of her house.

"Well, we're here," she said.

"I'll walk you to the door."

"That's really not . . ."

But Inky was opening her side and handing her out. John came around the car—too slowly, irritated with his stiff leg. He'd been sitting too much all day.

He took her arm, led her down the walk. "Did you lock up when you left?" he asked.

She nodded. "But, really..."

"Inky," he called, "take a look in Miss Hammill's house, will you?"

"John, honestly..."

"I'd feel better," he said. "Humor me."

She unlocked the door, and Inky went in. They stood there in the pool of light from a lamp. He could see that she was shivering a little.

"Nervous?"

"No." She gave a short laugh. "Chilly."

The lights went on in her house one by one. Inky came out. "All set, boss," he said, then retreated down the walk to the car.

"Thank you," she said, hugging herself.

"You can call me, you know. You have the number. Anytime day or night."

"I've already done that."

"If you hear anything. If you're afraid. Please call me."

She hugged herself and looked at him hard. He suspected she was getting ready to ask him in, to pursue what they'd been groping for all evening. To test her own courage. He sensed he was a challenge to her, a man and a challenge. The fact that he was impaired wouldn't matter to Kamisha at this point. He could acquiesce, enter her Victorian coziness and lose himself in it. For one night, one blessed night.

"John..." she started to say.

He took her hand and pulled it toward him, turned it palm up and bent his head to touch it with his lips. He heard her intake of breath.

"John..." she said again.

Yes, he could go inside with her, slip the shimmering silk from her shoulders, taste her. Still poised over her hand, he held her gaze for a pregnant moment. Her eyes were moist, her expression expectant. He knew that this was a game with Kamisha—a game she was accustomed to winning. Abruptly he didn't want to play.

He straightened and met her eyes again with his. "Good night, Kamisha," he said with more finality than he'd intended. He turned then, curtly, and limped down the shadowed walk to the waiting car.

CHAPTER NINE

THE ROSES WERE DELIVERED at ten o'clock, the scent of the two dozen red blooms filling Kamisha's office. She felt her cheeks grow as bright as the hue of the petals as she thanked the florist and watched him leave. On a clear plastic prong was a card. She closed her eyes for a moment, as if when she opened them she'd find the flowers gone, then took the envelope off the holder and stared at it.

What a mad, crazy charade they were playing, Kamisha thought as she pulled the card out. At the end of last night she'd have sworn he wasn't interested. For the life of her she couldn't figure him out. Still, for all her logic, her heart was beating wildly. She read the note again:

> Inky will be at your house at one with a Jeep. I hope it won't inconvenience you to join me on a ride.
>
> Yours, John

She smiled. He was asking her to take the afternoon off to be with him. And how could she refuse her boss?

All morning Kamisha rushed to get in a full day's work. She conned Rick's secretary into typing the letters to the celebrities she was asking to participate in the substance abuse event. She checked on the plumbing in the men's locker room and made calls to the Denver supply houses that provided soap and shampoo and razors for the locker rooms, placing next month's orders—she was a day late already. She checked with the Women's Forum president about next week's luncheon and arranged the menu with the chef. And still there were a couple of items left on her desk calender at noon. But what the heck, Kamisha thought, grabbing her zip-up sweatshirt and the flowers, the owner of the club had given her an order.

Leaving work, she felt carefree and young and deliciously guilty. Where would they go? The Maroon Bells Wilderness Area? To the top of Independence Pass? Maybe a walk along the Braille Trail. It was lovely and scented with pine, and you could hear the Roaring Fork River rushing, crashing down the steep ravines below. She wanted to show John everything. She wanted him to love her home.

In the rented car at the stop sign on Fifth and Bleeker Streets it occurred to her—how could she have forgotten?—that John was still the prime suspect in the murder attempt on her. What a perfect setup it would be to get her off into the wilderness alone. A convenient Jeep accident...

Yet her instincts told her he was a man of absolute integrity. She reached over to the passenger seat and brushed the tip of a ruby-red rose with her finger. A fleeting thought brushed her mind: the most perfect rose came with the sharpest thorn.

Kamisha pulled up in front of her house and spotted the bike leaning against the fence. Tracy's bike. And sitting on her front porch steps, the neighbor's cat in her lap, was Tracy. She looked absolutely miserable.

Concerned, Kamisha gathered up the flowers and her purse and stepped out of the car. "Hi," she called, "what a nice surprise."

"Hi." Sulkily.

"Cute cat. Isn't that Hogan from next door?"

"I guess."

Tracy looked enough like her mom to have been her sister, though she wore her honey-brown hair long and straight down her slender back. She was at an awkward age, too, thirteen and a little lanky, her front teeth still too big in her small mouth. There was a pimple on her forehead and one on her chin. Her eyes were swollen; she'd been crying.

Kamisha reached down and touched her shoulder lovingly. "Come on in. I've got to get these into fresh water. Come on."

"Can Hogan come?"

"Sure. But don't let him scratch my couch, button."

It was Kamisha who broached the subject finally. She was placing a rose in her crystal vase in the kitchen, Tracy sitting at the old oak table by the window, Hogan curled in her lap. "So, kiddo, what's new? You're looking mighty down in the mouth today."

Tracy sighed. "I hate Bullet."

"Oh. I see. Any particular reason?" Purposely Kamisha didn't look up, just went right on arranging the flowers.

"He's a jerk. He's always fighting with Mom and telling me to get lost."

"That's pretty nasty."

"I hate him."

"Did you tell your mom?"

"She doesn't care."

"Sure she does. She—"

"All they do is fight. And he makes my mom cry."

"Did this happen today?"

Tracy nodded. "Mom thinks he's got a girlfriend out in California."

"And I guess they must have fought about it, huh?"

"Yeah. And Mom was drinking, too, and Bullet broke her glass in the sink."

"This all happened this morning?"

"Yeah."

"I'm sorry, sweetie," Kamisha said, leaning against the counter, her arms folded over her sweatshirt.

Tracy looked up at her. "Can I stay with you? I don't want to go home."

Oh, boy, Kamisha thought. She took a minute to answer. When she did, she sat down at the table and put her hand on Tracy's knee. "I'd love to have you here," she began. "You know that. But we better reason this out, honey. It would only make things much worse. Your mom would be real hurt."

"I don't care."

"Right now I know you believe that. But in a day or two you'd start to feel awful and guilty, too. It would make it twice as hard to patch things up then."

Tracy hung her head.

"Honey, you'll have to trust my judgment on this one."

"What about Bullet? He doesn't want me there."

Kamisha sighed. "Listen," she said, "I don't think your mom and Bullet are going to be together that long. This is just between you and me. But I think that maybe if I have a heart-to-heart with Brigitte, she'll come around."

"You'll talk to her?"

Kamisha promised that she would, but just how she was going to accomplish it she wasn't sure. That fight they'd just had . . .

John arrived at one sharp, and Inky came to the door. "Jeep's all ready out front," he said, eyeing Tracy standing there in the living room. "John would appreciate it if you could drive."

"I understand," Kamisha said. She gave John a wave from the door. "I'll be out in a minute."

"I got lunch all packed for you," Inky called after her.

"Are you going Jeeping?" Tracy asked, surprised.

Kamisha was gathering up her jacket, just in case of rain, taking up her purse. "Yes, I'm going with a friend," she explained, "but we'll drop you and your bike off at home first. Okay?"

"I guess so."

She took Tracy's hand and led her out, locking up behind them. "Your mom will be fine, sweetie," she said, collecting Tracy's bike. "You'll see. I'll bet she misses you already." And then she added, "Your mom loves you more than anything in the world."

She loaded the bike into the back of the open Jeep and introduced John to Tracy, explaining they were going to drop her off.

"How do you do, Tracy?" he asked, turning around in the front seat to shake her hand.

"Inky," Kamisha said, "don't you want a ride back to the club?"

But it was John who answered. "We've taken the liberty of checking on your car over in Dillon. Inky can return the rental and pick up your Saab at the same time, if that's all right with you."

Kamisha looked at him for a moment. He certainly did take control. But it wasn't so bad. In fact, she realized, it was kind of nice to be taken care of for once. "Sure," she said, then turned to Inky, giving him the keys to the rental, "that would be great."

"My pleasure." He gave her that big white smile.

While Kamisha drove toward Castle Creek Road, she took the opportunity to glance at John from time to time. He was dressed today in blue jeans and a short-sleeved polo shirt, a khaki color. As always, his hair had been combed neatly back, but the wind had loosened it so that a big comma fell against his sunglasses, and the hair around his ears and neck wanted to curl up. He looked younger, wind-tousled like that, she decided, and somehow the cane that rested by his leg seemed terribly out of place. She imagined him as a younger man, in his twenties perhaps, and tried to see him with a frequent smile and a relaxed carriage, but the image wouldn't stick. Maybe he had never been a carefree youth. Maybe his father's "business" and Vietnam had robbed him of those good years.

She listened while he talked to Tracy, turning around, one hand resting casually on the back of her own seat. "Do you like school here in Aspen?" he was asking her.

"It's not as big as L.A.," Tracy replied, still sullen, "but it's okay."

"You have a lot of girlfriends?"

"Some."

And then a corner of his mouth lifted teasingly. "You have a boyfriend, Tracy?"

"Gosh, Mr. Leopardo," Tracy said, surprised, "I'm too young for that."

"Maybe," he said, "but you're a very pretty young lady."

And Tracy got all embarrassed and giggly and hid her teeth behind a slim hand. Kamisha was surprised, too, but it was a new side to John that had her thinking. He'd obviously sensed Tracy's discomfort and found a way to alleviate it. Amazing. It suddenly seemed a crime that he had no children of his own. But, then, neither did she.

"Here we are," Kamisha said, turning onto Brigitte's road. She wondered if she should go inside, talk to Brigitte for a minute. But then Brigitte was coming out, her bathrobe still on. She looked agitated, pale, hung over. Darn.

They only spoke for a moment, Kamisha explaining that Tracy had stopped by to say hello. "And John and I are heading up the mountain, Jeeping, so I thought I'd give her a lift home from town."

"Thanks," Brigitte said, eyeing both Kamisha and her daughter suspiciously.

"Well," Kamisha said, turning to head back to the Jeep, wondering if she should introduce John. But, no, Brigitte wasn't in the mood. "Look," she said, "I'll call you. We'll talk, okay?"

"It's your dime," Brigitte snapped. "So that's John. John Leopardo, I take it."

"Yes, um, he just got here yesterday and—"

Brigitte glared at her. "Aren't you afraid that man will kill you up there alone? I mean, what is this, Kamisha, another one of your cheap thrills?"

Kamisha bit her tongue. "We'll talk, Brigitte, when you're feeling better." She began to turn and head to the Jeep, but not before she saw Bullet standing in the big plate glass window, staring at the two women. *Jerk,* Kamisha thought.

Here are your BIG WIN Game Tickets, worth from $10.00 to $1,000,000.00 each. Scratch off the PINK METALLIC STRIP on each of your Sweepstakes tickets to see what you could win and mail your entry right away. (SEE OFFICIAL RULES IN BACK OF BOOK FOR DETAILS!)

This could be your lucky day – GOOD LUCK!

1 Scratch PINK METALLIC STRIP to reveal potential value of this ticket if it is a winning ticket. Return all game tickets intact.

LUCKY NUMBER

5E 582768

2 Scratch PINK METALLIC STRIP to reveal potential value of this ticket if it is a winning ticket. Return all game tickets intact.

LUCKY NUMBER

7Z 582768

3 Scratch PINK METALLIC STRIP to reveal potential value of this ticket if it is a winning ticket. Return all game tickets intact.

LUCKY NUMBER

2I 582768

4 Scratch PINK METALLIC STRIP to reveal potential value of this ticket if it is a winning ticket. Return all game tickets intact.

LUCKY NUMBER

6L 582768

5 FREE BOOKS — We're giving away brand new books to selected individuals. Scratch PINK METALLIC STRIP for number of free books you will receive.

AUTHORIZATION CODE

130107-742

6 FREE GIFT — We have an outstanding added gift for you if you are accepting our free books. Scratch PINK METALLIC STRIP to reveal gift.

AUTHORIZATION CODE

130107-742

YES! Enter my Lucky Numbers in THE BIG WIN Sweepstakes, and when winners are selected, tell me if I've won any prize. If PINK METALLIC STRIP is scratched off on ticket #5, I will also receive one or more FREE Harlequin Superromance® novels along with the FREE GIFT on ticket #6, as explained on the opposite page.

134 CIH ADNX (U-H-SR-01/92)

NAME _____

ADDRESS _____ APT. _____

CITY _____ STATE _____ ZIP _____

PRINTED IN U.S.A.

Offer limited to one per household and not valid to current Harlequin Superromance subscribers.

© 1991 HARLEQUIN ENTERPRISES LIMITED.

Carefully
detach card
along dotted
lines and
mail today!

Play
all your
BIG WIN
tickets
and get
everything
you're
entitled to-
including
FREE BOOKS
and a
FREE GIFT!

It was a six-mile drive back into Aspen and then across town to the Smuggler Mountain dirt road. But Kamisha had decided to show John some of the old silver mines that riddled the steep face of Smuggler. Many of the century-old shafts dropped a thousand feet into the ground, then turned south and headed directly under the town of Aspen toward the big ski mountain. It was said that a few of the old-timers could still find their way through the maze of shafts, but the shafts were old and dangerous, and Kamisha had never ventured into one. She wasn't going to today, either.

She drove and felt a cloud shadowing her former good spirits. It was, of course, Brigitte. And she wondered, too, just why she was throwing caution to the wind by heading off into the wilderness with John. Brigitte had a point. . . .

"You're awfully quiet," John observed over the drone of the Jeep's engine.

"Sorry." She slowed and steered cautiously around a boulder that forced the vehicle precariously close to the edge of the road. The drop on the driver's side was a good fifteen hundred feet.

"Nice road," he said, sitting up straight, looking over the edge.

"We'll be off this cliff in a few minutes. Then it's all woods and meadows. A few bad pitches, but we'll make it."

"And where are we headed?"

She glanced over and smiled. "The high country—God's country."

"Sounds interesting."

Kamisha wasn't sure just why John had arranged this get-together. She was accustomed to men being dazzled by her appearance, dazzled and distracted and held

at arm's length. It was how she managed men, and it
had always worked—until now. She stole a glance at
John; he'd braced himself against the dashboard with
one hand, a capable, square hand, a strong wrist that
swelled into his muscular forearm.

The rutted road rose and fell into a valley and rose
once more. They drove through deep stands of tall aspens and evergreens until they'd climbed above the altitude where aspens could grow. Then it was open
meadows and thick evergreen forests, the road wending its way still upward.

Kamisha was glad for the solitude. She was sure John
could sense her discomfort, though she wasn't quite
certain whether it was due more to Brigitte or him. She
knew one thing, however; she liked John's companionship a lot. Too much. She felt an odd sense of security
despite the little warning signs that kept blinking in her
head: *you can't trust him, not all the way.*

John was different from other men, fascinating but
difficult for her to handle. He kept throwing her curves.
Her usual techniques didn't seem to work with him. But
she knew no other way of dealing with men. Weren't
they all the same, really? Didn't they all want the same
thing from a woman, from her? John must, too. He was
just a little cleverer about it, a little more subtle.

Today she'd be able to manage him. She just needed
time to figure out what he was looking for in her.

They were crossing a warm, sunny meadow when she
felt his eyes resting on her. "Tracy seems like a nice
child," he remarked.

Kamisha avoided a chipmunk that had the audacity
to cross the road. "She's a good kid. I've known her
since she was born."

"She was upset today."

"Yes. A spat with her mom."

"A spat?"

He was drawing her out. She knew it. And normally she'd have retreated, but with John it seemed okay to open up a bit. "More than a spat," Kamisha admitted. "Tracy hates Bullet. He's that pro football star who—"

"I know who Bullet Adams is."

"Well, anyway, since Brigitte took up with him, Tracy's felt left out."

"I should imagine. And you, Kamisha, have you been left out, too?"

She glanced over. He was gazing at her solemnly, knowingly. "You could put it that way," she said. "But it's a lot more, too. Bullet brings out the worst in Brigitte. She doesn't need that...stuff in her life. She's always had a booze problem, and that guy only encourages her. He's a creep, if you must know. A real user."

"So I've heard."

"Anyway, Brigitte better get her head together, or Tracy's going to be permanently damaged."

"Are you two having a problem?" he asked, sincerely concerned.

"Yes. We had a fight. A real beaut."

There was a long, silent moment. "I don't suppose it had anything to do with me," he stated.

Kamisha raised an eyebrow. "As a matter of fact," she began, and then suddenly laughed. "Say, what's all this third degree, anyway?"

"Just trying to figure out who you really are."

She was suddenly, acutely uncomfortable. He was getting too personal. Her defenses rose automatically, and she raked a hand through her hair and tossed it

back over her shoulder so that it rippled like a banner
in the wind. She gave him a coy, sidelong glance and
smiled. But John just continued to regard her soberly.
Swiftly Kamisha switched her eyes back onto the road.

They stopped just below Warren Lake at the top of
the mountain. There was a campsite nestled in the forest at the northern edge of an alpine meadow—a hunt-
ers' camp that wouldn't be used for a few months still.
Kamisha got out the bag of food provided by Inky and
spread it on an old telephone cable spool that was used
by campers as a table.

"Um, chicken and potato salad. Want a soda pop?"
She turned to find John standing some thirty yards
away at the edge of the tree line where it met the sun-
splashed meadow. He was as still as the granite rocks
above, his weight supported on the cane, his head erect.
Sunlight filtered through the pine branches and dappled his head and shoulders. The majesty of forest and
meadow, the peaks beyond still capped with snow,
John's stillness, struck her motionless. The grandeur of
his surroundings diminished him, and he seemed so
mortal standing there with his cane in hand, so insignificant.

We're both human, she thought, and a sense of surprising peace pushed aside her anxiety for a moment.
Slowly she came up behind him. The summer wind
soughed in the green branches above. A billowy white
cloud cast the meadow in partial shade. She found herself whispering, "Lovely."

"Yes," he replied, unmoving, "it is lovely."

They ate their chicken and sipped the sodas, lazing
back against a tree, knees up, hands behind heads. All
the while Kamisha was so terribly aware of his constant, unwavering perusal. She knew her breasts pressed

against her shirt when she put her arms behind her head. She knew her legs were there for him to see, long, slim, tanned, stretched out in front of her. But John didn't steal secret glances at her, not like an ordinary man would. Even though he studied her, he seemed oblivious to her physical charms, and it made her nervous. He wasn't following the rules.

Eventually he stretched out on the soft pine needle floor of the earth and sighed. "I like it here."

"Um, me, too," Kamisha said. She couldn't help looking at him. His eyes were half-closed, one hand was behind his head, cradling it. He had a long body, she decided, lean and tapered in all the right places: belly, thighs, hips. A fly buzzed around his hand, and idly he shooed it away. How could she have ever thought that this man would harm her?

"You should spend more time in Aspen," she ventured. "Get rid of that city pallor."

"Would I look better with a tan?" he asked lightly, teasing.

"Everyone in Aspen has a tan. Year-round, in fact."

"Then my city white sets me apart." He turned his head toward her. "Is that so bad?"

"You like to be set apart, don't you." It wasn't a question. She tugged at an errant blade of dry grass, then plucked it, putting the sweet, reedy stem in her mouth. "Yes, John," she said, "I think you really like to be noticed, but in a low-key way. You're subtle but human."

"Oh, I'm human, Kamisha." He laughed lightly, mostly at himself. "In fact, I suspect I've got more than my fair share of frailties."

"You don't mean your leg."

"No, I don't. I mean problems, I suppose, personal problems."

"Care to share them?"

John shook his head slowly, still smiling. She found herself liking it when he smiled. "You can guess if you like," he said. "And you'll probably hit the nail on the head. I'm an open book, if you really want to know."

"So I'll guess. I'd say this rift with your family is one of your problems."

"A major one," he admitted, though there was a new edge to his voice.

"It's a shame."

"Isn't it."

"Seriously. My folks don't give two hoots about me. I know."

"That's not the way it is with me," he said. "It's quite the opposite."

"Do you care about them?"

"Very much."

"Can't your feelings, your problems, I mean, be mended?"

"No."

Kamisha leaned back against the tree and looked up at the sky that showed in patches through the branches of the evergreens. She chewed on the grass, thinking. Here they were—two mortals—darn close to bearing ugly truths to each other, so close that she began to quiver inside. It was rather like talking to a father confessor up here in the woods. In God's country, she'd said.

But that wasn't what she'd wanted at all. That wasn't what she'd meant to happen between them, and she wondered how he'd managed to turn the conversation to serious matters. Kamisha liked to keep it light, superficial, safe. With John she had to keep steering away from unpleasant subjects, and it kept her off balance.

She felt uneasy, not knowing whether to pursue the conversation or to let it drop. A part of her wanted to know all about John, to share his joy and hurt, to bare her own soul to him. But that wasn't *her*. It felt like a poorly fitted shoe.

She came to her feet and began to stroll around the campsite, kicking idly at pinecones. Here she was, up in the middle of nowhere, with an extremely attractive man, and all they were doing was talking.

She stopped and smiled. "Up over that ridge," she said, nodding, "used to be a real town."

"Up here?"

"Yep. On Saturday night the miners in Aspen used to hitch up the old wagons, climb on their horses, and hightail it up here for the good times." She found herself playing with her hair, tossing it, letting it drape over a shoulder loosely. She was aware that her movements became more provocative. It was a Kamisha she knew well and was more comfortable with than the one who talked about her parents and Brigitte to a stranger.

And John, seemingly, was playing along now. "And what did these miners find up here?"

True, she was comfortable with this side of herself, but she also hated it, the falseness, the sexual manipulation—and all because John had gotten a little too close. Tears pressed hotly behind her eyelids for an instant before she controlled them. She forced her smile; it was brittle and cold. "What did they do up here?" she said. "They came to enjoy themselves. You know, women, saloon women." The laugh she gave was short, nervous, too high-pitched.

But she couldn't stop herself. As if repeating lines from a long-ago failed play, Kamisha began to move toward John, tapping the blade of grass against her bottom lip. "Quite a trip just to let off a little steam, wasn't it?"

John had propped himself on an elbow. He was watching her acutely now, letting the drama unfold. His expression was impassive, but there was emotion in those secretive eyes and a watchfulness in the pitch of his head. She could see a muscle working in his jaw as she eased down onto the soft pine needles beside him. She was tired of talking, worn out. She had wondered before what it was that John truly wanted from her, and she was still wondering. It couldn't have been a nice afternoon chat. No. He'd arranged a Jeep trip to be alone with her, hadn't he? She wished he'd stop talking, stop requiring her to tell him things that were better kept quiet. She wished he'd make an advance—do something familiar, for God's sake, something she could deal with.

"Kamisha," he began, his tone odd, before she leaned closer, allowing the curtain of her hair to brush his cheek lightly before she, too, propped her head on her hand and faced him. She was so close to him that she could feel his warm breath on her neck. Yes, the talking was done. He'd pull her to him in a moment and she'd let him. She'd let him touch her and kiss her and press her against his hips until he couldn't think anymore. And then she'd be in control again.

"John," she said, a hoarse whisper, "I'm glad you came to Aspen."

"Don't."

"Don't?" Close, they were so close.

"This isn't what you really want."

"What do you mean?" She reached out with her free hand and ran a golden-brown finger along the inside of his arm. "You don't know what I want," she said softly. She knew she was lying because she'd never see it through. She never did. It was the old familiar game, an easy one, one she could win. John was just a man, after all, just another man. Maybe she hadn't quite figured him out yet, but she would. "John," she said, wetting her lips with her tongue, pouting a little, aware of the rise and fall of her breasts.

For a moment his dark eyes burned into hers, and then suddenly he was rising, reaching for his cane, coming to his feet. She felt utterly severed, out of control. What was he doing?

"John," she said, her breathing becoming uneven, a fear snaking around in her belly, "why are you...what's wrong?"

But all he said as he grabbed up their picnic litter was "Not this way, Kamisha, not this way." For an instant he stared at her and then strode away toward the Jeep.

CHAPTER TEN

KAMISHA COULD hardly wait to drop John off at his condo. She was barely able to meet his eye. He'd insulted her, humiliated her, rejected her. And in the back of her mind, somewhere in a deep, hidden place, she shivered with fear, because he'd seen through her act and recognized the falsehood of it.

She drove too fast down the bumpy, rutted road, but John didn't say a word about it. He sat beside her, quiet, unruffled, composed as ever.

Oh, God, she was so embarrassed. Why had she pulled that routine with John? She should have known better. He'd said over and over that he admired the truth, that he wanted only the truth between them. He'd been truthful with her. Yes, she was ready to believe that now.

She was through with his truth, though. It was too damn hard to live with. He was like someone from another century, some sort of knight errant with his outdated code of chivalry and honor.

"You don't have to try to kill us both," John said mildly after she skidded around a gravelly corner.

"I'm not," she said between clenched teeth, wrestling with the steering wheel, tasting dust in her mouth. "I just want to get home."

She pulled up in front of his condo building, stopping too short, lurching them both forward. John gave her a look but said nothing, only climbed out. "Why don't you take the Jeep home," he suggested, "until Inky gets back with your car."

"Fine." She wouldn't look at him.

But Inky, surprisingly, came out of the door of the condo just then. "Hey, boss," he said, his face grim.

"You can't have been to Dillon and back," John said, glancing at his watch. And Kamisha thought, Oh, great, now she'd be making the trip. Darn, why hadn't Inky gone?

She stared straight ahead, pretending not to listen.

Inky was saying, "Something came up, boss," and John was walking toward the black man. They spoke for a minute, heads together. Kamisha refused to look, tapping her fingers on the steering wheel in obvious impatience. She hoped he noticed.

But John seemed oblivious. She was aware that he was walking back toward her, of his cane rapping on the pavement. "Kamisha," he said, "something's happened."

She kept her gaze locked on the hood of the Jeep, tapping her fingers. She knew she was being childish, but she didn't care.

"Are you listening to me, Kamisha?" he demanded.

It was then that she finally turned and met his gaze and saw the bleakness of his expression. Her heart gave an unaccountable twang of fear. "I'm listening, John."

"Rick Simons is in the hospital. He's been badly beaten."

It took Kamisha a second to absorb the shock. Her eyes, wide with bewilderment, flew up to John's. There was no facade, no coolness or control or pretense. "Rick's been beaten up?" she whispered. "But who... why...?"

She was unaware of her hands gripping the steering wheel, her knuckles white. A quick, sickening image of Rick stabbed through her head: bruises, blood, swelling. Why in the name of God would someone—? It came to her in tiny jolts of realization, the flowers, the dinner, the Jeep trip, John's rejection just now. He hadn't asked her to show him the area to get her alone, to woo her, of course not. He'd been keeping her out of the way.

For a long moment she stared at him appraisingly, the disgust in her expression unconcealed. She knew he was reading her thoughts, too, and she didn't give a damn. When she mouthed the word, "You," it said it all to John. She didn't even need to finish. He'd used the Jeep trip as an alibi. He'd had Rick worked over because Rick had mishandled things.

She felt like laughing hysterically for an instant. She was the lucky one. John had spared her. But Rick's punishment would keep her silent, wouldn't it?

She stared into his eyes, tried to read what was there, but there was no expression in them, no message at all, neither sorrow nor anger nor surprise. He was absolutely closed to her.

Abruptly she gunned the accelerator, twisting the steering wheel, made a sharp turn in front of his condo and roared away, her heart pounding, her cheeks flaming.

She rushed up the walk to her house, grabbed the doorknob and twisted. Damn, it was locked. She'd forgotten. She'd only begun locking it recently. She had to fish the key out of her bag and struggle with the cranky old lock until it clicked open.

Oh, what a show! All that talk about the truth! And he'd been living a huge big whopper of a lie! And he'd used her to do it! John wouldn't dirty his hands. Of course not. He hired men, Mafia thugs. He probably didn't even let Inky dirty his hands, either. No, he just phoned his father and asked who was available, who could do a little job for him. Hit men. Contract killers. Oh, God.

And she'd believed him!

Kamisha sagged against the door, drained. She squeezed her eyes shut, but Rick was still there. Her imagination was running wild, tossing mental images helter-skelter into her head. Rick's jaw bruised. His eyes so purple and swollen they were closed.

She tried to take several deep breaths, to will the hideous pictures from her mind. But her breath caught in her lungs raggedly. And John. She could see him standing on the edge of the meadow, stock-still, contemplative. Oh, how she'd misread him. He'd been standing there, leaning on his cane, wondering if the job on Rick had been done yet.

She felt sweaty all over her body, hot and sticky. Burning. She pulled off her clothes and flung them onto the floor, stalking through her house. She got into the shower and turned it on hard, too hot, then too cold, then hot again. She washed herself all over, as if he'd touched her, as if he'd dirtied her. Her breath came too fast and her heart still thudded.

Then she put her face in her hands and stood there under the spray, sobbing, hurt and disappointed and ashamed to the depth of her being.

She sat in the dark later, not bothering to turn on the lights, unable to eat or sleep or read or call Brigitte to find out how Tracy was. The phone had rung several times, over and over monotonously, but she hadn't answered it. She sat there, hunched up, wearing an old red

bathrobe that was faded, with a tear in her sleeve. She
didn't care. All she could see in her mind's eye was
Rick—handsome Rick Simons, his face a pulp. No
matter what he'd done, how badly he'd messed up, he
hadn't deserved this.

It occurred to her to get up and lock her door. She
might be next. But a strange kind of perversity kept her
huddled in her spot in the dark. She'd been so damn
stupid, so blind that maybe she deserved the hospital
bed next to Rick's.

John Leopardo. She'd thought him the most wonderful thing to have come along . . .

She'd get over him. She'd let John impress her just a
little too much. She'd let him get inside her armor and
cause a breach in her walls. But she'd plaster the cracks
up and be as good as new. She'd make up with Brigitte.
Sure, things would go back to normal.

Or would they?

Sometime later she was faintly aware of a car driving
up and stopping in front of her house. She heard a
heavy door open, then thud shut. So he'd sent someone. So they were coming. She sat up and pushed her
hair back behind one ear. She wouldn't run. No, she'd
face them. She took a deep breath. There was a knock
at the door. She didn't move; she couldn't. Kamisha was
paralyzed with a crazy, mute fascination, anticipating
the worst. She actually wondered if she didn't deserve
it for her stupidity. Another knock. Maybe she was
mistaken. Maybe it was just an acquaintance, someone
stopping by. They'd see the house was dark and leave.
Go on, leave!

Another knock. Louder, more insistent. Then a
voice, "Kamisha." *His* voice, muffled by the door.
"Kamisha, it's John. Are you there?"

Maybe he'd leave if she just sat still in the darkness. She held her breath and hugged her knees to her chest.

She heard the doorknob being turned, heard him call to someone—Inky. "It's open. Wait a minute." She could hear his footsteps and the soft tap of his cane on the floor. A mumbled curse, then the click of the light switch and abrupt, blinding brightness.

For an endlessly long time John stared at her. There was absolutely no emotion on his face; it was purposely masked. But his eyes told a different story. She thought she could read in them a torrent of emotions: surprise, relief and something akin to fear.

Kamisha glared back at him over her knees. She felt drained, unable to deal with whatever new game he'd decided to play. When he took a step toward her, favoring his leg more than usual, she even flinched. She was at his mercy.

He finally sighed as his brow knitted. He swore softly. "Are you all right?"

Kamisha drew her tongue over her dry lips. "So far," she whispered, and felt the cool wall at her back as she pressed against it.

He seemed to want to reach out and touch her but then hesitated. "I tried calling you. I was concerned."

"I'll bet you were."

"Believe what you want. But I'd like you to listen to me for a minute. Will you give me that much, Kamisha?"

She only kept staring at him in complete distrust.

John sighed again. She could see him fight to control his anger. "Look," he began, "I didn't arrange to have Rick worked over."

Kamisha gave a short, bitter laugh.

John tried to ignore it, but she could see a muscle working furiously in his jaw. "For God's sake, use your head. Rick's up to his ears in something, but it doesn't involve me."

"Oh? Then who *does* it involve, John?"

"I wouldn't know. But I plan to find out. You can bet on that."

He was smooth; she'd give him that, all right. But she was learning, oh, how she was learning!

He was leaning on his cane with both hands now. She noticed inadvertently that his knuckles were white. "I spoke to the police, Kamisha. I made a full report. About the parties, about everything. The club's reputation isn't important enough to ignore this." He hesitated. "Do you think I could sit down?"

She made a distracted gesture with her hand, and he sank gratefully into a chair, rubbing a hand over his face. She got up finally, tired but restless, and pulled her robe tighter, yanking on the tie belt, walking on bare feet to the other side of the room.

"Kamisha," he said, "I'd like you to believe me."

"Of course you would."

"Look," he said after a moment, "it's been a long day. I—"

Kamisha spun around to face him. "A long day? Longer than Rick Simons's day?"

John made an obvious attempt to ignore her statement. "I saw Rick, as a matter of fact. He had surgery this afternoon. His jaw's broken, but he's going to be all right." When Kamisha made no reply, he went on. "I also arranged to have Joe Wilson fly on up and take over the club. He's a good man, my Florida operation."

"That's nice."

"Kamisha, listen, I'm going to do everything humanly possible to find out who did this to Rick."

"You mean you don't already have it figured out?"

"Not yet," he replied, a hint of anger and impatience in his tone. "If you'd have answered my calls . . . This isn't helping, Kamisha."

But she only shrugged, eloquently. "I haven't got anything to say to you."

"Then consider this. You could very well be in danger yourself. Whoever went after Rick is either desperate or totally ruthless."

"More *ruthless* than your family, John, the all-powerful Leopardo clan?" she said, facing him with narrowed eyes.

He was silent for a long time, his eyes shadowed, his expression unreadable, and Kamisha felt a spurt of unwanted guilt for her bitchiness.

"All right, Kamisha, you've said it. Do you feel better?"

She turned back to her window. She was aware that he was getting up from the chair, moving across the room. She refused to turn around, but her shoulders tensed in spite of herself.

"I would never harm you," came John's voice just behind her. "You're safe with me. I swear I had nothing to do with this business. How many times do I have to say it, Kamisha? What will make you believe me?"

She took a deep breath. "I don't know." The hairs on her neck prickled with his nearness. Her heart beat a wild staccato of fear and want. Then she heard his cane drop, and his hands came up to circle her neck, resting there lightly, ever so lightly, as if the wings of a bird touched her skin. Goose bumps broke out all over her body, and her breath stopped in her chest.

"I could, you know," he said softly into her ear, raising the hairs on her neck. "I could squeeze, just like this." His hands tightened imperceptibly. "You expect it. It would prove you were right."

She couldn't move. She felt the swift rushing of blood through her veins, the crazy juxtaposition of love and exciting fear, that sick self-destruct impulse. She just stood there, as still as a statue, waiting.

Then his hands were gone, and she sagged a little, released from tension.

"I had every opportunity to get rid of you, to shut you up, but I didn't. No one would have heard you or known." He put a hand on her arm and pulled her around slowly. "You made a mistake, Kamisha. You mistook who I really am."

He was so close, his face only inches away, his hand holding her arm hard, a kind of fierceness shining from him. "Do you believe me?" he asked.

"I...I don't know," she whispered.

"You flatter yourself. You're not so terribly clever. If I'd wanted to kill you, I could have, a dozen times between New York and here," he said angrily. "But I don't kill people. I'm not a Mafia hit man." He swung away from her and walked a few halting steps. "God, I'm tired of saying that. I'm so damn tired of having to say it."

Silence hung between them, filling the room. Her mind kept telling her to be afraid, to be cautious, but her heart felt pity and confusion. Her heart believed him.

A wrenching, unaccountable sadness gripped her. She saw his cane lying on the floor, and she knelt to pick it up, feeling the smooth burnished wood that his hand had caressed so often. She moved toward him and touched his arm from behind. He turned, tense, his eyes shadowed, his brows drawn.

"Here, John," she said softly, handing it to him.

He took it and searched her face for a time, an endless moment of recrimination and forgiveness and the faint stirrings of understanding. "Thank you," he said.

"Why did you come here?" she asked. "Why did you really come?"

He rubbed his hand over his face. "I don't know. I was worried about you, but I could have sent Inky. I guess I wanted to say what I just said." He looked at her. "Did it mean a damn thing?"

She nodded. A hint of self-consciousness came over her when she realized, for the first time, that she was clad in her old bathrobe with the ripped sleeve, her hair hanging uncombed, her feet bare. She pulled the robe around her protectively again.

"Look, Kamisha," John said then, quietly, with that gentle but unyielding authority restored to him. "I have to leave tomorrow. There's a Panamerican Trade Conference at my new hotel in Costa Rica. It's important. I should be there."

She felt disappointment wrap its tentacles around her. She tried to fight it off.

"I don't want to leave you here alone . . . for several reasons."

She remained silent.

He held her eyes steadily. "I want you to come with me."

"John, I couldn't," she said quickly.

"Forget your duties at the club for the time being. Joe's bringing a secretary with him from Florida.

They'll handle everything. I want you out of harm's way."

"You can't just order me around," she said, "and assume that my job isn't worth two cents."

"I'm sorry. That was hardly my intention. I'm worried about your welfare. I don't want you to end up like Rick. As owner of the club, it's my responsibility to see you're safe."

"Come on, John. Costa Rica?"

"Okay, I'll admit it's selfishness, too. I want to spend some time with you. Time away from here, away from everything. I want to prove my innocence to you once and for all."

She studied his face. "Is it so important to you?"

"Yes."

She looked down. "I don't know..."

"There'll be no strings attached. We'll have separate rooms. Do you understand? I'm not trying to seduce you."

"You have a way of being as insulting as the devil, John."

"I told you, I deal in truth. I mean that, Kamisha." He stepped close and tilted her chin up with one hand. "What do you say?"

She'd just been presented with the ultimate challenge—a man who stirred her blood, fascinated her, offered her danger and brand-new sensations, the lure of the unknown. Her curiosity was piqued beyond bearing. What did John really want from her? What was his "truth"?

"No strings," she said.

"That's right."

"But why? Why Costa Rica...with you?"

He seemed to have to search himself for the answer, for his truth. "I think I want you to get to know me."

She looked him square in the eye. Without hesitation she said, "Yes, I'll go with you."

CHAPTER ELEVEN

IT WAS A MAD RUSH to get ready for the sudden trip. Kamisha barely allowed herself the luxury of thought. She put from her mind the club and Brigitte and Rick— Rick, who was lying in the hospital. And there wasn't time, either to consider the danger to herself or even question Inky's substantial presence on the street outside her house. It was all so abrupt. It was downright crazy. John had come into her life and turned it upside down.

She stopped packing once, sat on the edge of the bed, her hands automatically reaching up to touch her neck—to touch the places where John's hands had rested, to feel his nearness and to wonder once again: what did he really want from her?

The flight south into Central America kept Kamisha's rapt attention. Her entire adult life had been spent in the cooler climates: the Rocky Mountains, the Canadian Rockies, the Swiss and Italian Alps, northern Japan, Sweden. She'd never seen a jungle or active volcanoes. But, as the 727 streaked across the blue sky, she saw that the land below was green and lush, the valley walls rising to surprising heights, jutting upward to where the green canopy met solid volcanic rock. She could look right down inside the craters of the necklace of volcanoes that were strung in a line down the Pacific Coast of Central America. There were few roads, the

Panamerican Highway being the only paved route south of Mexico. The land they flew over looked hostile, hot and steamy, uninviting to man.

"Different, isn't it?" John asked, closing the newspaper he'd been buried in.

Kamisha sat back in her seat and looked at him. "Sure I'm not going to die of the heat?"

"I hope not."

The flight path followed the Pacific Coast of El Salvador and Nicaragua, then headed inland, surprisingly low over the cloud-shrouded mountainsides of the Costa Rican interior. Then, up ahead, she could see a wide, lush valley and the spreading metropolis of San José, the capital city. The plane banked, easing its bulk carefully into the valley, in line with the small international airport.

"Is it a hassle at customs?" she asked.

He shook his head. "It can be, but my contractor is meeting us with a car. He'll have everything arranged."

She settled back, checked her seat belt; for all the hundreds of flights she'd been on, taking off and landing always made her a little nervous.

Flying could unsettle her, but strangely John no longer pushed those particular buttons. She was beginning to feel comfortable with him. She knew, too, that if she'd made love to John—if *he'd* allowed it—they would no longer have a relationship. It was an odd sort of foreplay, unlike anything in her previous experience, yet the sensation of his constant proximity held her as breathless as an intimate caress. She closed her eyes and took a deep breath. No man had ever stirred these feelings in her before.

"You aren't nervous, are you?" he asked, observing her, placing a hand gently on her arm.

"No," Kamisha said, turning to smile at him, praying he couldn't read her thoughts. "I'm fine."

It was hot and humid when they deplaned. Outside the airport, rumbling off the walls of the valley, was a thunderstorm. Rain pattered against the metal roof of the building, so noisy it was deafening. But, as promised, Juan Luis was there with a rental car for John, and they were miraculously whipped through customs and immigration while the tourists and businessmen waited in endless lines.

"That was convenient," Kamisha said, following the two men, glancing around. "Guess it pays to know the right people."

Her first impression of San José was how Mediterranean it appeared, not at all like Mexican cities she'd been to, but more Spanish, more European. They gave Juan Luis a lift into the center of town, and while the men talked about invoices and cost overruns and completion schedules, Kamisha sat happily in the back and took in the sights.

It was a cultured city, nestled in the cloud-covered mountains of Central America, sophisticated and clean. Theaters abounded, parks were crowded with exotic foliage. There were first-class hotels, exquisite restaurants and shops. The native Costa Ricans, or Ticos, as John had told her they called themselves, were well dressed and walked with pride in their step.

Like San Francisco, the city was built on hills that climbed both sides of the valley to steep, lushly green mountainsides. Cars went flying past them down the hills and chugged up the next ones. The downtown streets were teeming with shoppers, hawkers, tourists—a wealthy city—and bright colors assailed her eyes everywhere.

John dropped Juan Luis off at the rental car agency where he had left his van.

"Do you want me to drive?" she asked when the contractor had gone.

"I'll drive for a while. I don't get to very often," John said. "And it's an automatic." Unabashedly he tapped his knee with his cane before climbing into the driver's seat. "You just take in the sights. Relax. You're on vacation, Kamisha, and in Costa Rica the pace is slower. They don't like to display stress here."

"How far is the Montaña y Mar Hotel?"

"It's on the northern coast of the Nicoya Peninsula. As the crow flies, a hundred or so miles. But driving, that's another story. This could take us five or six hours, depending on traffic."

It wasn't long before Kamisha saw what John was talking about. Shortly after leaving San José, the road narrowed and began to climb a precipitous mountain-side. In the low-slung clouds myriad cars and trucks and buses crawled along, downshifting, spewing out exhaust.

Kamisha fastened her seat belt. "God, this is hairy."

"You get used to it."

John drove well, considering how seldom he chose to do so. And the car was peppy, a steel-gray Honda import, a model she'd never seen in the States.

The signs were in both Spanish and English, and when they stopped in a mountain village for lunch, she found that the menu was also bilingual.

"I thought I'd be floundering," Kamisha said, folding her arms on the wooden tabletop.

"The Costa Ricans are very well educated," he said. "They tell me there are twice as many teachers here as police. In fact, I don't know if I've ever seen a policeman."

"How often do you make this trip?"

"This is my eighth trip. But usually I fly up to the peninsula."

"You drove this time for me, then," she said, pleased that John had gone out of his way to show her the sights.

They both ordered fish. He told her that she should eat all the fish she could while there—it was some of the best in the world. Fresh, meaty, with names she'd never heard before. And each restaurant would cook it exactly the way she wanted. Over her cabbage and tomato salad she watched John in this setting that seemed to fit him so well. He could have been a Tico himself— dark-headed, olive-skinned, well-tailored in a lightweight khaki suit.

The fish was excellent, reminding her of bluefish. It was served with fried potatoes, hot and spicy, laced with peppers and onions.

They drove on, down out of the mountains to where the sun was shining brightly, and she could see the wide, deep blue waters of the Golfo Nicoya and the mountainous peninsula beyond. Then they turned north into the province of Guanacaste—cattle country, where the highway ran between two low mountain ranges and the valley was green and fertile, dotted with steers. It was a wealthy province. Sprawling haciendas graced the land, and Mercedes-Benzes, Audis and Volvos hogged the road. It could have been Texas—wide-open spaces with a bowl of lazy blue sky overhead.

Kamisha leaned back in her seat and let the balmy tropical air caress her face and bare arms. Languidly she asked, "Want me to drive?"

He shook his head and glanced over at her. He had one arm resting in the open window, the other draped casually over the steering wheel. "Maybe later."

"Leg not stiff?"

"Not bad."

They could have been husband and wife, Kamisha thought idly. A strange familiarity was growing between them. Yet behind the comfort was still that edge, that question: what, exactly, did John expect from her?

He drove, and she found herself watching him surreptitiously. Through half-closed eyes she took in the curve of his thigh muscles, his arms, the strength of his chin, the dignity of his carriage. He needed a shave. But she liked the dark shadow covering his cheeks and jaw and upper lip. She could imagine the burn it would leave on her own smooth face, that telltale red flush.

They turned westward now, leaving the main road. The country narrowed again, and the pavement gave way to a graded dirt road. And the jungle. It seemed to spring up around them on all sides, thick and lush and wet. Cloying and hot.

"Want the air conditioner on?" he asked.

Kamisha was well aware of the perspiration on the back of her neck and in between her breasts. The waistband of her tan slacks was soaked. Still, there was a feel to the jungle, a scent, that she hated to spurn. "No," she said, "it would ruin it."

John finally pulled over in a small farming village several miles from the coast. "Do you mind?" he asked, climbing out of his seat stiffly. "I'm cramping

up. And I don't know about you, but I'm dying of
thirst.''

"Whatever you're having, I'll take two.''

They sat in the shade at a tiny restaurant that con-
sisted of a tin roof, four supporting beams and a half
dozen tables. There were no walls, only the roof.

A lady in a spiffy white cotton dress appeared from
inside. Obviously her house was attached to the road-
side café. She wiped her hands on her apron and spoke
to John in Spanish.

"Dos Coca-Colas con Limón, por favor," he said.
Then, to Kamisha he said, "I'm afraid they don't have
plain soda water here. Is Coke all right?"

"It's fine.''

"You know, you can drink the water out of the tap
anywhere in Costa Rica.''

She looked at him doubtfully.

He laughed and made a cross over her heart.

"I won't get Montezuma's Revenge?"

"Not a bit of it. I promise.''

The village was filled with sound, Kamisha noticed.
Roosters crowed despite the afternoon hour, dogs
barked, birds screeched and squawked from deep in the
jungle. She asked John about the birds, pointing out a
small green parrot with a crimson head that sat in a
banyan tree across the road.

There were huge Wedgwood-blue birds scolding one
another down the way. John pointed out a family of
small brown monkeys resting in a tree. The jungle was
lush and exotic and scented by a dozen odors, all unfamiliar. Kamisha could smell beans cooking in cumin
and Tabasco from inside the woman's house. Flowers
crowded the small, wooden-framed bungalows and
grew in the jungle, up the sides of strange twisted trees,

clinging to vines. Their colors were brilliant: red, white, purple, yellow, fuchsia.

"It's almost claustrophobic," she said, draining her Coke.

"But different." He turned on his hard wooden seat and stared into the jungle.

"Not much like New York," she said.

"No, it's not." He turned back and looked intently into her eyes. "I don't know if a man could get used to it."

"Could you?" she ventured.

Casually, too casually, he shrugged. His Coke bottle was half lifted to his mouth. "Too much like another jungle."

Vietnam, she thought, of course.

John stretched his legs for a few minutes, walking down the nearly deserted village road. He stopped once and spoke to an old man who was sitting on his porch steps. Kamisha saw him gesture with his cane toward the coast and the old man reply and nod.

"What were you talking about?" she asked when John came back and climbed into the passenger seat, his cane resting on the floorboards.

"I asked how far it was to Culebra. The hotel's near there."

Kamisha put it in drive. "So? How far?"

"Ten kilometers. An *hour*," he replied, and they both laughed.

The coastal mountains were filled with the ubiquitous jungle and wild fruit trees, as well. There were coconuts and mangoes and pineapples, the fruit ripe for the picking. Kamisha stopped several times to gather up fruit that lay on the side of the road. He laughed at her.

She did like being in his company. And she was immensely glad she'd come along, although she still wasn't exactly certain why she'd agreed. After all, she couldn't be absolutely positive that John wasn't involved in the whole mess with Rick and the club. Of course, if he wasn't, she might have been in greater danger staying in Aspen.

But there was another reason she had to consider, another reason why she was making this crazy trip. John fascinated her. His words stuck in her mind: *I want you to get to know me.* She wanted to know John better, yes. Much better. She wanted to drive on through the jungle, just the two of them alone—on and on and on.

She glanced over at his profile and toyed with a novel idea. It was possible that she was actually falling in love.

It was early evening when they arrived at the hotel. Kamisha pulled into the parking lot reserved for employees just as a Sasha Airline flight was coming in, landing on a narrow airstrip carved out of the jungle. How easily they could have taken the small commuter flight, she thought. But then every minute they'd had alone together had been precious. John had known that, hadn't he? He'd called Juan Luis from Aspen to have the rental car ready because he'd anticipated those moments. The notion gave her a warm, spreading feeling deep in her belly.

Kamisha's room was luxurious. It was a suite, actually, done in pale pastels with blue-striped cushions on the living room couch. The carpet was rose, the curtains a paler rose. There were pastel seascape watercolors on the walls that were painted with the slightest blush of pink. The bathroom was white marble. The dressing room had a dainty little stool in front of the mirror. Every imaginable toiletry had been provided in a wicker basket, right down to lemon-scented soap from France.

But the view from the balcony was best. Her suite faced the turquoise-blue waters of the Pacific, overlooking a wide cove. Mountains stood at the entrance, green sentinels guarding the tranquility of the bay. She opened the sliding glass door and stood on the balcony, her hands on the smooth rail, and breathed in the salty air. She'd expected adjoining rooms in the spanking new hotel. But John's room was down the hall and faced the verdant mountainside. With the Panamerican Trade Conference scheduled to begin tomorrow, she assumed he'd been hesitant to take up one of the better rooms. It was a typical gesture, Kamisha knew, for an owner.

Despite the fact that one of the four wings was still not ready for occupancy, it was a lovely hotel. Nestled on the side of the mountain, its whitewashed structures gleamed in the tropical sun. There were two swimming pools, covered cabanas, tennis courts, exercise rooms, outdoor restaurants and lush gardens everywhere. A set of stairs wended its way down through the jungle to the beaches below. For the less hardy an open Jeep made the trip down the dirt road every fifteen minutes.

She took in one last breath of balmy sea air, then went back inside. It was too late in the day for a swimsuit, so she changed into loose white cotton slacks that she rolled up to her knees and a bright red tank top and sandals. She put her hair back in a patterned red scarf, then sat on the edge of the bed and picked up the phone, dialing John's room.

"Would you like to go for a walk on the beach?" she asked. "It would be good for your leg."

"I wish I could," he said, "but I've got a dozen obligations right here in the hotel. But you go. I'll see you back here for dinner at, say, nine. Is that too late?"

"Nine it is. And, John," she said, toying with the phone cord, "thank you for bringing me. It's absolutely beautiful here."

"My pleasure."

It was nearly sunset by the time Kamisha began the descent to the beach. From the stairs she could see the small fishing village nearby, a quarter of a mile to the north. But there were no buildings on the beach anywhere, only rows of tall palm trees and a sandy parking area. The Costa Rican beaches belonged to the government and to the people. It was unfortunate, Kamisha thought, that so many of the U.S. beaches were plagued with high rises and overcrowding.

Though the sun was setting, the sand was still warm on her toes. She walked to the water's edge to try out the temperature of the Pacific. Warm, delightfully so. And then she began to stroll at a lazy pace toward the village, checking her watch. It was seven-thirty. Plenty of time before dinner.

The sun finally dipped into the Pacific, casting the beach and the face of the hotel in magenta and gold. Above the building clouds clung to the jungle-clad mountainside, clouds tinged a deep lavender from the last rays of light. She couldn't fathom her presence in this Eden. At home in Aspen it would be cool already, cool and dry and absolutely cloudless. Club members would be just leaving for their after-work exercise program. And Rick . . . But Rick was in the hospital.

She swept a loose tendril of pale hair from her damp cheek and marveled at how easily she'd left the stress behind. John had been responsible for that. And somehow the problems at the club and Brigitte with all her nuttiness and troubles seemed far, far removed from this hidden corner of the world.

Ahead, several fishing boats were just making shore. Her stomach began to growl just watching the men unload the day's catch. She ventured close, smiling when they looked up to see her there. The boats were low and squat, and she moved closer, curious.

"What kind of fish?" she asked one of the men.

He gave her a broad smile. *"Pescado,"* he said, then shrugged. "Feesh."

"I know, but what kind?" she urged.

But he only smiled and pointed and said, "Feesh, *mucho* feesh *por la señorita."*

Well, they looked marvelous, anyway. And she could hardly wait to join John. What would she wear? And what would he wear? She adored him in summer white. His skin pale, his dark hair combed back smoothly. Would they dine outside by candlelight, the warm, tropical breeze caressing them? And then later. What did the evening hold in store?

She began to head back along the darkening shoreline, her sandals dangling from her fingers. There were a few other strollers out now, too, probably guests newly arrived. The beach was irresistible. Ahead she could see the stairs that led up to the Montaña y Mar Hotel. Lights had come on, illuminating the luxuriant hillside, displaying the palms and flowers. A soft, sea-scented breeze touched her back, cooling her.

Yes, they'd eat and talk and probably walk the scented grounds. And then maybe a cocktail from the lounge. But she'd insist they sit outside, perhaps by the pool where the palm fronds would click above their heads. Perhaps John would sit near. He might take her warm hand in his, stroke her fingers. He might even press his lips gently to her bare shoulder. She could almost feel it, her skin tingling at his phantom touch.

God, but I want him, she thought, and the idea was both frightening and exhilarating. She wanted all of him. If he'd take her to his room, she'd play no more games. She'd let him make love to her.

But would he?

There was still that reserve in John despite his easy conversation. For all she knew he didn't even desire her, not in that way.

Sandals still dangling from her hand, Kamisha began to climb the stairs back toward the hotel. Perspiration broke out on her neck and brow and upper lip. But it wasn't the hot, wet night. It was John; it was wondering and agonizing and second-guessing. What did he really want from her? And if she knew the answer, could she even provide it?

CHAPTER TWELVE

HE PHONED HER ROOM at 8:30 to say he'd be a few minutes late. "I'm terribly sorry," he said, "but the meeting's run over."

"Don't worry, I'm fine."

"Hungry?"

"Starved," she replied with a laugh.

"Hang on. I'll be there as soon as I can."

She wore a turquoise silk suit with full harem pants. The neck of the jacket plunged into a deep V, and Kamisha knew the color made her eyes look very blue.

It was a familiar routine: hair, makeup, shoes, accessories. She questioned for the first time in her life why she automatically went through the motions. But from the beginning she'd been trained to look her best. Women were valued above all for their appearance, she'd been taught. But as she wandered out onto the balcony and breathed in the fragrant air, Kamisha questioned that ironclad rule. John had seen her at her worst, with a torn bathrobe and uncombed hair, yet it hadn't appeared to matter to him. And, if what she looked like didn't matter to him, then maybe it was Kamisha herself that mattered to him. He'd seen through every smoke screen she'd thrown up, every subterfuge she'd attempted, and he still wanted her for...something. Companionship? Friendship? What?

It was such an odd, discomfiting sensation, to know a man wanted her for what she truly was, not what she appeared to be. And yet it was a great relief not to have to pretend anymore. She'd have to tell Brigitte when she got back... if Brigitte would speak to her. She wanted her friend to know, to understand this new discovery she'd made. It was important. Oh, god, Brigitte would *have* to forgive her and be her friend. They'd only had each other all these years.

But now, maybe, Kamisha had John. She looked out into the black velvet night, drew in a heavy, tropical air and smiled to herself. Yes, maybe she'd found a man.

His knock sent a shiver of excitement through her. She opened the door, and he stood there, impeccably dressed in a white dinner jacket, black trousers, a cummerbund.

"John," she said breathlessly.

"Sorry I'm late."

"It's all right."

He gestured at his formal clothes. "I'm still working, unfortunately. There's a banquet going on downstairs, and I've got to make an appearance."

"Am I going to be in the way? I mean, if you..."

He smiled. "I'm sure they'd rather look at you than me. These Latin men appreciate a beautiful woman."

She stepped out into the hallway with him and closed her door behind her. "What about you, John? Do you appreciate beauty?"

He took her arm. "Of course. Are you fishing for a compliment?"

"I would be with another man, but with you... I think I really want to know."

"You're beautiful, Kamisha. But that's not why I asked you to make this trip with me." He met her gaze frankly. "In a painting or sculpture there is only beauty. In a woman there is also passion and intellect and tenderness and need."

"And in a man?"

He nodded. "Yes, the same."

She walked beside him, slowing her pace to his, and felt his hand on her arm, keeping her close. She was proud to walk beside this man, bursting with a new-found joy, full of insane ripples of happiness and hope and gratification.

The banquet was being held on a covered veranda overlooking one of the pools. A large banner announced the Panamerican Trade Conference in English and Spanish, and there must have been three hundred people seated, being served by legions of white-coated waiters.

John showed her to a table near the door that led back into the hotel. "The getaway table," he said. "This dinner will go on for hours. Speeches and toasts, the usual."

"You don't have to stay?" she asked.

"God forbid. I'll be introduced after the meal, I'll stand and bow and say a few words. That's all."

Good, she thought. Then she'd have him to herself for the rest of the night. She'd have him to talk to, to look at, to touch—perhaps to hold hands or kiss. He'd never caressed her.

Huge tropical blooms hung over the veranda in teeming fecundity, almost artificial in their size and brilliance. Somewhere in the underbrush surrounding them howler monkeys chattered and rustled. Flowers adorned the tables in gorgeous masses, pearled with moisture.

Shrimp cocktails appeared before them, and their glasses were filled. "I hope you don't mind," John said. "It's a set menu."

"I don't mind. Your hotel is beautiful, John, and I'm sure the food is just as good."

"Looking at it professionally?"

She smiled. "No, I'm on vacation, remember?"

"Yes, I remember." He toyed with his wineglass. "I phoned Aspen a little earlier. I thought you might want to know."

"Rick?"

"He's doing all right. He can't be visited yet. Apparently he's told the police nothing."

"Um."

He reached across the table and took her hand. "Now, shall we forget all that?"

"Yes, all of it," she said fervently. "You said you wanted me to get to know you. All right, I'm willing. What should I know?"

He kept her hand in both of his and searched her eyes. "You know most of it. I haven't hidden anything. My family, the war, my business. I'm a very simple man, Kamisha. There are no secrets in my life."

She shook her head. "No, you're not simple. You're complicated. I never know what you're going to do or say or what you think. John, I don't even know what you think about me." She took a deep breath. "I don't know what you want from me."

"I want from you nothing except what you want to give me of your own free will."

"What? What can I give you?"

"Your friendship, your caring, your needs," he said carefully.

"That's it?" She drew her hand from his and sipped her wine.

"Yes."

"Why, John? Why me?"

He looked away from her for a minute, then turned back. "Because I see something in you that is good and fine, Kamisha."

She started to say something, but he held his hand up to stop her. "Not your body or your face, although they're lovely. I mean inside."

She drew in a quavering breath. This was difficult, wonderful, exciting, but so hard. "I'm a mess inside. Brigitte keeps telling me how I can't care for anyone because my parents didn't love me. I'm so afraid she's right, John."

He shook his head. "You're full of love, Kamisha."

"How do you know?"

"Trust me, I know."

Sudden tears burned in her eyes. She blinked, embarrassed, and felt one hot tear tremble on her lashes, then slide down her cheek. She raised a hand, but he stopped her and brushed it away with his own finger.

"See?"

Broiled fish arrived, with a béarnaise sauce, vegetables, rice. Kamisha ate a little, watching John all the time, noticing how he ate, seeing his hand on the fork, watching his lips, the muscles in his jaw when he chewed, his strong throat when he swallowed. The conversation rose and fell around them, the monkeys chattered, but she heard nothing, saw nothing but John's face and hands, the ruffled front of his shirt as it rose and fell with his breathing.

Her appetite faded. A feeling so powerful came over her that she could do nothing but give in to it. This was

no game. This was love and trust. This was absolutely
primitive—a man and a woman who wanted to be together, who needed each other, who fitted together like
the two halves of a whole.

"Kamisha," he asked, "are you all right? You're not
eating."

"I'm fine. I've never been better." She leaned across
the table and took his hand boldly. "Don't worry about
me."

It was late when the speeches started. A portly man
at the head table stood and welcomed everyone in ac-
cented English. "We wish to thank our host, Señor
Leopardo, for providing such a *marvilloso* hotel for our
meeting. John? Where are you, John?" the man said,
searching the crowd.

John stood up, raised a hand to attract attention,
smiled at the gathering. "Thank you, Señor Umberto,
it's my pleasure. Enjoy your visit here." Then he repeated his remarks in Spanish, and there was applause.
Kamisha clapped, too. She was proud of John. Oh, yes,
he was very special, a wonderful person, and he wanted
her. He'd chosen *her*.

The heavyset man went on, introduced someone else
who stood.

"Let's get out of here," John said quietly. "I retired
as of this moment."

"Yes, let's," she whispered.

It was as if she walked on air, or floated. John's hand
was at the small of her back, ushering her inside the
hotel. Where were they going? she wondered. What
would happen now?

A fine sheen of perspiration covered her as the humidity wrapped itself around her like a clinging veil. She
felt the warmth of John's body next to her, and she

knew she needed him beside her now, tonight, and tomorrow and always.

"Are you tired?" he asked.

"No."

He stopped, pulled her around to face him and held
both her arms. "You owe me nothing, Kamisha. Do
you understand? I will take nothing from you but what
you want to give me freely."

She felt herself melt and sag inside. "I want you," she
breathed. Then she just stood there, her eyes closed,
waiting.

He drew her closer, touched his lips to hers. Exquisite bursts of pleasure exploded inside her.

"My God," he said against her lips. "Kamisha..."

A group of people, laughing, chatting, were approaching. John pulled away from her, touched her
cheek and said, "Not here. It could be very embarrass-
ing." He smiled down at her. "But if you insist..."

"No, no." She was hot all over, dizzy. Her skin tin-
gled from head to toe and wild thoughts crowded her
mind.

He took her hand and kissed her knuckles, then led
her on, down corridors, around a corner. She was lost,
had no idea where they were. She followed, sure of
John, sure of herself, full to overflowing with her love.

Finally he stopped in front of a door. "This is your
room."

"Yes, yes, I..."

"Your key." He held his hand out.

She found it, gave it to him, saw him open her door
and hold his hand out to her.

"Come," he said quietly, and she went to him.

His lips were soft and hard all at once. She clung to
him, opening like a flower under his touch. He was

solid, hard-muscled all over, smelling of after-shave and wine. His arms were strong, holding her, his hands pressed her back, her buttocks.

She whimpered with her need and reached her hands under his jacket to get closer. His shirt was damp. She felt his fingers at her zipper. Then his hand was splayed on her bare back, his fingers kneading her flesh.

His tongue mingled with hers, and she could feel his heartbeat against her chest.

"Wait," he whispered. He pulled his coat off, loosened his tie, started taking the studs out of his shirtfront.

She helped him, fumbling at the studs. His skin glowed palely in the moonlight that came through the open balcony doors. Then her clothes dropped, sighing, to the floor, and they stood together, skin to skin, holding each other.

His beard was rough, as she'd imagined, but it felt good. His hands were gentle, knowing. They sat on the edge of her bed and kissed again, lingeringly, until he pushed her back and lay beside her.

He supported himself on one elbow and pushed her hair off her forehead with the other. "You aren't afraid anymore."

"No."

"I'm glad."

He leaned down to kiss her, drew his lips over her throat to find the spot where the pulse beat. Lower still his lips traced, finding a nipple, drawing it into his mouth until she moaned.

Outside the hot night wind rustled in the oversize fronds of the jungle, and a monkey scolded once, then was silent. Kamisha was in a foreign land, making love to a man who was a stranger to her. Yet his body was as familiar to her as her own. He fit against her and knew all her secret places, stroking, whispering, loving her. His fingers were light on her flesh, then demanding. He kneaded her hip and thigh as she lay next to him on her side. Feather-light, he ran a hand along the back of her knee until ripples of joy coursed upward, making her squirm and moan and twist her own fingers in his hair. He laughed gently, looked up into her eyes for a moment before his tongue again found a nipple. Kamisha arched her back and sighed in pure delight.

She had no shame, no self-consciousness. She loved John with her body, tasting, touching, wanting to give him as much pleasure as he gave her.

He entered her and filled her, rocking over her in a rhythm as old as time. Quicker, harder. She held on to him tightly and went with him, gasping, reaching . . . to the pinnacle, crying out her release, feeling him inside her, over her, all around her, loving him, adoring him.

Later she opened her eyes to find John propped on one arm again, watching her, smiling. His hair was mussed, and sweat gleamed on his skin.

"You were sleeping," he said.

"I wasn't."

"You were. Out cold." He drew his fingers through her hair that lay spread like a pale fan on the pillow.

She sighed happily. "I guess you must have tired me out."

"Go back to sleep," he murmured.

She nestled against him, drawing in his smell, feeling his damp skin, full of joy at his closeness. "Do you have to go back to your room?" she asked sleepily.

"No, not if you want me to stay."

"Stay," she whispered, closing her eyes again.

She woke to the sound of the shower on in her bathroom. The night came flooding back, and she lay there savoring the memory, utterly relaxed. John. The leopard. He'd attacked, caught his prey, devoured her. She was his now, part of him.

He came out of the bathroom, a towel around his waist, droplets of water on his skin. He looked young and happy, well rested.

"You're awake," he said. "Hungry?"

"Starved."

"You always say that."

She stretched, the sheet falling off. "I didn't eat much last night. I was otherwise employed."

He limped toward her, and she saw his knee for the first time. Yes, just as she'd imagined. A long, puckered ridge, shiny white scar tissue. Yet his calf below it was strong and curved, and above it his thigh swelled out against the white towel. His injury was part of him, just like his strong hands or the black hair on his chest or his thin, curved, sensitive mouth, and she accepted it, loved it just as she loved every inch of him.

He stopped, seeing her eyes on him, and looked down. "Pretty, isn't it?" he said.

"John. Come here." She held her hand out to him.

He moved toward her and stood looking down at her, his eyes shadowed.

"It's beautiful," she said, tracing the scar with her finger. "It's part of you, and I think it's a beautiful knee." She tugged at his hand, pulling him down next to her.

"Oh, God, Kamisha," he said, "where have you been all these years?"

"At your club in Aspen. Didn't you know?" she asked facetiously.

"I knew. I knew. But—"

"Shh." She ran a hand over his flat stomach and felt him tense up. "Are you ticklish?"

"I don't know. Try me."

She ran her fingers along his ribs. "Well?"

"A little. Maybe you should try lower."

"Naughty, naughty." She kissed him full on the lips, then drew her hand back. "Will anyone be looking for you? I mean, in your room. Do you have to go to work this morning?"

He glanced at the bedside clock. "Not for an hour."

"Oh, good."

She took his head in her hands and covered his face with kisses. He moved against her. "Ah, Kamisha," he said, "I wish..."

"What?" she whispered against his skin. "What do you wish, John?"

"For this, that's all, just for this."

She knelt over him, her hair hanging down like a curtain. His towel fell away, and she lowered herself onto him. He was ready. He filled her, grunting with pleasure. She rose over him and fell back, again and again, watching his face as the ripples of passion washed across it. She felt enormous power because she gave him that pleasure—her and no one else. She was full of strength and exultation and fertility, a primitive earth goddess.

It came on her suddenly, a wave of pleasure so intense that she nearly fainted. "Oh!" she cried out, surprised, lost. "Oh!"

Collapsing on him, she lay there, breathing hard, exhausted. She became aware of his hand stroking her back, up and down, up and down.

He loved her, too. He must. She had to be careful, though, not to assume too much, not to push him. John was a man who knew what he wanted, and he'd made it clear he wanted her. When he was ready to commit to something more, he'd tell her. There was time, lots of time. All she had to do was love him and wait.

"Do you have to go yet?" she asked, turning her head sideways on his sweat-slicked chest.

"Not yet," he said.

HE'D NEVER FELT this way in his life. He'd spoken to the chef and the maître d'; he'd checked with the head housekeeper, and made a call to Juan Luis in San José. He'd worked hard all day, doing his job, making sure the hotel ran like clockwork, touring the unfinished wing with the workers. But he was only going through the motions. Inside he ached for Kamisha and thought about her every moment.

He'd only had time for a quick phone call after the formal luncheon.

"Hello," she'd answered breathlessly.

"It's me," he'd said.

"I know." She'd laughed. "Who else would call me here?"

"What are you doing? Bored?"

"No, I'm as happy as a clam. Reading, relaxing. I miss you."

"I miss you, too. Damn, I just can't get away until this afternoon."

"I know. Listen, I'll go down to the beach later. If I'm not in my room, that's where I'll be. Come down and join me when you're done."

"And get some sun on my city pallor?"

"Sure, risk it all."

"Kamisha..."

"Yes, John?"

"Nothing. I'll talk to you later. As soon as I can. Be good."

"Oh, John, I'm so glad you brought me here. I'm so happy."

"Look, I've got to go. Later, all right?"

"All right."

Impatience tore at him all afternoon, but things kept cropping up. A shortage of a certain vintage of white wine, a problem with the laundry, a new brochure to look over, an employee who was stealing. A million small, nagging details that inundated him, drowning him in aggravation.

At six he phoned her room. No answer. She was down at the beach then. He hurried to his room, threw off his clothes and pulled on a bathing suit. God, he hadn't been to a beach for years! Not since R and R in Vietnam. No, he'd been too busy, too tied up, too damn mature to put on a bathing suit and lie on a beach.

A shirt, open in front, sunglasses, his cane. Ridiculous, a bathing suit and a cane. He didn't care. Kamisha was waiting, as impatient as he was, her long, lean body awaiting him. Her love warming him, resurrecting his dead heart. He felt young again, a boy who was going to meet his girl. This time it would be different; this time he wouldn't lose his woman to the voracious hunger of the press.

It had been ten years since he'd been crazy about a woman. Ten years since Jo, the girl he was going to marry. Oh, yes, it was going to work, he'd assured himself then. She'd been young and innocent and pretty, like a china figurine, but, oh, how she'd run when the TV cameras started following her and John around. She'd gotten hurt and frightened and left him cold.

Down the stairs to the beach. Damn his knee; it slowed him. Across the warm, giving sand. The sea sighed and splashed, blue, as blue as Kamisha's eyes.

Not many people were left on the beach; the sun was low. They were all resting in their rooms, showering, changing for dinner.

Where was she?

He walked with difficulty through the sand, his cane sinking into the softness, searching the beach, impatient.

"John," he heard. There, over there. She sat on a big red towel, her knees crossed Indian-fashion, wearing a black tank suit, her skin as smooth and tan as satin.

He waved and limped toward her.

"Hi," she said. "It's about time."

"Sorry, I got hung up."

"I know. I'm a workaholic, too. Only now I'm on vacation."

He sat on her towel and put down his cane. "What a day."

"Relax. Lie down. I'm so relaxed I think I'm going to melt." She laughed at herself. "Listen to me."

He leaned over and kissed her. "I'm glad you're enjoying yourself."

"I'd be enjoying myself even more if I had you to myself every second of the day."

"Selfish."

"Yes," she said. "Very."

"There's another dinner tonight."

"Oh."

"We don't have to go."

"Don't let me keep you from something important."

"I won't." He fingered a lock of her hair that lay on her shoulder. "I know my priorities."

"Work."

"I may rethink that priority."

She smiled and lay back on the towel, her eyes closed, her hand resting lightly on his knee. "I love it here," she said, sighing, and he recalled her sighs of pleasure the night before.

"Um." He sat there and looked at her, simply looked, drank his fill. He couldn't fit his mind around the reality of her there with him, giving him the precious gift of her body and her love.

He'd said he wanted only what she chose to give, and it was true. But what he'd received was so much more than he'd imagined. It was as if a dam, an emotional dam, had been broken in her, and the water was flooding over it, drowning everything in its path, a sea of passion drowning them both.

She tapped his knee. "Lie down, relax. Stop staring at me."

"How do you know I'm staring?"

"I can feel it."

"Your eyes are closed."

"It doesn't matter."

He stretched out next to her. The sea gurgled and whispered to itself, and the sun was still warm.

"I've been here for hours," she said lazily.

"What do you want to do tonight? Eat in the restaurant, walk to the village? There's a disco, too."

Her lips curved deliciously. "How about room service?"

"That can be arranged." He rolled over onto one elbow to see her better.

"Your room or mine?" she asked.

"Yours has a better view."

"What will the hotel staff say, John?"

"Nothing."

"But you're the owner. You're acting disgracefully." She was smiling, though, teasing.

He shrugged, but she couldn't see that; her eyes were still closed. "Does it bother you?" he asked, tracing a finger down her jaw, her throat, her chest.

"No."

"Me neither."

She sighed and rolled over onto her stomach. "Do you want to go swimming?"

"Is the water warm?"

"Chicken. Warm as soup. I bet you've never been in the water here, and you own the hotel."

"You're right. But I'm a good swimmer. It's part of my physical therapy program."

"Come on then." She sprang up and held her hand out to him. "Come on."

He took it. She braced herself and pulled him up, and they walked down to the water's edge, hand in hand. She let go then, ran in and flung herself into the waves, turned onto her back and paddled there, afloat.

John walked in, up to his knees, then his waist. He made a clean dive and felt the water surround him, support him. He surfaced and stroked out to where she floated on her back.

"Nice, huh?" she asked.

"Great. Now I know what to tell the guests." He floated, too, looking up at the sky.

"You can stand here. It's shallow," Kamisha said. She stood, sculling her arms to stay upright.

He jackknifed and dived underwater. Her arms and legs were greenish and wavering. He put his arms around her waist and pulled her under with him. She felt cool and slippery, and her arms came around him as they kicked to the surface together, bursting through to the air, laughing, gasping, splashing.

"No fair," she cried.

"Sure it is."

They clung together, sleek and wet. Her hair was plastered to her shoulders, her skin smooth and silky, warm above water, cool below. She entwined her legs around his, and he held her up like that, buoyed by the seawater. Bending his head, he kissed her, long and thoroughly. Her hands clasped his shoulders and her body pressed to his. She tasted of saltwater and sweetness. He tried not to think, tried to wipe his mind clean and take the pleasure as it came. Exquisite, blinding pleasure.

"Oh, God," she whispered, against his mouth. "You feel so good."

"I won't be able to get out of the water," he said lightly.

"No one will notice." She smiled impishly. "No one but me."

Eventually they returned to the beach. It was empty. The sun was setting over the ocean, washing the sky with tropical hues. They flung themselves down on the towel, dripping water, breathing hard.

"It'll be dark soon," he said idly. "And I bet you're starved."

"Salty and sandy and starved."

"We should go back," he said.

She rolled over on top of him, pinning his entire length to the towel. Her hair hung down, heavy and wet, tickling. She gazed into his eyes, leaned down and touched her lips to his. "You make me feel very special, John. I've never felt this way before. I'm afraid it's addictive."

He put his arms around her, loving the feel of her weight on him. "You are special."

"This isn't...I mean..." She looked away for a moment, serious suddenly. "This isn't a one-night stand for you, is it?"

"No, Kamisha."

"You're sure?"

There it was, that vulnerability again, the little girl lost. He hugged her tighter. "I'm sure."

"I won't let you go easily, John. I'm warning you."

"Be careful, lady. You're scaring me to death."

The sky was fading to purples and grays when they climbed the stairs to the hotel.

John felt as though his skin were sensitive—from the sun and sand, he supposed. But it could have been from Kamisha's nearness. He felt sensitive all over, inside, too, alive to all kinds of new possibilities.

Even Kamisha with her tan was a little red. He could see a line of white skin that followed the curve of her bathing suit straps and also along her thigh where her suit ended. Abruptly he wanted her, there and then, wanted to strip her suit off and see the white skin underneath.

He was out of control, spinning in the midst of new, remarkable sensations. But it was good, fantastic. It was life as it was meant to be lived.

There was the door to her room. She was opening it, turning to him. "Are you...?" she began.

He stepped in with her, set his cane against a chair and took her in his arms. Hot and sandy, gritty, salty, they stripped off their wet suits, let them drop to the floor, clung and caressed and whispered and loved each other.

CHAPTER THIRTEEN

JOHN WOKE AT DAWN to the cacophony of jungle noises outside the screened door and the swishing of the off-shore breeze in the palm trees. He lay there for a time, savoring the moment—the feel of a woman next to him, the scent of her body, the soft soughing of her breathing. He couldn't remember the last time he'd awakened like this. Maybe he never had.

He felt happy, a singular and unfamiliar sensation that took him a minute to recognize and acknowledge. Not just physically sated but content inside. He lay there, his hands folded behind his head, and grinned up at the ceiling.

Eventually he rolled over and kissed her shoulder, breathing in the scent of her skin, feeling its softness. He was being selfish; he should let her sleep, but he couldn't wait another moment.

She stirred and murmured something, then her eyes opened sleepily.

"Wake up, Sleeping Beauty," he said.

She stretched, lithe and catlike, and turned onto her side to face him. "Hi," she whispered.

"I'm sorry I woke you. I couldn't help it," he said, smoothing her hair back. "I feel like we have so little time together."

"Do we have to go back soon?"

"No, well, not today, anyway."

"Good. Do you have to work today?"

"Not much. A couple of things." He kissed her nose.

"You need a little R and R. I can see that. Just lie around and relax. The beach maybe," she said lazily. "And room service."

"We never ate last night."

"I know." She laughed a little, her eyes sparkling. "My stomach's growling."

"Let me listen." He put his ear to her smooth, tanned stomach and listened, then turned his head to kiss her bare skin there.

"John," she whispered, and he felt her muscles tighten. "You better not do that."

"Why not?" he murmured against her belly.

"Um, you know."

He straightened and lay half on top of her, feeling her long, taut length against him. "I know, Kamisha, but what I'm not sure of is if you can perform on an empty stomach."

"I don't know," she answered, moving against him. "Should we find out?"

She entwined her legs around his and arched against him, her skin warm, soft satin sliding over muscle. He felt himself growing aroused, his breath quickening. His hands roamed her body. He kissed her everywhere, drawing response from her like a maestro on an instrument. And all the while he watched her, drank in her sleek beauty like a man too long denied water. Pale morning sun that filtered through the jungle mist fell in patches on her flesh, highlighting a hipbone, bringing forth a curving breast from the shadows. He touched the precious curves with his lips until her flesh quivered. Lightly, lightly, he drew his tongue across a nipple, pausing only momentarily at its crest before he moved lower to her belly.

He entered her finally, fighting for control, wanting to give her pleasure, to satisfy her as she'd never been satisfied before. He was poised over her, his breathing ragged, his eyes closed, and he felt her gather under him. She moaned and drew in her breath and cried out, and then he could release his own passion into her, his body hard and strong and absolutely fulfilled.

When she stirred under him, he sighed and rolled aside. He lay propped on an elbow and studied her face.

"Penny for your thoughts," she said.

"Not much going on in my head right now," he replied.

"Um. This is nice. Better than nice."

"Kamisha." He paused, unsure of what he wanted to say.

She touched his face with her fingers. "Ask me anything."

"Did you . . . I mean, have you . . . dated much?"

She smiled. "You want to know how many men I've slept with, don't you?"

"No, no, it's none of my business."

"It is. Everything about me is your business. John, I want you to know everything. I've never been honest with a man in my life, but I will be with you." She hesitated. "I was married for almost a year. Josh and I were kids playing at house. I don't think he was a very passionate man. He was too selfish. I guess I wasn't very knowledgeable about men, so I didn't know any better. Now I know, though, and when I remember—"

"You don't have to tell me," he said.

"I do. I have to be honest with myself, too. I haven't had many men, John. Since Josh, very few. I flirt with men. I'm good at that. I control the relationship that way, but when it comes to sex, I back off. I guess...oh, I don't know... Maybe it's my way of getting back at men."

"You're so beautiful. How can you blame them?" he said, holding her hand, kissing her fingers one at a time. "You should pity them."

She shook her head. "All my pity was reserved for me. Men always looked at me, sure. But they never put any value on what was inside. A homely woman, she has a chance to be loved for what she really is, but not me. I suppose it's sort of like being rich. Then you're always on guard against men who will love your money and not you."

He thought for a minute, grateful that Kamisha could confide in him. Maybe all the pain he'd endured was worth something, after all; it had made him sensitive to her and able to recognize what lay under her brittle surface. Maybe everything in his life had prepared him for this time, this place, this woman.

"Am I making any sense?" she asked, searching his face.

He nodded.

"Okay, Dr. Freud," she said, nestling against him.

"What about your parents?" he asked. "Did you ever tell them this?"

"You're kidding." She ran her fingers through the fine hair on his chest. "I didn't even know myself, and they wouldn't have listened. They would have said what they always did, 'Kamisha, we did the best we could for you.' And it's true, you know. They did the best they were capable of. It just wasn't good enough. But, you know, I've come to terms with that."

"Do you see them much?"

She shrugged. "Not much. They drop by Aspen once
a year to ski. Unless the snow's better in Europe. We
speak on the phone. It's all very polite. Civilized. I
might never have learned there was anything more to
life."

He stroked the back of her head as it lay on his chest.
"You knew."

"Maybe. I missed something. I didn't think it was a
man, though."

"How wrong can a person be?"

"Very, very wrong," she said.

"Funny, my folks are just the opposite. Lots of wailing and fighting and loving. Typical Italian emotional
outbursts. I loved my dad when I was a kid. He was a
good father, and being the only son I was spoiled rot-
ten, I guess. It was when I realized what he did, what he
really did—I was in high school—that I turned away
from him. It must have killed him, and my mother. I
was very young and hard then, and you don't realize
what pain you can inflict."

She lay there in his arms, quiescent, listening.

"When I look back, I think that's why I joined the
army. I wanted to get farther away from him, as far as
I could get." He paused, remembering. "I certainly
succeeded."

"What was it like over there, John?"

"Hot, sweaty, smelly. Scary. You were scared all the
time. You lived hard, played hard. Everyone had his
own way of coping. It was a dirty war." He took a deep
breath. "I made sergeant because I was the one with the
most seniority, and our sergeant got blown up in front
of me. There I was, a nineteen-year-old recruit, a college kid, in charge of a platoon of filthy, terrified men.
You've got to wonder..."

"And Inky?" she said.

"He was in my outfit. My right-hand man. He knew more than anyone about war. Somehow you just knew Inky was a survivor. He was a lifer, but hadn't made sergeant yet. He kept getting busted. Fighting. Usually with his superiors."

"But not you?"

"Hell, no, *I* always listened to Inky."

"I wish I'd known you then," she murmured.

"No, you don't. I was a brash kid. You would have hated me. Besides, you were too young. You'd have been, let's see, eight years old."

"I would have adored you."

"You're prone to exaggeration, lady."

"And Inky, tell me how he ended up with you."

"Well, when the war was over, Inky decided the Special Forces were no fun anymore. That's the word he used—fun. He left the army, and we'd kept in touch, so he showed up one day. Just showed up. It was a time when I was low, feeling sorry for myself. My knee was giving me a lot of trouble. So Inky took over. He started me on a weight program. He...uh...he did me a lot of good."

"Friends are important," she mused, her fingers playing idly across his chest.

"Brigitte."

"Yes, good old Brigitte. I know how she looks to you, to the world. But she's the sweetest, most spontaneous person I've ever met. We were roommates in the Taos School. Both of us were outcasts, poor, lonely kids. Her parents sent her there because they couldn't handle her getting into trouble, and mine sent me to get rid of me. All in the name of doing what was best for their daughters. Maybe it was the best, because I met

Brigitte. I couldn't have made it through without her. After my divorce, she took me in. Her marriage was pretty shaky at the time, but she took me in, sat up nights crying with me. And then when Freddy divorced her, she came to me. We've taken care of each other over the years.''

''But you've taken care of her a little more,'' John suggested.

''I don't know. There are different ways of taking care of a person.''

''Yes, there are.''

''And I feel really bad about this fight we had. I can't understand why she got so upset at me telling you about the parties. It was almost as if she thought they weren't wrong, as if she were defending them. That's crazy, though. I know Brigitte, and if there were kids involved . . .''

''She'll come around.''

''I hope so. Sometimes she gets so out of control that I get scared.''

''Forget Brigitte for now,'' he said. ''Remember, you're on vacation.''

''Um, okay. I'll just lie here and listen to the birds like this all day.''

''No beach? No room service?'' he teased.

''Just you.'' She snuggled closer against him.

''Fine with me,'' he said into her hair.

She lay there, slender and warm in his embrace, and he thought that nothing had ever felt so good. He turned his head to say something to her and realized that she had dozed off. He smiled to himself and watched her for a while, drifting on a sea of pleasure, holding on to the perfection of the moment.

When he woke later, the sun was bright, the palms still, the morning offshore breeze at rest. He saw that Kamisha was awake, still buried in his arms, her mouth curved with a languid amusement as she watched him.

"Lazybones," she said.

"I'll show you who's lazy."

He found the tiny little spot on the column of her neck that held her pulse. He kissed it, then he drew his tongue downward, across her shoulder and collarbone, lower, to taste a breast again.

Kamisha sighed and squirmed gently as his hands moved beneath her and pressed her body to his. With infinite care John placed his lips between her breasts, kissing the hollow.

"Um," she said, "that feels so wonderful."

He smiled into her sleep-warmed flesh.

"Aren't you famished? We still haven't eaten since—"

"Hungry for you" was all he said, and it was true.

Kamisha turned his head up to her face and laughed. "I'm out of fuel, John, I'm going to have to eat something." She stirred, attempting to get up.

"All right," he said, propping his head on an elbow, "I suppose I shouldn't starve you."

"But you don't have to get up. I'll go fetch us some sweet rolls and juice and coffee."

"Call room service."

"I need to eat now. Not in twenty minutes. I'm faint."

"Are you always this famished?"

"'Fraid so. I'm such a pig."

"An active one."

He watched her pad across the room, the long thigh muscles in her legs curving femininely, her buttocks round and firm. She leaned to pick up her clothes, and her breasts hung deliciously. Naked, Kamisha was a centerfold, not as endowed as some, but beautiful to behold.

He hated to see her get dressed, and she teased him, tossing the smooth, silky curtain of her hair over a shoulder as she combed it out.

"Hurry back," John said. "I'm getting hungry, too." He smiled at her knowingly.

The room felt empty without her presence. Yet the aroma of their lovemaking lingered, a sweet male-female scent. He wanted her back. He wanted her soft warmth beneath him again. He was ready. And he was amazed at himself. Even as a young man he hadn't had this stamina. But then he hadn't known Kamisha, either.

It was a full ten minutes before he heard the key in the lock. He'd showered and shaved quickly and was standing in the steamy bathroom.

"John?" she called.

"In here. I'll just be a minute. Were they helpful in the dining room?"

"Oh . . . yes," she said, sounding strangely distracted.

"You brought coffee?"

"Ah, yes."

"Something wrong?"

There was no reply, and he wondered. When he came out of the bathroom, he saw her standing by the window, looking out. There was a tray of rolls and coffee and juice on the table, a folded newspaper. But Kamisha wasn't eating. She was frowning.

John's brow furrowed. "Thought you were starved."

"Oh," she said, turning to face him. "I am. I was."

He cocked his head, pulling on the white robe that the hotel supplied. "I get the feeling—" he began, but Kamisha interrupted.

"Oh, God, John," she said, her shoulders sagging, "I wasn't going to show you this. But you'd see it eventually." She reached down and picked up the newspaper, unfolding it. "Here," she said, walking to him, holding out the day's edition of the *Miami Herald* that was shipped abroad routinely the evening before.

"So?" he asked, taking it, looking at her.

"Read page two. Go on. Oh, John," she said, and there was a break in her voice.

John studied her strained face for a moment longer, then went over to the table, pouring himself a coffee, sitting down before he opened the paper. From the look on Kamisha's face he already knew he wasn't going to like this.

He turned to page two, shook the paper, folded it. The headline jumped up at him: "Aspen Love Nest, Mafia Involved. Mob running brothel in Aspen, claims Joanna Stern, wife of Senator Luke Stern of California."

John swore, then looked up at Kamisha. There were tears in her eyes. He tried to keep his cool.

"It gets worse," Kamisha whispered, and sank onto the bed. "Oh, John..."

With controlled effort he sipped on his coffee, then began to read the article. His fingers clenched the paper tightly:

At a Washington press conference today Mrs. Stern, 41, told reporters she was filing for divorce in California. Mrs. Stern claimed knowledge of "disgusting parties at Aspen's posh Ute City Club involving underage girls."

Mrs. Stern was quick to point out that the club's owner is none other than New York and Miami's John Leopardo, the son of famed Mafia kingpin Gio Leopardo. When asked if Senator Stern attended any of these parties, Mrs. Stern referred reporters to her lawyer.

John let out a deep, rasping breath. His rage made the print blur, but he forced himself to read on:

Mr. Leopardo could not be reached for comment today, nor was Senator Stern available. But this reporter learned that the manager of the swank Aspen club, Rick Simons, formerly of Miami, is currently in the hospital in Aspen.

Mr. Simons's doctor, John Freeman, told reporters that his patient received a bad beating at the hands of an unknown assailant. The assault raises several questions. Did Rick Simons threaten to go to the police with details of these parties? Has the self-proclaimed black sheep of the Leopardo family, John Leopardo, finally come back into the fold of brutality and vice?

For a long time John sat staring out the window, the paper drifting to the floor. It was happening again, all over again. The look on Kamisha's face—exactly the same. It was the nightmare that had come back to haunt him again and again over the years—the headlines, the filth in the papers, the tears and recriminations and, finally, the excuses, the severing and rejection.

He couldn't go through it again.

"John?" he heard her saying. "John, are you all right? John?"

He looked at her, and already the pain smote him like a bludgeon. "Yes," he forced himself to say, "I'm fine."

"How can they do this to you?" she asked, pacing the floor like a sleek, agitated panther. "It's so unfair."

He shrugged. "The press isn't in business to be fair."

"But you'll tell them the truth, won't you? Don't let them get away with this. If you tell them—"

"The truth," he mused, turning from her. Hadn't Jo said the same thing?

"It's horrible, horrible. Why are they doing this? Why can't they leave you alone?" Kamisha asked.

But he held up a silencing hand and then picked up the telephone. "Front desk," he said. He waited, his jaw clenched. "Have a bellman up to room 207 and room 220 in ten minutes. No, everything's fine, Alvarez. I've got an emergency at home. And arrange to have my rental car returned to San José. That's correct. When is the morning flight due in? All right, have them hold it. Thank you."

John replaced the receiver and put his hands on his hips, frowning.

"We're leaving?" Kamisha asked.

He had force himself to acknowledge her. "Yes. The commuter flight is due in twenty minutes. Can you be ready?"

"Well, yes, of course I—"

"All right. Twenty minutes, Kamisha. I don't want to miss this plane."

"We're going to Aspen today?"

"As fast as I can get there."

JOHN KNEW that from Kamisha's point of view he was being unreasonable. And cold. But he'd never been able to pretend. Anyway, he thought, she'd have to realize that they'd made a mistake in Costa Rica. Perhaps, though, it hadn't been a mistake. Rather, they both would do well to view it as an interlude, a brief affair. He'd been foolish to think otherwise even for a moment.

Now he was back to the real world.

They sat in a coffee shop in the New Orleans airport, waiting for the connecting flight to Denver. Kamisha sipped on a soda while John stared out the window at the tarmac. It was drizzling out, hot and steamy. Low, grainy clouds hung over the city. The weather suited his mood.

"John," he heard her ask, "can we at least talk about this?"

"There's really nothing to say, Kamisha."

"But there is. I'm a part of this, too."

He lifted a dark brow. "Are you?"

"Yes, I am."

"I don't think so. You have no idea what my life has been like."

"So am I supposed to pity you? Are you feeling sorry for yourself?"

"I was stating a fact."

"But you aren't your family. You aren't your father."

"Tell that to the press."

"What do you care *what* they think?"

"I don't care. Not for myself."

She was silent for a moment. "Is it...me, then, you're worried about?"

"Can we drop this subject?" he said, then turned away and looked back out the window.

The flight to Denver was no better. Kamisha kept trying to get him to open up, but John had closed her out, coldly, deliberately. His walls were back up, firmly in place. Kamisha Hammill barely existed to him. When they reached Aspen, he'd put Inky in charge of watching over her. She'd be safe until he got to the bottom of this. And then it was home to New York, home to try to repair the damage caused by Rick Simons and God knows who else.

Damn, John thought. All those years of distancing himself from his father, from his entire family. All the years of living a practically celibate life because, after Jo, he could never ask a decent woman to share his family's name. The dozens of times he'd dodged the press. The Internal Revenue Service audits every time his father had faced a Senate investigation. Oh, sure, he'd thought about changing his name. But a stubborn kind of pride had kept him from doing so. And besides, John knew, the press wouldn't have been fooled for more than a day.

Despite it all, however, he'd darn near succeeded in living a solitary life where the media couldn't really get to him. Four beautiful health spas, twenty years of hard work and careful planning. And now *this*. Again.

The long line of barrier mountains, the Rockies, rose to the left of the plane. It was evening, the sun just setting behind the great mountains that formed the backbone of North America. As the plane banked, turning two degrees west toward the city of Denver, John could see a blanket of twinkling lights glowing softly in the growing dusk.

He felt a heavy sadness. This morning he'd been near true happiness. It had been like entering a dream, living a fantasy. He supposed now that he'd known all along it couldn't last, but he'd let himself go for once, let himself drift right into the middle of that Shangri-la. The foolish thing was to have taken Kamisha with him.

John looked directly ahead, but he was still aware of her sitting, straight-backed, next to him, leafing through a magazine. He wondered if she could see the pages, or if she was accusing him in her thoughts, blaming him for dashing her dreams.

He could explain to her. He could tell her that life with him would be a living hell. Oh, maybe not at first. But eventually she'd tire of the press hounding her. She'd get fed up with the questions: what was it like marrying into a Mafia family? And children. A man owed a woman her own family. How could a child be expected to put up with the teasing and jeering, the humiliation, a lifelong trauma? He could tell her about Jo, lovely, warm, naive Jo, whose love had shriveled up and died under the spotlight of the press.

Sure. He could tell Kamisha what the future really held in store. But she wouldn't believe him. She hadn't already lived it as he had. It was best to let it drop. Let her think what she would. She'd get over it faster. And, maybe, so would he.

What had she said as they'd departed New Orleans? *John, talk to me. For God's sake, let me help.*

He'd answered her in steely silence.

The landing gear thumped down beneath their feet. The stewardess in first class was saying something. John glanced at the beautiful woman who sat next to him and felt regret stab him in the breast.

CHAPTER FOURTEEN

KAMISHA LIFTED her hair off her neck, feeling its dampness. Her nerves were scraping together. She glanced out the window of the commuter flight and saw the lights of Aspen twinkling at the end of the valley below. In a couple of minutes the plane would land. Inky would be waiting with the car. They'd drop Kamisha off at her house, and they'd pull away, severing the single, fragile thread that existed between her and John. She knew in her heart that this was the end of their relationship. She wanted to cry.

When they deplaned and walked in silence through the cool mountain air toward the terminal, Inky was indeed there. He was standing by the double glass doors, unmistakable in his loose khaki trousers, casual pink shirt and leather jacket. He wasn't smiling this evening, she noticed. Probably all of Aspen had either read about John Leopardo and the scandal at the club or they'd heard the gossip by now.

"Good flight, boss?" he asked.

"Uneventful," John replied.

"You want I should get your bags while you wait in the car?"

"Sure, that will be fine."

Then he turned to Kamisha and said, "By the way, Miss Hammill, I finally picked up your car for you."

"Thanks, Inky. I appreciate it," she said unenthusiastically. Her car. Once, she would have been overjoyed to have it back, but that was before. Before John, before something truly mattered in her life.

The interior of the limo seemed too big, too hushed, too hot with the engine running and the windows closed. Kamisha sat across from John, facing the rear. The panic twisting in her belly made her breathing shallow. She needed to talk to John, to get him to talk to her. There were only a few more minutes before Inky would be there with their luggage—a few minutes to tell John that she loved him and was going to move heaven and earth to get them through this ordeal.

If only he'd listen.

"John," she began, "can we look at this reasonably? Can we talk about it?"

He shifted his gaze to her for a moment. "There's nothing to be said."

"But there is. I want to help. I want to help find out who put Rick in the hospital. I want to go to the press, tell them who you really are."

He only made a distracted gesture with his hand.

"I have connections with the press," Kamisha said. "I can get them to listen."

"Don't be naive."

She sighed. "I don't think I am. John, I care about you. I care about *us.*"

And then Inky was there, and the panic welled up inside again, coiling and writhing in her. John had become a stranger.

They dropped John off at his condo first, both men insistent that Kamisha not stay alone in her house.

"Inky can drive you to Brigitte's," John began. "I insist that you—"

"I'm not staying there," she said. "I'm going home."

"You can't stay alone, Kamisha. Not until I clear up this business with Rick."

Wearily she shrugged. She knew he could ask her to stay at the condo with him. She also knew he wouldn't. "I just want to go home," she stated, and once again felt herself biting back tears.

He hesitated, and through her misery she could see that he really was worried about her, that he was weighing possibilities, alternatives. Somehow the fact that he cared so much about her physical safety seemed unimportant, almost insulting. If he really cared about her, if he *loved* her, he'd talk to her. He'd stay with her. He'd care for her feelings, not the physical shell.

"Okay," John said, "but lock your doors and windows. I'll send Inky with you to check things out. Don't take any chances. Call me immediately if you—"

"Oh, for God's sake, John," she said wearily.

"All right, fine. You're tired. We're both tired. Just be careful," he said. "I mean that, Kamisha."

"Don't worry. You won't have me on your conscience," she said darkly, then watched his form as he walked, limping badly, toward the condo. She waited for him to glance back, to at least lift a hand—something. But he never did.

SHE TRIED TO SLEEP that night, wept a few hot, bitter tears into her pillow and got up to pace and sit by the bedroom window. And there, out on the street, a long, pale sedan cruised by once, then twice, then again. John's car. Inky.

Oh, God, she wished he cared as much for her soul.

Kamisha phoned John the next morning to let him know she was all right. She'd been tempted not to but decided to be mature about it.

Inky answered. "Glad to hear you're fine," he said. "John's in the shower right now, Miss Hammill."

"Can you have him call me back, please?"

"Well, we were going to the hospital to see Rick as soon as John's dressed," Inky said hesitantly.

John was avoiding her. Inky had been given directions. He was cutting her out of his life, like an irritating bill collector. She swallowed and took a deep breath, forcing the lump in her throat down. "I think that's a great idea. I'm coming, too. Pick me up, will you?"

"Well, Miss Hammill, I—"

"I'll be ready, Inky. Don't forget me." Then she hung up quickly.

The sedan pulled up at her curb precisely half an hour later. So he'd decided to give in on this matter. Perhaps in the name of fairness or out of some misguided desire to let Rick face his accuser. She didn't care. It was enough that he was there, in her reach, in her sight. Close to her.

"Did you sleep well?" he asked politely. Sunglasses hid his eyes. He looked pale. Perhaps it was true what they said, that one's tan faded on the airplane on the way home from a vacation. Her heart squeezed, remembering the sun of Costa Rica, the sand, the tropical air...and John.

"Yes, thank you," she lied. Her own sunglasses hid her expression from him. The two of them—back to square one. How pathetic.

She heard Inky swear softly as they started up the long drive leading to the hospital. "The press is here," he said harshly, putting on the brakes.

"Damn." John sat up straight, his body tensed.

Kamisha could see it then, a van with a satellite dish on top and News Star 4 on the side. Word had certainly gotten out fast. Aspen was in the news again.

"Inky," he said, "turn left, yes, there. We'll go through the emergency room door."

The emergency room was empty. In the winter it would be full of skiers with injuries, but now the one nurse sat behind the counter reading the *Aspen Times*.

She looked up, took in the two of them, obviously uninjured, and eyed John with suspicion, then dawning recognition.

"Excuse me, but who are you looking for?" the nurse asked. "Visiting hours aren't until noon."

Kamisha's back bristled, and she was about to say something when she felt John's warning hand on her arm.

"I'm terribly sorry," John said smoothly, "but I'm trying to avoid the reporters in front of the hospital. I'm Rick Simons's employer, and I would very much like to see him."

His aura of gentle but absolute command worked like a charm. "Room 107," the nurse said promptly. "Just don't be too long."

They found Rick propped up on pillows in a bed near the window that overlooked Maroon Creek Valley and the glistening white peaks beyond. If one had to be in a hospital, this was the place. Still, he was far from comfortable, his eyes bruised and swollen, his jaw wired shut. A chocolate milk shake sat half-finished on the movable table. CNN News was on the TV.

"Hello, Rick," Kamisha said tentatively, approaching the bed. "How do you feel?"

He looked them both over, obviously ill at ease, then snorted. "Lousy," he said, the word a hiss coming through his clenched teeth.

"I'm sure you are," Kamisha said, then looked at John.

"Hello, Rick."

There was a mumble through the wires that held his jaw in place.

"Look," John said, "you can guess why we're here."

"I won't," Rick managed to say. "Won't tell you."

John studied him for a minute. "I understand. But do you want to live in fear for the rest of your life?"

"I want to *live*," he said. "Period."

And then Kamisha tried. "Rick," she began, "wouldn't it be smarter to tell us who did this to you? We can go to the police. If you don't, you'll always be looking over your shoulder."

But Rick shook his head adamantly. "Leave me alone," he muttered.

"Okay," John said, "we will." He grasped his cane and took a few steps toward the door. He stopped there, turned and assessed Rick one last time. "With or without you," he said, "I'm going to find out who's responsible for this. When it all comes out, Rick, it would go better if you cooperate. Think about it. You know how to reach me."

"He's frightened," Kamisha said as they closed his door.

"He should be" was all John muttered.

She supposed she should be afraid, too, but somehow the matter of the parties and Rick and even Senator Luke Stern's involvement paled in comparison to her inner pain. What she wouldn't have given to melt that frozen place in John's heart. If he'd just talk to her, listen for a minute.

They began to head back toward the emergency room where they could exit without running into the News Star 4 team, but it seemed luck was against them. Coming down the corridor was a reporter and his cameraman.

"Come on," Kamisha said, tugging on John's arm, "let's just go."

But by then the reporter was already hurrying toward them, his mike on. John had stopped abruptly and was shrugging off Kamisha's grasp. His brow was creased in anger.

"John," she began, but was interrupted by the newsman.

"Mr. Leopardo," he was saying, "Mr. John Leopardo, isn't it?" Then suddenly the cameraman was switching on the light on top of his handset and positioning himself alongside the reporter.

John's posture stiffened. "That's correct," he said. "I am John Leopardo."

"Would you comment on allegations being made as to your club's involvement in—"

"No comment."

"And what about Mr. Rick Simons, who is now lying in a hospital bed?"

"I had nothing to do with that," John stated.

"Your father is Gio Leopardo, isn't that true?"

"That is correct." John's entire body had grown rigid.

"And the lady with you here," the camera swung to Kamisha, the light hot and bright in her eyes. "You are Miss Kamisha Hammill?"

She nodded.

"And you work for Mr. Leopardo at the—"

"I really don't have anything to say to you," Kamisha interrupted, "except to inform you that you haven't done your homework. Mr. Leopardo—"

"Are you suggesting—?"

"This interview is over," John said abruptly, and he took Kamisha's arm, leading her down the corridor.

Behind them Kamisha could hear the reporter saying, "You heard it here first. Miss Kamisha Hammill has insinuated . . ."

"God, I hate those people," John said flatly.

"Maybe the way to handle them," she began carefully, "is to tell them everything."

"It never works that way."

"It could. I know. I was the object of their lust when I divorced Josh," she said, striding alongside him through the emergency room door.

"It's hardly the same thing."

She let it drop. He'd been hounded all his life, accused of crimes he'd never committed, stared at, discussed. It was an open wound inside John, a problem he had no control over and thus one he'd never come to terms with. She could tell him that, but he wouldn't listen.

John was silent on the ride back to Aspen. Kamisha tried her best to reach him, but she felt as if she were talking to herself.

"There's somebody nearby," she said. "That's why Rick is afraid to talk. Somebody who can get to him."

"Um."

"Well, that's good to know, isn't it?"

"Um."

She could barely remember what he'd looked like when he smiled, when he made love, when he told her she was beautiful. Or had she only imagined those things?

"John—?" she started to say.

"I want you to stay with someone," he interrupted. "Just to be safe. Can you stay at Brigitte's?"

She sighed and looked out the tinted window. "I suppose. Although I would hardly call Brigitte's safe. It's a madhouse."

"I want you away from this mess and away from reporters. You're on vacation until further notice," he said coldly. "Can you call Brigitte and make the arrangements?"

It was something Kamisha supposed she had to do, but she didn't relish the confrontation with her friend that was bound to come. For a moment she was about to tell John she could look after herself, but that would have been childish.

"Yes, all right," she finally said to John when they parked in front of her house. "I'll call her."

"Inky can take you out there," he began, but Kamisha put her foot down.

"*I'll* drive myself, John. I can't go around afraid all the time. I *won't.* I'd rather end up like Rick."

"No," he said quickly, "don't even think that. I'm going to get to the bottom of this, Kamisha. I promise you."

She got Brigitte immediately when she called, but she wasn't quite ready to face her. Their fight had been the worst they'd ever had, and it had left scars.

"Oh," Kamisha said, switching the phone to her other ear, "it's you."

"Who did you expect?" Brigitte's tone was guarded.

"Tracy, I guess. How is she, anyway?" Neutral ground, Kamisha thought. What a chicken she was.

"She's fine. She's off riding."

"Is, ah, Bullet around?"

"He's been in L.A. for an overnight. He's due in on the six o'clock."

"Oh."

There was a long, uncomfortable minute of silence.

"Listen," Kamisha said, sighing finally, "I feel like hell."

"Me too."

"We were both being really childish. I miss you, Brigitte, and I apologize for the stuff I said."

"Yeah, well, I guess I do, too."

"Friends?"

"Friends."

"Good, then I better tell you I need a big favor."

"Shoot."

"Can I stay with you for a while?"

"Of course you can. Kamisha, is everything all right? I mean . . ."

"Everything's fine. Well, not everything."

"John Leopardo?"

"Yes," she admitted, "it's John."

"We need to have a talk, huh?"

"A nice long one."

They never quite got around to that talk, though.

By the time Kamisha arrived at Brigitte's, Tracy was there, the stereo was blaring, and Brigitte was already into a bottle of wine, wringing her hands over Bullet, as usual.

"Some goddamn bimbo called here at two," Brigitte said, pacing the living room. "It was long distance. I could tell. The little tramp said she was an old friend, but I knew."

"Maybe she..." Kamisha began, but Brigitte was working herself up, spilling her wine on the wet bar, tears beginning to squeeze out beneath her long lashes.

"When that louse gets home, I'm going to scratch his eyes out."

And then Tracy came out of her room, saw that her mom was getting drunk and slammed her bedroom door so hard that a china plate fell from the corner cupboard in the dining room and shattered.

"Damn it, Tracy! You get your butt out here!"

"I'll clean it up," Kamisha said, rising. "Tracy didn't mean to—"

"The hell she didn't!" And Brigitte collapsed into a sobbing heap on her beautiful white sofa.

It was Kamisha who cooked dinner. And while she and Tracy sat in the kitchen, choking down their food, Bullet arrived from the airport, swaggering, tie pulled loose, biceps and shoulders straining his shirt.

"Oh, God," Tracy remarked, rolling her eyes. "The legend is home." She got up from the table, went to her room and shut the door.

Kamisha didn't know whether to ignore him, try to be friendly or do the same thing Tracy had done—retire. The decision was taken out of her hands when Brigitte leaped off the couch and started in on him.

Kamisha couldn't escape the scene, as much as she wanted to; they were between her and the guest room. She heard Brigitte's accusations, every wounded, wailing, drunken one. She heard Bullet's nasty replies, heard the disgust in his voice.

"Shut up," he said, towering over Brigitte, his size dwarfing her. "You're drunk. Go sleep it off."

"I am not! You listen to me! One more of your *friends* calls here and we're through! Through! You're

making me crazy, Bullet! You can't treat me like this!"
Brigitte wailed.

"Listen, sweets, I can treat you any way I want. For
God's sake, pipe down. I'm hungry. Did you fix anything tonight?"

Finally Kamisha escaped outside to the deck. She
could still hear them arguing, but at least it was muted.

She stood on the deck, leaning against the rail, hugging herself and watching the sun go down behind the
mountains. She couldn't stay here in this house, she
thought; she couldn't bear it. Brigitte's pain heaped on
top of hers. Tracy's youthful anguish. Bullet's cruelty
and selfishness. She stared out at the darkening mountains and thought of John—his calmness, his love—and
ached for him. He was so close, a few miles, and as
lonely as she was. The irony of it.

She stayed there on the deck until it was cold and
dark, and she had to go back inside.

Bullet was in the kitchen, alone.

"Where's Brigitte?" she asked, shivering a little.

"Ah, she went to bed."

He'd fixed himself a sandwich and was perched on a
stool, hunched over the counter. He was big, a broad,
heavily muscled man. Some women, Kamisha supposed, would find his blunt features boyish and attractive. She didn't.

"You fix this tuna salad?" he asked, smiling a
mirthless smile, a bread crumb at the corner of his
mouth.

"No. Brigitte must have made it."

"Amazing."

"Why is it amazing, Bullet?"

"Oh, you know, she can't do anything right lately."

"She does okay," Kamisha said icily.

"Excuse me," he quipped. "I forgot what good buddies you two are."

"That's right." Kamisha put her hands on her hips and faced him. "And you know what, Bullet? I think *you're* her problem."

"That's really none of your—"

"It is my business. She's my friend."

He grinned at her. "You've got a big mouth on you, Kamisha," he said. "If I were you, I'd quit poking around in other people's affairs."

"You know," she said, her back stiff, "I don't like you, Bullet Adams."

"Well, lady, I don't much like you, either."

She tried calling John. She wanted to hear his voice, to lose herself in his calm reassurance, but John was with Joe Wilson, Inky told her, and wouldn't be in till late.

"You'll tell him I called?"

"I sure will," Inky said, "and hang in there. Things will work out."

But she was beginning to doubt it.

She lay in the guest room bed that night and tried to still her ragged breathing. The turmoil around her had taken on the quality of a living entity. It seemed to beat and pulse in the night air. She felt helpless. John's anguish seemed so hopeless in the silence of the night. And Brigitte. How was she going to help her? She'd promised Tracy days ago to have a talk with her mom, but when? Brigitte wasn't going to listen. And Bullet. It was true. She thoroughly disliked him. He was using Brigitte, sponging off her to achieve a lavish life-style in Aspen that he couldn't really afford.

Kamisha closed her eyes and tried to will her limbs to relax. The day before yesterday, on that beach with John, she'd been in heaven. What had gone so wrong?

For the next few days it was impossible to reach John on the phone. Either his line at the condo was busy or she'd get Inky and he'd tell her that John was over at the club. She was going stir-crazy at Brigitte's. They'd finally had that talk—about John and Kamisha's feelings—but Brigitte had seemed distracted, worried about something, and she was unwilling to go into it when Kamisha began to pry.

Tracy buttonholed her several times, afraid that her mom was going to get sick. At Tracy's age she didn't truly comprehend a nervous breakdown, but Kamisha did. And Tracy was right: Brigitte was sick, getting worse by the day.

Bullet was a constant source of dissension in the house. Brigitte nagged and he made sarcastic remarks back. Tracy cried and Kamisha merely tried to stay out of the way. She couldn't go home, couldn't go to work full-time. She was bored, miserably disgusted with Bullet and her friend. She couldn't bear much more of that house. She'd give it, maybe, another day or two.

"I don't see what all the fuss was about," Bullet said at dinner that night. "Who cares if some prominent folks want to blow off steam?"

"God," Kamisha said, "don't you realize what was going on in that condo?"

"Good times." He shrugged, forking pasta into his mouth.

"There were young girls there," Brigitte put in. "That's not right."

"Probably of their own free will," he said, and grinned.

It rankled that officially Kamisha was on vacation. She made daily trips to the club, anyway, but it was as if Wilson's secretary needed her advice less and less. Invariably Inky would see Kamisha there and then follow her back to Brigitte's. But she never ran into John.

She took long hikes in the woods behind Brigitte's house. She went bicycling with Tracy—if Inky had seen that! She tried to keep fit and busy. But it was hard killing time, wondering, waiting, hoping.

Why hadn't he returned her calls?

She tried to put Costa Rica and the sweet interlude out of her thoughts. But inside a terrible fear and loneliness lurked, hiding in a shadowy corner of her soul, ready to spring into the light without warning.

John's rejection was killing her.

It came to her in the middle of the night. She awakened with a sudden knowledge, and she knew how she could help John.

Carin McNaught. The sheriff's daughter. The kid would never confide in her father. No. But if she could get the girl to talk to John, in confidence, of course, then maybe John could get a handle on some of the prominent men who regularly attended those parties. He could then get in touch with them, perhaps obtain more names. Eventually someone would talk. Whoever had beaten Rick Simons had surely been to at least one of the affairs. Someone would know. Someone would come clean. Maybe even Stern.

She lay in the dark and felt much better. In the morning she'd see John. She'd park her butt on his steps all day if necessary. Her idea had merit. He'd have to listen. And maybe they could talk about themselves.

INKY OPENED THE DOOR, a surprised look on his face. "Kamisha. Is something wrong? You okay?"

"I'm fine. Is John in?" She tried to peer past his great bulk into the hushed interior.

"He's...ah, here. But he's on the phone. Can I...?"

"I want to see him. Please, Inky."

His wooden countenance softened finally. "Come on in. Boss won't mind."

John was indeed preoccupied. He was talking on the telephone, pacing, the cord reaching its distance before he turned around. He looked tired and haggard. When he saw Kamisha, he seemed to pause, his dark eyes full of emotion until he quickly masked it. While he nodded for her to be seated, he spoke into the phone again. "All right, Ken, I understand," John was saying. "I know you've got a reputation to uphold. Yes, well, so do I. You think it over. Any help you can give me on this matter will be greatly appreciated. All right. Thanks." And he hung up.

"Ken?" Kamisha asked, curious.

"Kenneth Whelps," John replied, still distracted.

"Whelps Manufacturing? Isn't he a frequent guest at the club?"

"Yes, Kamisha, he is. He spends half the year in Columbus, Ohio, the other half here."

"You asked him if he'd ever been to one of Rick's parties?"

"Yes."

"And?"

"And nothing. This mess with Luke Stern's wife has everyone nervous."

"Um," she said.

John sat down and rubbed his jaw pensively. She could see tired circles under his eyes, circles made darker in contrast to his pale skin. He must have been on the telephone for days, using the master guest list from the club as his only source of information. Clearly no one was talking. It occurred to her that if John's father were doing the asking, maybe the results would be better. Who would have the guts to tell a Mafia don no? But then John wasn't his father; John would never push or threaten.

She crossed one leg over the other, absently smoothing her khaki pants, wiggling her toes in the open sandals. On the drive over she'd felt confident that John would welcome her suggestion about Carin McNaught. Now, looking at him, at his pale face and the drawn brow, she wasn't so certain.

"John," she said with care, "have you gotten anywhere?"

He let out a breath. "I've been told by a friend and associate in L.A. that there's some pretty big money involved. Big names and big money."

"And no one wants to rat."

"Exactly."

"What if you pushed a little harder?"

His gaze shot up to hers. "What are you suggesting?"

"I . . . never mind." She bit her lower lip. This wasn't going at all the way she'd imagined. He was so closed to her, a stranger. It was as if Costa Rica had never happened. She felt a stab of pain knife through her stomach. "Listen," she said, "I've got an idea. Will you hear me out, John? Will you try not to shut me up?"

He seemed not to notice her discomfort. "Sure," he said, "whatever."

"Remember in New York how I told you about this young local girl, Carin? She was the one who first put me onto Rick."

"I recall."

"Well, I was thinking. She's afraid to go the authorities. Her dad is sheriff of Pitkin County, in fact. But I bet I could convince her to talk to you. She could give you all sorts of names, and—"

But John had come to his feet and was shaking his head, holding up a hand. "Forget it."

"But—"

"I *said*, forget it."

Kamisha felt tears sting hotly behind her eyes. "Why?" she demanded.

He spun around to face her angrily. "She's a kid is why! Hasn't she been through enough?"

It was Kamisha's turn to get mad. "Come off your high horse, John," she said hotly. "Carin knew the score. She got paid plenty to attend those parties. It's time she faced up to what she did."

"She's an innocent victim."

"Girls her age aren't stupid, John. She's not a bad kid, don't get me wrong. But she still needs to learn that what she did is wrong. She could give you those names."

"I said no. The subject's closed."

"Everything's *closed* with you, isn't it?" she said before she could control her anger. "You won't listen. You won't let anyone help. John Leopardo against the cruel world! Well, I'm sick of it!"

For an instant he seemed about to respond, but just as quickly the expressionless mask covered his features again.

"John," she said, her voice cracking, "please. Please let me help."

"I'm sorry," he said, "but it's no good, Kamisha. I'm accomplishing nothing whatsoever here. I'm flying out this afternoon."

"You're ... leaving?"

"Yes."

"But ..."

"Inky's staying in Aspen. He'll watch over you."

"Damn it, John!" she said. "I don't need a body-guard! I don't want one!"

"Your safety—"

"I'm going back to work, anyway. I'll stay at Bri-gitte's. But I need to be working."

"You'll be careful."

"Of course I'll be careful. It's all out in the open now, John. No one's going to bother with me."

"Still."

"John, please. I ..."

But already he was ushering her toward the door, dismissing her. He was as cold as granite. "I am sorry," he said. But his voice was without emotion. "It's over, Kamisha. I made a mistake. A relationship can't sur-vive the press. I've been through this before. Believe me, I—"

She stiffened. "What do you mean, John?"

He stared her right in the eye. "I was going to get married once. Be a normal guy. Unfortunately my father's activities hit the news just then. They came af-ter me ... and her."

"And she left you," Kamisha said, feeling the blood stop and freeze in her veins. "She couldn't take the heat and she left you."

"It was a long time ago. I don't blame her. But I won't do that to anyone else again. It's a promise I made to myself."

"But, John, I'm not her. I've been through this myself. I can take it. John . . ."

He was opening the front door, steering her gently but firmly. "If I caused you pain, I'm sorry. But my life doesn't have room for—"

"For what?" she demanded.

"For these kinds of interludes. Forgive me." And then he was closing the door, shutting her out.

She stiffened her arm for a moment and held the door open. "I don't forgive you, John. I'll never forgive you," she said, and then he was gone, the gleaming wooden door staring her in the face blankly.

For a long moment she stood there in disbelief. Her hands were fists at her sides, her chest was heaving. When she finally found her legs, she almost ran down the wooded path to where her car was parked. She left a patch of rubber on the drive and raced away, the wind tearing at her hair. She drove and drove, needing the fresh mountain air on her face and the hot sun on her shoulders. She didn't care where she drove or if anyone were following.

Silent and withdrawn, Kamisha finally made her way back to Brigitte's. She felt numb, in shock. If anyone said a word to her—Brigitte or Bullet—she'd burst into tears. All she wanted to do was be alone. She could let the tears come then, in privacy. Later, maybe later, she and Brigitte would talk.

She almost made it to her room.

"Oh, Kamisha," Brigitte said, coming out of the kitchen. "Oh, God, I'm so glad you're here. We have to talk."

Vaguely, through the haze of her anguish, Kamisha was aware of Brigitte's agitation. Her friend seemed sober, but she was wringing her hands, nevertheless. Her cheeks were pale and pinched-looking, and Kamisha made a fleeting assumption that this had to do with Bullet. Another spat.

"Kamisha, oh, Lord, *please*. I hope you'll forgive me."

For a moment Kamisha hesitated. "Not now, Brigitte. Not now," she managed to say, and then brushed past her and headed to the guest room. She was aware of Brigitte calling after her, of the urgency in her friend's voice. It didn't matter. Kamisha closed the bedroom door, locked it and sagged into a chair.

CHAPTER FIFTEEN

JOHN STOOD at the window in his office and looked out at the city. It was hot and hazy, not the awful heat of the month before, but pretty uncomfortable, nonetheless. The sky was white, not blue, and a brownish pall hung over Manhattan, as if the grime of the city rose from its streets and clung to the skyscrapers.

He stood there and stared, unfocused, battling his thoughts—thoughts about Aspen, about a magic little town nestled in the Rockies, thoughts about a woman. Unwelcome thoughts.

"Damn," he muttered, letting out a breath.

It would be cool in Aspen, with a clean snap to the summer air and a sky so blue that it was unbelievable. The mountains would, perhaps, have a dusting of early snow on their peaks, an army of white giants crowding the narrow green valley. The streets would be tidy and charming, the tourists strolling the downtown malls, stopping at outdoor cafés that were nestled in flower beds and groves of aspen trees.

He imagined the scene, down to the details of color and sound and smell, and then despite his better judgment he imagined Kamisha there. She'd moved back to her house, Joe Wilson had informed him, claiming that she was in no danger now that Senator Stern's wife had let the cat out of the bag. At any rate, no one was going to run Kamisha's life for her. He could see her as if

he had mysteriously transported himself to be close to
her. In her quaint living room, the sun filtering through
the Victorian lace curtains, falling softly on her rich
silver hair, warming it to his touch. Or at work, charming the club's guests, playing tennis, her long legs
flashing in the brilliant mountain sun. She'd be busy,
too, working on the upcoming substance abuse event,
leaning over Joe's desk, her voice soft and just a touch
husky, so close to Joe the man would notice her scent,
would see the delicacy of her slim, sun-browned wrist.

Abruptly a stab of jealousy knifed through John. For
an insane moment he wanted to call Joe and tell him to
get the hell back to the Florida club—crazy, because Joe
was still needed in Aspen. Rick, whose fate John still
hadn't decided, was in Florida now himself, recuperat-
ing, on a paid vacation. John couldn't leave the club
without management.

But Joe Wilson. Single, forty-one years old. Handsome. A smooth operator. Did Kamisha find him attractive? She'd come alive in Costa Rica, a butterfly
emerged from a cocoon of self-imposed hibernation.
Did Kamisha find Joe a new challenge?

Damn.

His dark musings were interrupted by Martha buzz-
ing him. He forced himself back to New York, to the
heat and haze and wail of sirens below on the street.
"Yes, Martha," he said, pressing the button.

"Mr. Leopardo, I thought you might want to know.
Miss Hammill from Aspen called again. I told her you
were in conference, as per your instructions."

"Very good. Thank you, Martha."

He released the button and stood over the phone,
staring at it as if it would tell him something. Kamisha
had tried to phone him several times over the past few

weeks, but Martha had followed instructions. Though, for some perverse reason of her own, Martha insisted on letting him know whenever Kamisha called. He smiled grimly. He supposed it was his very efficient secretary's way of showing her disapproval. She'd done the same thing years before when John's father had tried to call him. But eventually Gio had given up. So would Kamisha.

Sitting at his desk, John started going through reports from each of his clubs. Figures, columns, numbers. The Amalfi club was a little slow. He'd fly over and take a look, although he was sure his manager there was quite competent. Nevertheless, it didn't hurt to have the owner drop in. Yes, he'd do that. It would be good to get away.

The intercom buzzed again. "Mr. Leopardo, there's a man on the phone from the *Boston Globe*. He'd like an interview."

"Tell him the usual, Martha," John said tiredly.

"Yes, Mr. Leopardo."

Good God, they'd never stop! There were still stories circulating about the "love nest" in Aspen and Senator Stern, whose presidential hopes appeared dashed, and the Ute City Club and the Leopardos. The *Los Angeles Times* had even dug up an old photograph of John when he was ten, holding his mother's hand in front of a New York courthouse, greeting Gio as his father emerged from one more trial or indictment or grand jury hearing.

He tried to study the weekly reports again, but his eyes wouldn't focus, his mind wouldn't concentrate. Kamisha. He'd had to leave her. She had her safe, protected life in the little town where no one paid the least bit of attention to celebrities. Where the media was tol-

erated but not admired and not necessarily believed.
She'd moved there, she'd told him, partly to get away
from the prying eyes of the world, as did so many other
celebrities, and Aspen had accepted her without fan-
fare, judging her on her abilities, not her reputation.
She had her life and her friends. She was surrounded by
beauty. Her job satisfied her, and she was good at it.
Yes, she had a fine life.

He'd known the moment he'd seen that paper in
Costa Rica. The words had been so sickeningly familiar. Everything had come back to him, rushed in on
him. He could never ask Kamisha to share the sordid
life the press had created for him, to hide from cameras, interviewers, to hide from his own family, for
God's sake. It was better he'd realized that in the beginning, before he'd made her any promises he couldn't
keep.

He could live with his decision. He could live without love, without Kamisha, but it was hard. He could
do it, though, because the alternative was worse. She'd
despise him if he dragged her into his orbit. Sooner or
later it would get to her, and she'd hate him. Only it
would be messier, and it would take longer for her to get
over it, and the press would have another weapon to
attack with, to smear and twist the knife in the wound
until he squirmed in shame and agony as Kamisha suf-
fered with him. He could see it now, a media event as
dreadful as Donald and Ivana Trump's breakup. No, he
couldn't do that to Kamisha.

The buzzer sounded. "Mr. Leopardo, it's Harry in
Coral Gables."

"Put him on, Martha."

"Hello, John. How's it up there?" Harry Kahn was
the assistant manager of the Sea Star Club.

"Hot and dirty. How's it going, Harry?"

"Hotter but cleaner. I spoke to Joe just now, had a few questions. We're having some problems with the kitchen help, but it's slow down here now, so it's no big deal. I wanted to check with you on your policy of hiring Cubans, John. For the winter, you know."

"If they have papers, Harry. Real papers. We can't hire illegals. I'll stand firm on that."

"That's what Joe thought. Okay, but we may have some trouble filling all the spots."

"Joe always worries too much. You'll see that there'll be a seasonal influx of workers come fall. You have time. Besides, Joe will be back by then. It'll be his headache."

"He makes me do the hiring, John. My Spanish is better."

"Didn't I tell everyone to learn Spanish?"

"Joe hates languages. Says he failed Latin in school."

"I'll talk to him about it."

"Hey, don't tell him I told you. I gotta work for the guy." Harry paused. "Did I tell you I've been getting a lot of calls from the papers, John? They want to see the club, write us up."

John massaged his forehead. "Just tell them no, Harry."

"It's good publicity."

"Not the right kind."

"You sure? You know what they say, there's no publicity that's bad publicity."

"I'm sure, Harry. They're just fishing. They want dirt."

"Okay, you're the boss." There was another moment's hesitation. It was obvious Harry had more on his mind than Cubans and the press. Harry was smart enough to handle those details without bothering John in New York.

"Look," John said, leaning back in his chair, "if there's something on your mind, I want to hear it."

Harry cleared his throat. "It's Rick Simons. He stopped by this morning."

"And he wants his job back, right?" John said. "So he figured you could put a word in for him."

Harry sighed. "We worked together, you know, for four years, Mr. Leopardo. You understand. And, well, I really think the guy learned his lesson."

"I'll be the judge of that," John snapped, irritated.

"Of course. I just thought..."

"It's all right, Harry. Enough said." John hung up shortly and steepled his fingers. He believed Rick had indeed learned a tough lesson, but the fact remained that Rick was still withholding the name of the man behind the parties, the man who had undoubtedly beaten him up. John didn't consider Rick a criminal. But Simons owed it to his position, to the club, to come clean. And until he did John had no intention of allowing him back to work.

It infuriated him. His temper flared every time he thought about the condo filled with big-name power brokers fondling young women—the booze and God knows what else flowing. But no one was talking. And until someone did talk John was going to be on the hot seat. Of course, Stern's wife was still talking. And every other word out of her mouth was Aspen. The Ute City Club. John Leopardo. Last week's scandal sheets had covered it all over again, the headlines changed, naturally, but the same muck: "Mafia Love Nest in the Rockies."

Goddamn it.

He wondered how Joe Wilson was handling it. His new manager there hadn't said. And John wondered, too, if the press was bothering Kamisha. There was certainly a human interest angle—the Silver Lady, they'd named her when she raced in the Olympics. He supposed it was too much to hope that they'd leave her alone. He could just imagine the questions they'd ask her. Were you aware, Miss Hammill, that the owner of the club you work for was connected to the Mafia? Do you know John Leopardo very well? What do you think of the parties that were held here, Miss Hammill? Did you ever attend one? Would you still vote for Senator Stern for President, Miss Hammill?

His intercom buzzed again. "Mr. Leopardo."

"Hey, boss, it's Inky. I got something for you."

"Send him in, Martha."

"Yes, Mr. Leopardo," she said very correctly, registering her disapproval of Inky's familiarity.

Inky sauntered in, holding a rolled-up copy of a newspaper. He shook it at John. "You might want to take a look-see, boss. Front page, bottom."

"What is it?"

"Today's *New York Times,*" Inky handed him the paper and stood there, folding his huge arms.

John unrolled the paper and spread it out on his desk. His eyes traveled to the bottom of the page. "Leopardo Son Alienated from Mob Family," read the headline, "by the Associated Press. Don Gio Leopardo, longtime leader of one of the most powerful Mafia families on the East Coast, made an unprecedented statement to the press yesterday."

John gripped the paper, his mind whirling. Pop making a statement? He looked up at Inky, who stood there, smiling smugly, arms still crossed over his massive chest.

"Read on, boss," Inky said. He grinned more broadly.

"My son, John, is a law-abiding American. He fought for his country in Vietnam," the elder Leopardo said. "He won a Bronze Star and a Purple Heart. My son distanced himself from the family many years ago. He has nothing to do with the family's business concerns, and John Leopardo's health clubs are in no way connected to the family's business. In fact," Gio Leopardo said, "I have not heard from nor seen my only son in over eleven years. John is a Leopardo in name only." It is believed that the Don made this statement as a result of the allegations brought against his son's health club in Aspen, Colorado, where the manager was beaten in a bizarre string of events. . . .

It went on, reiterating the whole ugly tale, but John stopped reading. He sat at his desk and stared at the print until it danced in front of his eyes. His father had gone to the press of his own free will! The man who hated reporters and publicity, who had more reason than most to shun it. The man who over the years had been indicted for dozens of crimes but never convicted, a Mafia boss, a criminal—he'd endangered his own position to go to the press and tell them that his son wasn't connected to his own illegitimate dealings.

"Unbelievable, huh, boss?" Inky said.

John leaned back and whistled through his teeth. "My God." He furrowed his brow. "Why?"

Inky moved to one of the black-and-chrome chairs in front of the desk and sat. "To help you."

"Pop?"

"Sure, he's trying to help you."

"But do you know what this does to him? He's practically admitting what he is."

Inky nodded.

John shook his head. "I can't get a handle on it. I can't figure it."

"Hey, boss, it's simple. He's your dad." The big man shrugged heavy shoulders. "He's taking care of his son."

John just stared at him, incredulous.

The phone rang all afternoon. Martha turned the calls away with a quote of "no comment," but even she began to get frazzled by five.

When he left the office, John had Inky take him to his health club for his routine workout. He was still dazed, thrown completely off balance, but he thought it would do him good to work up an honest sweat.

His father, going to the press of his own accord—to help his son. It boggled his mind. Gio put the organization first; he always had. He'd never endanger his operation, never be disloyal to the family. That was his first commandment. And yet he'd done this for his son. John could come up with no other conceivable reason for Gio making that statement.

John took a towel from the attendant. "Thanks," he said absentmindedly, heading for his locker.

He swam a half mile. Every stroke reminded him of the beach in Costa Rica, the warm water, Kamisha, wet and sleek as a seal, the feel of her body, silky and slippery against him. Would he ever forget?

He pulled himself dripping from the pool and sat on the edge, chest heaving, remembering too much.

The weight room was busy these hours after the working day was over. It was, as usual, hot and damp and faintly smelly, despite the overlay of eucalyptus the attendants used to clean the place. All gyms smelled the same, he guessed, even the Ute City Club. He wondered if Kamisha worked out there. Yes, probably. He could see her in a leotard, tight-fitting as her tanned skin, all her muscles taut, sweat on her face, on her chest, between her breasts. He knew every muscle in her body, had stroked and kneaded every long, curved sinew. His hands itched with the feel of her, as if she were there and he could reach out and—

"Hey, John, how's it going?" A man he'd seen there for years was greeting him. He could have sworn the guy's tone was different, his eyes more assessing. Maybe he'd been following the stories in the paper.

"Okay," John replied. "And yourself?"

"Not bad, considering."

John did his curls, his bench presses, working hard at it. His arms and shoulders and chest were pretty good, but when it came to his legs—well, he was lopsided. He used machines to exercise his legs, but he always pressed more weight with his good leg than his bad one. Still, he kept at it, and his knee had become stronger over the years. It ached a lot, and it seized up at times, but at least it was still there. There had been a time when he thought they'd have to amputate his leg. There had been a raging infection . . . .

Why in hell was he thinking about that now? He lay on his back on the leg press machine, pushing the plate, first the bad leg, then the good. Breathing hard, push-

ing. The muscles in his thighs bunched up, then relaxed, bunched up again. Sweat beaded on his forehead.

Why had Gio done it?

He'd said further on in the article that he was retired
now, a law-abiding citizen like his son. Retired. Gio. It
was probably a lie, but maybe Pop *was* retired. It could
be. John didn't even know. He couldn't even remember exactly how old his father was. Seventy? Seventy-
one?

He spoke to his mother a few times a year, but they
never discussed Gio, not a word. They talked about his
sister, about her three children, John's niece and neph-
ews. But never a word about Gio.

My God, he *had* utterly alienated himself. He had no
family, no friends but Inky. He'd gotten rid of the one
woman he'd cared for, wounded her deeply.

For years his mother had begged him to talk to his
father. *You're his only son, Johnny. Just call him once
in a while. Please, Johnny.*

But he'd so detested the business his father was in that
he'd refused. It was all mixed up with his brush with
death and the war and youthful idealism. But he was
older, and things that had mattered then didn't seem to
matter as much now. He was so damn alone, so lonely.

Of course, it was Kamisha who'd made him reassess
his situation. He'd just never noticed before how alone
he was. He'd prided himself on being in control, but
he'd so carefully isolated himself that he had no one to
control, so it had been easy. Now it was hard. Now he
knew what it felt like to be happy.

And the truth hurt.

He got his weekly massage from Thomas. The man
had magic hands, and he spent a lot of time on John's
bad leg, kneading and stroking, digging deeply to relax

the stressed muscles and increase the blood supply.
Usually Thomas's ministrations allowed John to empty
his mind completely, then emerge fresh and ready to
focus on problems.

Not tonight. He was impatient under Thomas's
hands, tense, unable to escape the thoughts that plagued
him.

"Hey, Mr. Leopardo, relax," Thomas said.

"Sorry, I'll try."

"You got business problems?" Thomas inquired.
"Everyone does. Forget 'em for now."

Sure, he had business problems. But it was other
kinds of problems that were torturing him. He felt the
masseur's hands on his leg, pressing each muscle slowly,
stretching each sinew. He closed his eyes and willed
himself to relax, to forget. But his mind recalled Kamisha's hands touching him in the same places, touching the scar on his knee gently with one finger, looking
up at him and smiling a lazy, sensual smile. Damn it all.

"Boy, are you tense today. Come on, Mr. Leopardo," Thomas said chidingly, still working on his leg.
"I bet I know what's bugging you. I heard there was
something in the paper, your father, something about
him. I don't wanna be nosy, but how many guys get
their dad mentioned in the *New York Times*? That's it,
isn't it?"

Thomas had known him for years. There was no
sense getting angry with him. "Might be," John allowed.

"Listen, take it from me. Parents, they can drive ya
crazy, ya know? But they're your folks and they mean
well. What are ya going to do? Ya forgive 'em. Ya live
with 'em. They aren't going to be around forever, you
know."

"I guess so."

"Nobody said it was easy."

Inky picked him up at seven outside the club. "So, boss you goin' home?"

"Yes, home."

Inky watched him in the rearview mirror for a time. Then, finally, he spoke. "What are you going to do about your dad?"

"*Do?* What can I do? I can't even figure out what he meant by it."

"Come on, boss, you aren't dumb."

"Stop mothering me," John snapped.

"Sometimes you need it," Inky shot back. "Don't be a damn fool, John. He's getting old. Says he's retired."

"Sure, retired."

"You gotta trust someone," Inky said darkly.

John ate alone. The cook had left something for him, but he couldn't have said what it was a minute after he finished. He sat and chewed and looked out his window over the city that was just being touched by dusk.

After he ate, he pulled the *Times* out of his briefcase and read the article again. He was still too stunned by Gio's uncharacteristically selfless gesture even to begin to weigh its implications. All he knew was that he hurt inside. He was in pain, and his father and Kamisha were connected somehow in his mind. He couldn't figure out how or why, but he knew they were. What he didn't know was who in the hell he, John, was. He'd thought he knew, but the certainty was gone now. He was floundering, lost, unsure of everything. All the rules of the game were changed, and the players were acting illogically.

What are you going to do about your dad? Inky had asked. *Ya forgive 'em. Ya live with 'em,* Thomas had said. It was as if the world were pressing in on him from every direction, poking, prodding, turning him from the way he wanted to go, forcing him to rethink, reassess, walk a new path.

Gio had done something utterly unexpected. Unasked, he'd tried to help his son. It was more than John had done or was willing to do.

He stood and roamed around his living room, looked at the blueprints on his table, turned on a lamp, picked up a magazine, put it down. He limped, leaning on his cane, tired, drained of all his energy.

Suddenly, overwhelmingly, he wanted to pick up the phone and talk to his father. "Hey, Pop, thanks, that was a nice article, a nice thing to do. I appreciate it, Pop," he'd say.

"Well, son, it was the least I could do," Gio would say. No, a normal father would say that. He could no longer even guess what *his* father would say.

He limped to the window and looked out at the lights coming on all over the city. Lights in people's apartments. Kids turning on lights, mothers and uncles and aunts clicking them on. Lovers turning on lights, talking, touching each other.

Abruptly he threw his cane across the room. It hit a table with a sharp sound, bounced, lay on the carpet, a dead brown stick, a useless prop.

He was powerless. Powerless to deal with his father, powerless to treat the ills of his beautiful club in Aspen, to defend himself from the greedy press, to mend his relationship with his family or to accept Kamisha's love. Powerless.

John put his face in his hands, took a deep breath, then looked up. There was no deliberate decision, no thought, no rationalization. He headed straight for the door of his apartment, closed it behind him and took the elevator down to the lobby.

"You want I should call Inky?" the doorman asked.

"No, uh, no, he's off tonight. Just get me a taxi."

"Yes, sir, Mr. Leopardo."

It wasn't until the cab was halfway across the Brooklyn Bridge that he realized he'd forgotten his cane.

THE HOUSE LOOKED THE SAME, the shrubbery fuller, but otherwise the same. It was full dark now, and lights showed at the windows behind the draped lace curtains, old-fashioned curtains. It had been eleven years since he'd been there.

It was a mock-Tudor house, solid stone and stucco between dark beams, set on a street of similar enduring houses, each with a large, landscaped lawn. Well cared for and comfortable. Around the back, at the end of the curved gravel driveway, was a garage, and his father's Cadillac would be neatly parked inside.

John took a quavering breath. What was he doing?

"You gettin' out or what?" the cabbie asked.

"Ah, yeah, sure. How much do I owe you?"

The driver nodded. "It's on the meter."

The walk to the house was difficult. He told himself it was because he lacked the habitual support of his cane. He felt as if he was faltering. By the front door, in the shadows, was the ubiquitous guard. John had spotted him, or at least the glowing tip of his cigarette, immediately. The man moved into the light slowly as John approached. His back straightened, and John could see him flick the butt of the cigarette down the drive. Slowly his now-free hand moved up toward the breast of his dark jacket. It was all very familiar to John, though at one time the man would have greeted him and tousled his dark hair.

John neared. "It's Gio's son," he said, stopping for a moment. "Is that you, Mario?"

"John?"

"Yes, it's me."

"Well, I'll be damned."

He managed a smile for Mario, the man who had been his father's personal bodyguard for thirty years. He felt his hand clenching and unclenching at his side, automatically gripping a phantom cane. He reached out then and shook Mario's hand, noting the thick mop of gray hair on his head, the heavy jowls.

"It's nice to see you, John," Mario said.

"You, too." And then John stared at him hard. "Pop still needs a guard, huh?"

"A man can retire," Mario said, "but his enemies never do." He stepped back into the shadows and reached into his pocket for his pack of cigarettes.

John stood there for a moment and gazed at the door. He could feel his knee throb and his heart pound too heavily against his ribs. He wanted suddenly to turn and go. But he'd come too far.

His mother was inside that house, watching TV maybe or playing cards. Gio would be in the study or on the phone. Did he watch TV with Mom these days? Were they an ordinary aging couple?

The windows were open, and John could hear faint strains of music. Italian opera—*Rigoletto*. Familiar music that he'd heard his entire childhood.

Slowly he walked up the stone steps to the broad front door. Should he ring the bell or walk in?

Eleven years. He pressed the bell and heard it chime inside. A familiar sound. How many times...?

The front door opened. His mother. Older now. Gray-haired, plump, in an old-fashioned house dress. She looked at him, peered through her glasses, then turned pale and put her hand over her heart. "Johnny?" she gasped.

"Hello, Mama."

"Johnny. Oh, dear Lord, Johnny. What is it? Are you okay? Come in, come in."

He entered the house, the dark hallway exactly the same, the smell, the feel, the very air of his childhood exactly the same.

"I'm fine, Mama. I'm okay. I just thought..." God, his knee hurt.

"Let me look at you." She held his hands and cried and laughed, hugged him, wiped her tears. "Oh, Johnny, it's so good, so good."

A voice came from down the hall, a familiar, irascible voice. "What's going on? Such a noise. Lucille?"

A bent figure shuffled out into the hall, an old man, balding, white-haired, slight. But the voice was the same. "So, Lucille? What the—?"

The figure stopped, thrust his head forward and blinked. His mouth opened, then hung there.

John tried his voice. He wasn't sure what he said, something stupid. His throat constricted. In the shadows of his consciousness he was aware of his mother saying his name over and over, of her tears. And then his father, so old now, so very very old, was moving down the darkened hall toward him. An old, worn man.

CHAPTER SIXTEEN

KAMISHA SAID GOOD-NIGHT to Joe Wilson, checked in at the front desk to let them know she was leaving, then left through the back door to where her mountain bike was locked to a cottonwood tree.

She took a deep breath of the evening air. There was a snap to it already; autumn was setting in. Not even the second week of September and she could feel it—winter was just around the corner. On the noon news today the weatherman had said the East Coast was due for a September heat wave. It would be hot and grimy in New York. How could John bear it?

She pedaled the mile and a half to her house, trying to enjoy the ride and the fresh air, but inside her belly was a gnawing anger. It was that old biddy Martha.

I'm sorry, Miss Hammill, but Mr. Leopardo is tied up in a meeting. I'll give him your message.

How many times over the past weeks had Martha said those same words? Of course, John had given her instructions to put Kamisha off, so she shouldn't be angry with Martha. She knew that. But still...

She got off her bike in front of her house, walked it around back and locked it to the fence. She turned the sprinkler on the waning garden and realized that the flowers had lost their summer spark. But then so had she, Kamisha thought. She went in the back door, replacing the key over the ledge, and stood with her hands on her hips in her tidy kitchen. The house seemed empty, so picture-perfect and sterile. But that was how she'd wanted it, wasn't it? Since Josh had left those many years ago, she'd purposely lived that sterile existence—until John Leopardo.

What a fool she'd been. When she was young, she'd set goals and sometimes achieved them. But that was youth. A person could overcome an endless flow of troubles and keep going. She'd lost her energy now, though, and no longer had the strength to strive.

"Great," Kamisha said.

She pulled out the iced tea pitcher from her refrigerator and took a long drink. John had beaten her. Even Martha had her cowering. Once, she'd had the guts to fly down a steep ski slope with the icy wind in her face, and they'd hung a Silver Medal around her neck. The Silver Lady. Well, now the lady was tarnished.

THE SHRILL RINGING of her bedside phone startled her out of a deep sleep. It took a long moment to orient herself, to wake herself out of another lousy dream.

"Kamisha?" It was Brigitte. *What now?* Kamisha wondered, glancing at the clock—7:30 a.m.

"What's up? It's really early, Brigitte."

"Oh, I couldn't stay in bed. I've ah...I'm not drinking and... Well, I'm sort of nervous. Do you think we can go to lunch today? It's Saturday. You're off, aren't you?"

"Sure. Where? You want me to pick you up?"

"No, I'll, ah, drive."

"That's a novelty."

"The new me." But Brigitte sounded tense.

Kamisha arrived at the restaurant late. An unscheduled crisis at the club. There was always something,

though, and a day off, a full day, was an impossibility.
She spotted Brigitte sitting at a table near an open window in the dining room of the Hotel Jerome and gave
her a quick wave.

"Sorry," Kamisha said, breathless, pulling out the
chair across from her friend. "I had to run over to the
club."

Brigitte smiled at her, a swift, forced twitch of her
mouth. "That's okay."

She looked wan, scared, and the very pale freckles
that usually didn't show were evident on her skin. She
had no makeup on, and her soft, curling brown hair was
simply pulled back in a ponytail. Kamisha noticed that
instead of the usual glass of wine, a cup of coffee sat in
front of Brigitte.

"What's up?" Kamisha asked, taking a menu from
the waitress.

Brigitte shrugged, her eyes shifting away. "Everything's up, I guess. I'm trying to get my act together."

"The, ah, drinking?" Kamisha asked carefully.

"Yes. That and... Well, some other problems, too.
You know."

"We all have them," Kamisha said. "Is it Tracy?"

"She's okay." Brigitte shrugged again.

"Bullet?"

"Oh, I don't know. Really I don't."

Kamisha studied her friend for a moment. "Do you
want to talk about it?"

Brigitte's eyes switched to hers. "Do you want to talk
about John Leopardo?" Her tone was defensive.

It was Kamisha's turn to shrug. "There's not much
to talk about." Even the mention of his name was
enough to prod the open wound, but Brigitte knew that.
She had no secrets from Brigitte.

Her friend sat silently, assessing Kamisha. There was still that anxiety in her eyes, though, but Kamisha chalked it up to alcohol withdrawal. "So," Brigitte said, "has the lout answered your calls?"

"No." She tried to make light of the situation with little success.

"I feel so bad for you," Brigitte said, twisting a ring on her finger.

"I'll live." She could say the words, but she wondered if they were true. She didn't feel alive at all. Inside, she felt dull and dead.

"Oh, God, Kamisha, I know how it is. To love a man and have him shoot you down like that. Oh, I know how it hurts."

Kamisha bristled at her friend's automatic comparison of Bullet and John, as if they were equals, as if Bullet were fit to lick John's boots. But she held her tongue; Brigitte needed help now, not another quarrel. She reached a hand across the table and patted her arm. "Guess it's just you and me, pal, and to hell with men."

"Yeah, you and me. Like at school." Brigitte tried to smile, but her eyes were shiny with moisture. Quickly she looked down again until Kamisha could only see the top of her head.

"What is it, Brigitte?" Kamisha asked again, praying it wasn't another fight with Bullet, another infidelity or girl phoning long-distance or . . .

Brigitte looked at her then, her fingers twisting the ring, tendrils of her fine honey-brown hair lifting in the breeze from the lace-curtained window. "You'll hate me," she whispered. "You'll never speak to me again."

"Come on, what is this?"

"I'm sober, Kamisha. I want you to know that. I haven't had a drop all day, I swear." Brigitte's brown eyes were huge, her heart-shaped face pale and solemn.

"I believe you."

"I have to tell you something."

The waitress arrived to take their orders then, and Brigitte clammed up, but Kamisha could see her lips quivering. They ordered salads, and the waitress had to ask Brigitte twice, because she spoke so quietly that she couldn't be heard.

Kamisha studied the woman across from her, the woman who had been her friend for over half her lifetime. She *was* different today, scared and depressed, not drunk, and Kamisha was abruptly worried. Something was really wrong, something different. Maybe Tracy had been right. Maybe Brigitte was sick. Maybe she was going to have a breakdown.

"Tell me, Brigitte, what were you going to say?" Kamisha said carefully.

Brigitte bit her lip until it turned white, then she took a sip of coffee and set the cup down, spilling a little in the saucer. Her hands were shaking.

"Come on," Kamisha urged gently, "what are friends for?"

But Brigitte had turned inward, and it was no use. All through lunch, which neither of them finished, Kamisha had the feeling Brigitte was holding back on her. They talked about Tracy. They discussed Brigitte checking into the Betty Ford Clinic for a forty-five-day alcohol abuse program. They even discussed Bullet in a reasonable manner, and the fact that Brigitte knew in her heart that he'd been using her all along—her connections, her house, her money. But they never truly got to the heart of Brigitte's troubles, Kamisha suspected. And she wondered about that.

It happened when Kamisha got home. She should have known the attention of the press would turn to her eventually. But she hadn't expected the woman from the *Insider* to be parked on her doorstep.

"Excuse me," Kamisha said, "but this is my home. Call me for an appointment at the club."

"Just a few questions, Miss Hammill," the woman said, rising, ignoring Kamisha. She licked the end of her pen as if words were going to rush out magically onto the notepad. "Now rumor has it that you were in Costa Rica at—"

"I'm allowed a vacation, aren't I?"

"Then you aren't denying—?"

"Listen—" Kamisha began.

"And that while you were gone Senator Stern's wife walked in on her husband at a party where—"

"*That's* a lie."

"And furthermore," the woman went on, "you were the one to arrange these affairs and—"

"Oh, God, will you please listen?"

"You *are* PR director at the Ute City Club, Miss Hammill, and therefore responsible for—"

"*Lady,*" Kamisha said in a quavering voice, "if you want the truth, then why don't you listen to it?"

But the woman never did stop firing inane questions in her face, and the only way Kamisha escaped was to go inside and lock her door.

Damn, she thought, throwing her purse onto the sofa and gritting her teeth. It had to stop! And just what was John doing about it? Hiding in New York? She couldn't believe that of him. He was a lot of things, but not a coward. Still, it was obvious no one was talking about the parties. Not Rick Simons, certainly not Senator Luke Stern or his cronies—no one. And neither the police nor the sheriff's deputies had gotten anywhere. She knew that because they'd called her and asked a lot of questions after Rick's beating. She'd told them everything she knew, which wasn't much, everything except the fact that the sheriff's daughter had been at some of the parties.

It occurred to her then: she couldn't go on working at the club under this cloud of suspicion. And another thought followed on the heels of the first. There was a way—Carin McNaught. She knew John had disapproved of using an underage girl to get their information, but it was starting to look as if Carin was their best bet.

It struck Kamisha that if John returned her calls, she'd run the idea past him one more time. Then just as quickly she realized there was little chance of that happening. Instead, she sat down and looked up the McNaughts' phone number. A few names, that was all she really needed from Carin, and no one ever had to know where the names came from.

But, by the next afternoon, Carin hadn't responded to the message Kamisha had left with her mother. She jumped every time the phone in her office at the club rang, positive one of the calls would be Carin or maybe, just maybe, John. She alternated between hope that Carin would help them clear the club's name and despair that John had so utterly rejected her. At one time she might have rejoiced in the challenge, but no longer. John had done that to her; his search for the almighty truth had made her see herself in a new light. No, she didn't need any more challenges. She didn't need to lay her life on the line for a cheap thrill, not anymore. Now she knew what made her happy, what fulfilled her, what gave her that emotional high. She knew what she needed. She needed John.

It wasn't until seven-thirty that evening that Carin finally called. "We've got to talk, Carin," Kamisha said.

"I can't. Really, my parents would kill me." The girl sounded scared, half crying.

"You have to, and they won't kill you. They'll understand once they know the truth. I'll be there with you. I'll explain everything. We need you, Carin."

"Miss Hammill, I don't dare!"

"Listen, I'll meet you somewhere private. Just hear me out. You'll be protected, Carin, because you're a minor. Just listen to me."

"Oh, I can't."

Kamisha pulled the last stop. "I'll have to go to your dad then, Carin. But wouldn't it be better if he heard it from you first?"

The next afternoon, on her lunch hour, Kamisha bicycled down the hill to the Roaring Fork River where the bicycle path began. She had her fingers crossed that Carin would show up, as she'd promised, that the girl wouldn't back out.

She stood, one foot on either side of the bike pedals, arms resting on the handlebars, waiting for Carin. John still hadn't called, she thought again. She'd been at work all morning and he hadn't called. She couldn't believe he was doing this to her—to himself. Why? What had wounded him so terribly that he had to defend himself even against her?

Carin pedaled up, only a few minutes late. She was a pretty girl, very fair, with strawberry-blond hair and a mature body for her age. She looked worried, though, and upset and awfully young to be mixed up in this messy affair.

"Hi," she said shyly.

"Thanks for coming, Carin. I mean that."

"Miss Hammill, will I have to tell how I got paid and went to the parties?"

Kamisha put a hand on the girl's arm. "Hey, it won't be so bad. No one's accusing *you* of anything. You're a witness, that's all. The police may need your testimony to put a very bad person behind bars, Carin."

"Who is it? You mean Mr. Simons? I mean, I know he got beat up. God, the rag sheets at the grocery stores are still featuring all that stuff on the front pages."

"Mr. Simons was involved, yes, but he had a partner, the man who put him in the hospital."

"Oh, my gosh." Carin paled. "Who...who was it?"

"That's what we need you for, Carin," Kamisha said gently. "We've tried and tried to find out who was working with Mr. Simons, but everyone's afraid to talk."

"But I don't know who."

"I know you don't, honey, but you must remember a few of the names of the men who went to those parties."

"I..."

"Carin, just a couple of names. No one will ever need to know you told."

"I don't want to be a rat, Miss Hammill."

Kamisha sighed. "In school maybe it's called that. But this is the real world. The man who put Rick Simons in the hospital is dangerous. He could have killed Rick, Carin."

"But my dad, he'll be so mad at me."

They walked their bicycles across the road and started pedaling slowly down the shaded bike path along the river. Kamisha kept silent, allowing the girl to think.

"Will I have to, you know, testify in court?" Carin finally asked.

"I don't think so. And besides, at your age it would all be private, anyway. What I'm hoping," she said, "is to find out who beat Mr. Simons, and then Mr. Simons won't be afraid to come forward with the truth."

"Miss Hammill," Carin said, "is it really true?"

"Is what true?"

"The stories in the papers. You know, about the Mafia and all that stuff?"

"No, honey, it's a bunch of garbage."

The girl finally came up with several names—names no one could fail to recognize. At the parties had been a basketball star known as P. T. Malloy, the all-time three-point king in the NBA. And there had been a well-known news anchorman, a Canadian, who worked for a national television station. But the most formidable figure Carin remembered had his face on the covers of at least three nationwide publications a week—Rory Dustin, a world power broker who owned hotels and casinos in thirteen countries and was estimated to be worth thirty-five billion dollars.

"He has a house on Red Mountain," Carin said, her head bowed. "He invited me and another girl, one of the ones from California, up one night after this party. But I didn't go, Miss Hammill. Honest."

"I'm glad you didn't. What a creep," she said under her breath, remembering a couple of tennis matches she'd played with him. She'd won, too, and now was damn glad she had. "You know," Kamisha said, shaking herself mentally, "we've got to tell your dad about these men."

"Oh, God."

"I know. It'll be hard. But I'll be right there beside you. And when it's over, Carin, you'll feel much better."

"He'll kill me."

"He'll *love* you for being truthful."

But the girl only hung her head.

CHAPTER SEVENTEEN

"MR. LEOPARDO," came Martha's voice over the intercom, "Mr. Rick Simons is on line two."

John's hand stopped short on its way to the phone. Rick. Well, well. How interesting. "Put him through, Martha. Thank you."

The line was obviously long-distance, with echoes and the sound of static.

"Mr. Leopardo?"

"Speaking."

"Uh, Rick Simons here."

"Yes, Rick, what can I do for you?"

"Look, I want to apologize for the way I acted in Aspen. I...I was upset and scared. I want you to know I appreciate you giving me a paid vacation like this."

John said nothing. He could almost hear Rick's quick, nervous breath, see his pale, sweat-slicked face.

"I...wondered if we could...talk."

"About what, Rick?" John kept his voice very even, but his hand tightened on the receiver.

"About those...the...uh...parties."

"The ones you had nothing to do with?"

"Well, Mr. Leopardo, that's not exactly the way it was."

Silence vibrated on the line between them.

"Go on, Rick," John said softly.

"Okay, I was wrong. I shouldn't have done it. But, you know, I figured it didn't hurt anyone. I swear I didn't know about the age of those girls, the kids."

"Why are you telling me this now?"

"I figure it's gonna come out. I mean that Stern woman, the senator's wife, well, she blabbed it all over. It's still in the papers. There's going to be a Senate investigation."

"I've heard," John said. "What exactly did you want to tell me, Rick? So far you've said nothing I don't already know."

"I think we can make a deal, Mr. Leopardo. I figure I'm pretty much finished with you, but I don't want to do time. If I talk, if I go to the police and clear your club, if I tell who was really behind the parties, I figure I can make a deal. And I'd like to know you won't bring charges against me in the middle of all this."

"It sounds reasonable, Rick. I can't speak for the authorities, of course, but if you cooperate fully with the investigation, I will allow you to resign."

"Sounds okay to me, then. I trust you, Mr. Leopardo. You've always been fair with me, and I'm sorry this all had to—"

"Fine, Rick, but I'd like to know who you were working with," John said in a curt voice.

There was a long, silent moment. "Bullet Adams."

The realization struck John cold. Bullet, Brigitte Stratford's boyfriend, the sports announcer, the one Kamisha didn't like at all. Hell, he'd just seen him announce a preseason NFL game on cable TV.

"Mr. Leopardo?"

"Okay, Rick. I appreciate this. I'll take care of everything from here on. Is Bullet the one who—?"

"Yeah, the son of a— Yeah, he did it. He likes to hurt people. He's one dangerous dude. Too damn many steroids in his football days."

"You'll have to testify against him, depositions, probably at a trial, too."

"It'll be a pleasure," Rick said grimly.

"Where are you, Rick? The authorities will have to get in touch with you."

"I'm still in Miami. At my folks. Joe at the Ute City Club has my address."

"You'll stay available?"

"Yes, sir. There's nowhere I can run."

"All right, Rick. You'll be hearing from me. Thanks again. And I take it you're feeling better?"

"Yeah, it only hurts when I laugh," he said bitterly.

John put the receiver down very carefully. Bullet Adams. He conjured up a mental image of the man from the many times he'd seen him on television, and the brief glimpses he'd gotten of him at Brigitte's that day he'd gone Jeeping with Kamisha. Big. Not so tall, but broad and heavily muscled with the bull neck of a linebacker. Blond and good-looking in a blunt-featured way. John recalled that he'd been a favorite with the young groupies, teenagers really, in his football days. And hadn't there been some problem when he was in college? An assault charge or a rape or something? Yes, he thought, there had been.

Bullet had married some starlet, gotten a divorce, married another and gotten another divorce. An unsavory character, and Kamisha's instincts were right about him.

No doubt it had been a lucrative enterprise, arranging those parties. And Bullet must have been infuriated when Kamisha had caught on and cut off his supply of

easy money. He'd evidently tried to get Rick to go on
with them, Rick had declined, and Bullet had beaten
him up. A violent man, shrewd but not too bright; his
beating of Rick had been patently ill-advised.

Bullet Adams.

It occurred to him without a bridging thought. He
had to let Kamisha know. My God, she'd been staying
at Brigitte's house! Bullet could have done something
whenever he'd wanted, gotten her alone. But now Kamisha was back at her own home, thank God. Maybe
he should have left Inky there, after all, to watch over
her. But after Joanne Stern had held that press conference, he'd believed she was safe. By then it had been too
late for the instigator of all this trouble to save the situation.

Of course, there was always revenge. Would a man
like Bullet resort to revenge, physical revenge, even if it
gave him away? Was he capable of that?

John dialed Kamisha's number. It was midafternoon
in Aspen, and he suspected she wouldn't be home, but
he tried, anyway. He let it ring and ring. No answer.
Damn! Why didn't she have an answering machine?

He tried the club then. "I'm sorry. Miss Hammill's
line doesn't answer. Can I take a message?" the girl at
the front desk asked.

"Do you know where she is?"

"No, I'm sorry. She's out of her office right now."

"Leave her a message, please. Tell her to call John in
New York right away. It's important."

"Yes, sir, I've got that. Do you want to leave a number?"

"She knows it."

He stood and paced, thinking. Worry coiled within
him, and he cursed the two thousand miles that lay be-

tween him and Kamisha. He was helpless and hated the feeling.

There was nothing he could do right now. The sheriff and the police in Aspen would have to be informed, of course, but he wanted to reach Kamisha first—warn her and get her out of danger. Then he'd call the authorities, or maybe she'd want to do that.

He could probably get her at home around five, Aspen time—in two hours. Damn.

The console buzzed.

"Yes, Martha?"

"Inky is here for you."

"I'll be right out."

He'd go to his health club, have a quick workout, then try her again. "Martha," he said when he reached her desk, "have the answering service pick everything up after you leave. I'm expecting an important call."

"Yes, Mr. Leopardo."

"All set, boss? The club?" Inky asked.

He told Inky about Rick Simons's call on the way to his club.

The black man whistled. "So what now?"

"I've been trying to get hold of Kamisha, but she isn't available. I don't like the idea of that man on the loose around her."

"He'd be nuts to try anything, boss," Inky said.

"Yes, he would."

"But..."

"Yes, but."

From his club John checked with the answering service; he was standing in the steamy locker room, in sweat-soaked shorts, a towel around his neck.

"No calls, Mr. Leopardo."

"No calls," he repeated.

He dialed Kamisha's home number again. It rang and rang, echoing ominously in his ear. He pictured her lying there, like Rick Simons, her jaw broken, her lovely skin scraped and bruised. The image caused a hot wave of nausea to rise in his gut, even though he knew Adams had had plenty of opportunity to get to Kamisha already. Most likely she was safe, totally safe. But still . . .

At home he tried again, both the club and her house. She'd never picked up the message he'd left at the desk earlier. The new girl at the desk thought Kamisha had been in a tennis tournament at the Snowmass Club, and she'd probably gone straight home from there.

But where was she?

He felt a fist of fear tighten in his belly. He was turning a molehill into a mountain, he told himself again. Kamisha didn't have to go straight home from work. She didn't have to report in. She was a mature, single woman. She could be anywhere. *Relax,* he told himself.

By eight o'clock he gave up. He couldn't let this go on any longer. If he wasn't able to reach Kamisha, he'd have to contact someone in Aspen to do it for him.

Sheriff McNaught. He was going to have to call the man, anyway, about Bullet Adams. He'd wanted to tell Kamisha first, but he couldn't gamble, couldn't wait any longer.

He got the number from the operator. The Pitkin County Sheriff's Department. He dialed, tapping his fingers impatiently until there was an answer.

"Sheriff McNaught, please."

"He's gone home for the evening. Can I connect you to another deputy?"

Damn. "No, I need to talk to him. This is John Leopardo, owner of the Ute City Club. I have some information that he's been wanting."

"I'm sorry. Would you like to talk to—"

"It's an emergency. There's a possibility that someone's life may be in danger," John stated flatly.

Ed McNaught's wife answered the phone. She sounded irritated when she heard what John wanted, as if her husband was disturbed at home too often for her taste.

"Ed McNaught here."

"Sheriff, I'm calling from New York. I just found out something today that I think you'll want to know. It has to do with the assault on my club manager, Rick Simons."

"Well, I'll tell you, Mr. Leopardo, any help you can offer us in the case would sure be appreciated."

"I know who got to Simons. The same man who was throwing those parties at my club."

"The parties?" The sheriff's tone became wary, as if John had touched on a nerve.

"That's right," John said. "I intend to press charges against the man in Pitkin County, but I'm afraid you may come second to the Senate investigation that's due to start soon."

"You mean Senator Stern's involvement?"

"Exactly."

"Well," McNaught said, "we'll see about that. This is my territory here, Leopardo."

"That's your business," John said, a quick image of future headlines dashing through his head: Aspen Sheriff Battles Federal Government over Extradition...

"So who's this man?" McNaught was asking.

John tapped a pen slowly on his desktop. "Before I give you his name I want it understood that Simons came forward with this information. I won't press charges against him, Sheriff. He'll most likely be a friendly witness for the government at any rate."

"*Who* beat up Simons?" the sheriff asked sharply.

"Bullet Adams."

"The sportscaster?" came McNaught's incredulous voice.

"That's your man. He also supplied the young girls."

"Bullet Adams," Ed McNaught was saying slowly, as if savoring the name.

"Yes," John said impatiently now. "He's the one." But then suddenly John knew why McNaught sounded so tense—the man already knew about his daughter's involvement. Somehow, either through Kamisha or his daughter, he knew. John wondered about that but kept silent. It wasn't his problem.

"Look," John said, "I'm concerned about Kamisha Hammill. She came to me in the first place about her suspicions and—"

"I know," the sheriff broke in. "I know all about that. *Now*."

"I see."

"Have you spoken to Miss Hammill?"

"I've been trying to reach her all afternoon."

"And?"

"No luck. I'm hoping you'll send a car out to her place. It's also possible that she may have gone to her friend's—"

"Brigitte Stratford."

"Correct, Sheriff. I don't think Adams is going to try anything at this stage, but—"

"I wouldn't put it past him," McNaught said darkly.

"You'll send a car then?"

"I'll go myself," the sheriff said, and John didn't like the sound of the man's voice. Not at all. The helplessness, the fear for Kamisha, began to twist in his gut like a knife.

KAMISHA DIDN'T ARRIVE home from the annual Snowmass Club tournament until after six. She threw her tennis bag onto a chair and then searched the refrigerator for something to drink. She was tired and thirsty and hungry, still in her sweaty tennis clothes. She was going to eat, then take a long, hot shower. Then bed, early.

Just as she was pouring herself a glass of grapefruit juice, the phone rang. Holding her glass, she answered it, tucking the receiver between her ear and her shoulder.

"Kamisha!" A man's voice, perturbed.

"Who is this?" she asked.

"Bullet. God, Brigitte's on the floor. I can't...I can't wake her up!"

"Bullet, wait a minute? What's going on?" She straightened, put the glass down, grabbed the phone.

"It's Brigitte! We had a fight. I left for a while. Just got back. She was on the floor, unconscious. A bottle of whisky, pills all over. I'm afraid—"

"Oh, no! Oh, dear Lord. Did you call the ambulance? The hospital? Oh, God, Bullet, is she...is she...?"

"I don't know! She's just lying here."

"Call for an ambulance! Right away. You hear me, Bullet? Nine-one-one. I'm hanging up. I'll be right over. You hear me?"

"Yes, okay, I'll call!"

She slammed down the receiver and grabbed her car keys, raced outside, started her car up, stomping too hard on the accelerator. Her heart was beating like a trip-hammer. Brigitte! Brigitte! Oh, no, it couldn't be!

Tears burned in her eyes, but she forced them back. No time. The hospital was close to Brigitte's house, though. They'd have her there in a flash. Oxygen, IVs. She'd be all right.

It only took her ten minutes to get to Brigitte's. She burst out of her car, leaving the door open. Her mind registered momentarily that there was no ambulance there yet. Oh, God, where was it? Soon. It'd be here soon. She'd be okay. Brigitte would make it.

She raced up the walk to the door, flung the door open, panting, her heart threatening to explode. "Bullet!" she cried out. "Where is she?"

"Here, Kamisha," came his voice.

The kitchen, he was in the kitchen.

"Bullet!" she gasped, running through the living room. "How is she? Did you—?"

She stopped short. Bullet was leaning back against the counter, a tall drink in his hand, a smug half smile on his face.

"Hello, Kamisha," he said coolly.

"Where's Brigitte? What...?" She felt as if something was wrong, as if she'd made some awful, irreversible mistake. Her eyes fixed on the glass casually held in his hand.

"Brigitte. Yes, well, she's gone with Tracy to a horse show."

"But you said...you called me..." Inadvertently she began backing away from him.

"Come in, relax, sit down."

"Where's Brigitte?" Kamisha asked, harshly now.

"I told you. She's at a horse show with Tracy. New-castle, I think."

"Why did you call me then? Why did you...lie?"

"I wanted to talk to you," he said nonchalantly, up-ending his glass.

"You could have talked to me on the phone." Her heart was beating slowly and heavily now, a familiar rhythm, the one with which Kamisha met danger.

"I wanted to talk to you in person."

"About what?" She'd keep talking, keep her eye on an escape route—the kitchen door, the living room, the front door. If she showed fear, then like an predator, Bullet would strike.

"What do you want with me? Why did you get me over here?" she asked angrily. "You almost gave me a heart attack."

He smiled, his all-American, snub-nosed features turning malevolent. "You did me a bad turn, lady."

"What are you talking about?" Kamisha folded her arms and glared at him. In a minute she'd casually turn and leave, walk out the door, tell him she had to be somewhere.

"You and Rick Simons."

"*What?*" Knowledge was creeping upon her like a sickness.

"You stopped my lucrative gigs, Kamisha. You went running to the owner and got me into lots of trouble."

"*You?* You had the parties?" Her mind whirled diz-zily, seeking support, and all the while she knew it made perfect sense—Bullet, the party boy, the jock who knew everybody, Rick's tennis partner.

Bullet straightened, placed his glass down carefully and took a step toward her. She moved backward, try-ing desperately to regain her wits, to think.

"Yeah," he said, "the parties were my idea. A great setup, good money. But you had to go and ruin it all."

Kamisha unfolded her arms and drew herself up. "You're damn right I did it. I'd do it again. You're a pimp, Bullet, a disgusting pimp."

"I told you once before about your big mouth, lady."

"All right, Bullet, you've had your say-so. I don't like your company very much, so I'm leaving. Save your stories for the police." Now was the time. She turned, watching him out of the corner of her eye, her muscles tensed, her pulse pounding that slow, deep cadence.

"Not so fast." His voice boomed at her, and she almost flinched, but she kept moving, steadily, toward the front door.

One step, two steps. Her breath rasped in her throat. She kept telling herself that he wouldn't dare touch her, wouldn't dare do anything. Three steps. The white living room carpet sank under her feet. Four steps, another.

A hand came down hard on her shoulder, and he thrust his face up close to hers. "I said not so fast," he rasped. He smelled of alcohol, and his eyes were bloodshot.

"Let me go," she said icily.

"Like hell I will."

She reacted instinctively, swinging her other arm, slapping him on the side of his face, yanking away at the same time. He grunted but kept his grip. Then his hand exploded against her face.

Shock, pain, fury crashed in her head. She must have cried out. He must have said something, too. But she didn't hear. She twisted, fighting him, clawing at his face, panting like a beast, but he held her at arm's length. He was grinning, his teeth showing. He hit her again, a glancing blow that made her sob with rage.

He was strong and quick, and he wasn't afraid of hurting her. She almost panicked, her breath coming fast, her face hot and pulsing with pain.

She doubled over, pretending to collapse. His grip loosened, and she lurched up, bringing her knee up to his groin, hard.

Suddenly she was free, gasping, heedless of the pain in her face, backing away, watching him on the floor as he writhed. *Good*, her mind told her. *Good.*

She ran then, across the white carpet, flung open the door and fled outside into the cool dusk.

But there was a car pulling into the driveway, a Pitkin County sheriff's car, and it was stopping, a man was getting out. She stood there, breathing hard, half dazed.

"Kamisha! Good God! What's going on?"

It was Ed McNaught. She took a step toward him, drew in a quavering breath. "Bullet," she tried to say, clearing her throat. "Bullet. He's in there."

"Are you all right?" The sheriff took her arm and looked at her closely.

"He hit me," she said.

"He's inside?"

"Yes, he's ... in there."

"Okay, I'm calling for backup. You come here, sit in my car. Does he have a gun, a weapon?"

She shook her head.

The sheriff used his radio while Kamisha sat there, stunned. The fury had died, and in the aftermath she felt absolutely drained, shaky.

"Now you stay here. I'm going inside to talk to Adams. You okay?"

She nodded.

Within five minutes two more cars pulled up, their red lights rotating, sirens dying. They saw Kamisha, asked where Ed was. She told them, pointing, noticing that they unsnapped the flaps of their holsters as they went toward the house. She sat there, oddly incurious, and the revolving red lights of the deputies' cars pulsated in the autumn dusk.

She was still sitting like that when Brigitte drove up, just as the three men led Bullet out of the house. He was handcuffed, his shirt torn, a smudge of blood on his lip.

"Oh, God!" Brigitte screamed, bursting out of her car. "What happened? Bullet?"

But he never even looked at her, just ducked his head under the deputy's hand and got into one of the cars.

She saw Kamisha then, sitting silently in the sheriff's car. Running, she dragged the door open. "Kamisha, what's going on?"

"Miss Stratford," Ed McNaught said, "Mr. Adams assaulted Kamisha. He resisted arrest, too. I'm afraid he's going to be in some trouble here."

"Bullet?" Brigitte, eyes huge in her small, pallid face, looked from the sheriff to her friend, back and forth, searching for succor.

"Brigitte, he was the one running those parties," Kamisha said quietly.

"Oh, God" was all Brigitte said.

It struck Kamisha that her friend sounded more despairing than surprised. "You knew?" she whispered.

But Brigitte didn't answer at first. Her eyes welled over with tears, and she put a finger out to touch Kamisha's face where Bullet had hit her. "I'm sorry," she said in a broken voice. "Oh, I'm so sorry."

"You knew," Kamisha repeated.

Brigitte sobbed, put her face in her hands. Her shoulders shook. "I tried to tell you," she said, her voice muffled. "But you didn't listen. That night when you were upset about John and at lunch that day. I tried. Oh, Kamisha, I'm so sorry. I was afraid."

"You knew and you never told me. Oh, Brigitte, how could you?"

"He threatened me." She dropped her hands and looked at Kamisha. "I wanted to, oh, God, how I wanted to. I'm so sorry. I never thought...I never, never thought he'd hurt you."

"You knew he'd beaten Rick Simons?" Kamisha asked.

"I...I guessed."

"Oh, Brigitte."

"I know. Now I've really messed up. I was just so scared. Kamisha, I'll do anything I have to to make it up to you. Anything."

"We'll talk about it later," Kamisha said. "Okay? Later, Brigitte." She felt immeasurably sad.

"You won't hate me, will you? You'll forgive me? Please, Kamisha..."

"Don't worry, Brigitte. I'm just so tired now."

"Do you want me to drive you home, Kamisha?" Ed McNaught asked.

"Uh, no...I'm okay, really."

"I'd say it's a good thing Mr. Leopardo called me when he did. Can't tell what might have happened. Glad I drove right on out."

"John?" Kamisha's head snapped. up. "*John* called you?"

"John Leopardo, yeah. Said he tried getting hold of you, but you weren't home. He got worried, so he called me."

Kamisha held her head with both hands. "John tried to call me?"

"Seems like. Anyway, it's a good thing he did. Guess he was right to be worried."

"John," she said, hugging herself around the middle, sitting in the sheriff's car while the red lights flickered over their faces eerily.

"You okay, Miss Stratford?" the sheriff was asking Brigitte then.

"No," Kamisha heard her say haltingly. "No, I'm not okay. I'm a mess."

"You want me to call someone?" he asked.

"No, no." Kamisha looked up and heard Brigitte say, "You don't need to call anyone. My best friend in the whole world is right here." And Kamisha felt a single, hot tear finally squeeze from her eye and slide down her cheek.

CHAPTER EIGHTEEN

KAMISHA CALLED late that night. John snatched up the phone on the first ring. His gut was churning, as it had been the whole evening since he'd spoken to McNaught, but hearing her voice now, knowing she was safe, he felt like an expectant father—out of his element, afraid, happy she was on the other end of the line and wary, too. Yes, he was still very much on guard with this woman.

They spoke in monosyllables. About Bullet, about Rick Simons, about the upcoming Senate investigation of Luke Stern and his trysts at the Ute City Club. The conversation was stilted, awkward, and John wished to God he could handle it better.

"Well," she was saying, "I know it's late in New York, but I haven't been able to get through to you at your office, and—"

"I'm glad you called," he said. "I was truly concerned about your safety."

"Well, thank you, but everything's all right now."

"Yes, finally."

"Well . . ."

"I'll be talking to you soon, I'm sure," John said, "and you take care."

"Oh, I will." There was a pause, then she said, "John, listen, I—"

"Please, Kamisha," he broke in, "we'll talk another time. It's late here. I have appointments in the morning."

"Oh, I'm sorry, well..."

"Good night, Kamisha," he said, and hung up abruptly. For a long, long time he sat in the dark in his room, his head bowed, his stomach knotted, his heart beating too fast. There was a moment when he nearly picked up the phone and called her back, but the instant passed, fleeing into the dark corners of the room.

Inky sauntered into his office the next day in the middle of the afternoon. "Thought you might want to go home early today. You know, after that mess last night," he said, perching one large thigh on the corner of John's desk.

"Doesn't Martha screen my visitors anymore?" John asked irritably.

"Not me. Besides, boss, she thinks you need some rest, too. Said you were hard to please all day."

"That's ridiculous."

"How well did you sleep last night? Come on, tell me."

"It's none of your goddamn business, Inky. Will you lay off?"

Inky looked him square in the eye. "You been down, boss, since Aspen."

"I've been busy. Preoccupied."

Inky shook his head. "Man, I've never heard you lie to yourself."

"Knock it off, will you?"

"I'd like to, boss, honest I would," he said. "Just yesterday I promised myself I wasn't going to mention a thing, but—"

John held up a hand. "You're pushing, Inky."

"Yeah? And I'm gonna go right on, too."

For a long moment John eyed him furiously, his temper boiling.

"When you gonna admit you blew it, man?" Inky said, unperturbed.

"Blew *what?*" John whispered dangerously.

"Blew it with Kamisha."

"I won't discuss that with—"

"Yeah, man, I'd say you ruined the best shot you ever had at happiness."

That did it. John exploded. It was as if the past few weeks of tension and misery came spewing out in a gush. "You want me to go through that again? You think I should do that to Kamisha, too?"

"Geez, boss," Inky said, calm, "maybe you should've asked her."

"She doesn't know a damn thing about it, what it's like."

"Sure she does."

"Inky," John grated out, his face hot and flushed, "just go wash the damn car or whatever it is you do. Leave me the hell alone."

Inky did leave then, but he was grinning.

"Damn it!" John said to the echoing emptiness in his office. He was fed up with Inky's aggravating mothering, fed up with Martha and her silent disapproval, fed up with himself. He stood at the window and watched the frenetic movement on the streets of the city below and knew that his life would never be quite the same again. It was as if he were a rock that had been shaken to its very core and cracked, irreparably cracked. He might live like this for his lifetime, weathering the storms, but he was changed forever.

He snatched up his cane and left the office, walking stiffly past a surprised Martha. "I'll be back in the morning," he said. That was all, no explanation.

He walked, bumping shoulders with hordes of shoppers and businessmen and street people for hours, it seemed. He found himself, finally, down by the East River, on the same path he'd taken with her. It was as if her shadow moved alongside him, a phantom in the bright September sun; he'd never be rid of that memory. He'd never be rid of that empty spot that she'd once filled. The yearning, the ache in his heart, was something entirely new for John. He felt like a man who'd been blind all his life, whose sight had been miraculously restored and then abruptly snatched away.

Inky found him on a bench. It was past 6:00 p.m.

"Goddamn, boss! I been looking for you for hours!"

"How did you find me?" John asked, only mildly curious.

"Well, hell, I looked every place else in this city, then I thought, Where would the boss go if he needed to think?"

"I feel like hell," John admitted, his knee throbbing to beat the band.

"I bet you do. Come on. I'll drive you home. Come on, John."

But he had to tell Inky. He was sick of the lie. "You were right," he said, looking up into the wide black face. "I did blow it."

"I know," Inky replied slowly. "I know, man. When you're lucky enough to have someone love you, you learn to live with whatever problems come up. Love's too special to dink with, boss."

"Is that so?" John asked, smiling tiredly.

"That's about it, I guess."

"Is that why I feel like hell? Is it love?"

"That, boss, and maybe there's this stranger inside you, too, this man that's afraid to come out 'cause it might hurt too much."

"Too risky, huh?"

"Yeah, I suppose."

"Have you been reading psychology books, Inky?"

"Naw. It's just common sense."

"Maybe for some," John said pensively. "Maybe for some."

The next day he flew to Aspen.

He waited in the Denver airport impatiently. He boarded the small jet that flew into Aspen impatiently. He was nervous, unused to this feeling of being unprotected, raw, his emotions so close to the skin that any small nick or bruise could make him bleed.

What if she had another man? What if she no longer wanted him? What if she laughed at him, scorned him, raged at him? She might have been hurt too much, wounded too deeply, to ever forgive him.

The plane banked, circling the green valley, and John could see the glint of the Roaring Fork River below, twisting along next to the ribbon of highway that connected Aspen to the outside world.

She didn't know he was coming. He hadn't had the courage to let her know. Or maybe he'd been afraid she'd have time to steel herself against him. No, it was better to just appear, to be there, to judge her reaction.

He wondered what she thought of him after that last awkward conversation two nights ago. She'd tried to break through his rejection, but she hadn't been able to. She'd tried before, but he hadn't listened to her then, either. She'd begged him to let her help him, but he'd turned from her with a hopelessness born of stubbornness and fear. He could hear her voice, taut with anxiety, asking him, *John, can we talk about it? I care about you. I care about us.*

And he'd turned away.

Aspen after Labor Day was a different creature: calm, sedate, quiet, a small town once again. The air was clear, the sky blue, the branches of the aspen trees hung with dancing golden coins. The driveway of the club was littered with fallen leaves, which a girl in cutoff jeans and a Ute City Club T-shirt raked into piles.

He had the taxi drop him at the door of his condo. It was getting late, nearly five, and he wanted to catch Kamisha at work, in a more neutral setting than her own house. Hurrying up, he left his bag in the middle of the floor and turned to leave again.

He hesitated. He could phone the front desk and ask her to meet him. But, no, he wouldn't; she could leave, refuse to see him. No, he had to walk in, no Martha or Inky to smooth things out and prepare the way. This he had to do himself.

He walked down the path toward the main building, concentrating on moving easily. A pair of tennis players passed him, laughing, red-cheeked with exertion. Two men jogged by, dressed in bright-colored shorts. A breeze rustled in the golden leaves and caressed John's skin, teasing, promising.

He limped across the narrow wooden bridge that spanned the river, which tumbled by, bright and clear, laughing at his slow progress.

The path rose slightly, making its way to the front door of the club; he felt his heartbeat respond to the altitude and his nervousness. His hand gripping the cane was slippery with moisture.

People were coming out of the club, carrying gym bags, their hair still damp from showers. Healthy, vibrant people. Kamisha's kind of people. She belonged here, he thought. But did he?

He saw her the instant he stepped inside the lobby. She was leaning over the counter of the front desk, conferring with one of the girls. She wore a jade-green leotard and matching headband, and tendrils of her hair were lying on her neck, damp with sweat. Her skin gleamed.

He watched her for a time, held motionless by uncertainty. He felt old and haggard and foolish standing there with his cane, dressed in a business suit. He could do nothing. He felt as if the situation was out of his control now, rushing to some kind of conclusion that fate had chosen for him—for them. And he'd relinquished control utterly. It was a frightening feeling but strangely one of relief, too. At last, finally, he'd given up and the burden was lifted from his shoulders.

He watched her until she sensed his presence and turned abruptly. It was then that he saw the bruise on her cheek, the dark smudge left there by a man's hand— Bullet's hand. His fingers clutched his cane, and he took a deep breath to control himself. He should have been there. He should have been with Kamisha.

Their eyes met. Hers widened, and he saw a flush rise on her skin. Her back grew rigid. It was as if the thin mountain air was suddenly sucked from that place, and he could barely breath.

She said something to the girl at the desk, straightened and came toward him. Her lips quivered into a half smile as she stood before him.

"John," she said, her eyes searching his.

"Hello, Kamisha."

"I didn't know you were coming."

"Neither did I."

They were being so careful with each other, as they had been at first, two people who were afraid to say what they really meant, two people with carefully constructed facades, unable to penetrate beyond the banality of their words. He ached to tell her how sorry he was that he hadn't been there to protect her from Bullet Adams. He wanted to tell her that she'd never be alone again, never.

"Well," Kamisha was saying, "you're here. I am glad, John. Did you get my message? There are going to be a lot of things for you to take care of. Bullet and a press release and—"

"We can discuss all that later," he said, cutting her off.

"All right." She stood there, waiting, slim and poised, waiting for him to say something, anything.

"I should have taken your calls," he said.

"Your Martha was just too efficient for me," Kamisha replied coolly.

"Martha," he said, "disapproves of how I've been acting lately."

"Oh?"

"She thought I should take your calls, too."

For a moment she looked surprised. Finally she nodded in comprehension. "Martha was right."

Silence hung between them awkwardly.

"John—" she began.

"Can we go somewhere and talk?" he asked quickly.

"Yes, of course. Just let me get something...." She gestured at her leotard.

She was back in a moment, a long shirt over her aerobics outfit. They went outside to the far corner of the deck and sat at a table under a big umbrella. He was so terribly aware of her proximity, the reality of her that had only been a dream for these past weeks. He wanted to say so many things, but the words never reached his lips.

"How is it in New York?" she asked.

"Muggy. Kamisha..." He hesitated, looked out over the tennis courts. "Look, I came here to...apologize, I guess."

She just looked at him for a heartbeat of time, then said, "I thought you came because of Bullet. I thought..."

"No, I came because of you, Kamisha."

A tremulous smile curved her lips. "John, you mean that, don't you?"

"I mean it."

She looked down. "You must have known how I felt about you. I didn't try to hide it. You hurt me, John."

"I know and I'm sorry. I'm not sure you can forgive me, but I guess I'm here to ask you to."

"Oh, John..." She reached out a hand and put it over his. "This role of penitent doesn't suit you very well. You're lousy at it."

"I don't have much practice," he said stiffly.

"And I'm not making it any easier, am I?" She smiled and then looked away. "I don't know. I'm just getting over the shock of you being here. Give me a little time." She gave a short laugh. "Let me figure out what I feel. I'm not even sure."

"Of course, that's fair." What had he expected, that she'd fly into his arms, swearing eternal devotion? He swallowed his disappointment and put a good face on it. He had time.

She leaned forward, elbows on the table. "Speaking of apologies," she said, "I owe you one myself for going to Carin McNaught when you were against it. John, I—"

"Kamisha, don't. You don't owe me an apology for that. I was being stubborn that day, so sure of my own power to solve every problem on earth. I was wrong."

She smiled and nodded. "As it turned out, Carin won't have to give a deposition or anything."

"That's good."

"Yes. It's enough she's working things out with her dad. And then just this morning— Oh, wow," Kamisha said. "I almost forgot to tell you, but Sheriff McNaught called and said the FBI searched Bullet's house in California and found not only all kinds of drugs and paraphernalia, but young girls living there— runaways, John, from all over the place. It looks like the government is going to have an ironclad case against him."

"I'm glad."

"So am I. He deserves it. You know, he was the one who arranged to have my brakes tampered with at the Denver airport."

John lifted a brow.

"Brigitte told him what I was doing. It wasn't her fault, though. She didn't realize—"

"Of course she didn't. Will Brigitte testify?" he asked.

"Yes, she already gave her statement to the FBI. She left this morning for the Betty Ford Clinic. She quit drinking."

"I'm glad to hear that. I hope she sticks to it."

"Oh, she will. This time she really will. I think she realized what she was becoming. It had to do with Bullet and the parties and Tracy. With all that."

John stood restlessly, aware of the other people sitting on the deck, tanned, fit people who were eyeing him with curiosity, the same bone-chilling curiosity that he'd tried to escape all his adult life. Would he always be so sensitive to strangers' scrutiny?

"Do you mind if we take a walk? I've been sitting too much today," he said, cognizant of Kamisha watching him, too, watching, weighing, wondering.

They made their way along the tree-shaded bike path, treading upon the crisp fallen leaves. He was aware of how effortlessly Kamisha matched her pace to his. Above their heads the leaves whispered, and at their feet the river rushed, dancing in the sun. But John still felt restless.

"I've talked to my father," he said, as if to himself.

Her step faltered for a split second. "Yes?"

"It was very strange after all this time."

"I can imagine. How is he, John?"

"He's an old man, Kamisha. That's what surprised me so. Old and defenseless."

"Was he...uh...glad to see you?"

He nodded. "Yes, grateful and glad."

"I envy you."

"My father has done terrible things in his time. I can't condone what he's done, but now, I think, I can overlook it. We're still family. I was wrong to deny that."

"It must have been hard," she said softly.

"Yes." He walked on for a time, comforted by her presence. "I learned from you, you know."

She regarded him in surprise.

"You taught me that love and loyalty must transcend a person's faults."

"I...um, don't really think..." Her voice died away. "I missed you, John."

"Yes, I missed you, too."

"I tried to call. Well, you know that."

"Yes, Martha made sure I knew every time."

"You never answered."

"I thought I was doing you a favor."

"Oh, God, John, how could you think that? I love you!" she said abruptly.

Pain gripped him. Pain and elation. His hand tightened on the cane until his knuckles turned white. Slowly he stopped and faced her. "I've taken everything you could give me. I took your love and your trust, even your strength. It was because of you I spoke to my father. I don't know...I still don't understand the connection, but somehow, in my mind, I couldn't love one and spurn the other. I've used you and given you nothing back."

"John, you've given me everything."

He shook his head. "What about you? I love you, but I can't ask you to share a life with me. Do you want to be thought of as a Mafia wife? Do you want to be questioned, followed, hounded? I can't ask you to share that with me, Kamisha. I saw what it did to Jo."

"Was that her name?"

"Yes."

"I feel sorry for her."

"She couldn't take it, Kamisha. It hurt her, nearly destroyed her."

"Did you love her?"

He paused. "I loved the idea of her—squeaky-clean, innocent, pretty. We might have been happy."

"She was weak, though. She didn't love you enough."

"I suppose so."

"I'm not Jo. I'm tough, John." She looked at him, her eyes glistening with emotion. "Oh, John, why didn't you ask me before you put us both through this? I can stand it. I've stood it before. I've been through the worst they can throw at me. Don't you realize? You can't hide from the press. That just makes it worse. You've tried to hide all these years when you should have been open. If you talk, if you tell them everything, be absolutely frank, they'll get bored and leave you alone. I know. It happened when I divorced Josh. Once they have the facts, they're satisfied."

He stood there looking at her, torn between disbelief and hope.

"Oh, John," she whispered, "is *that* why... is that the only reason you left?"

Then she was in his arms, and he held her tightly, cradling her head against his chest. She turned her face up, and he saw that she was laughing and crying at the same time. He touched her cheek where the bruises marred it. "You got this because of me," he said sadly. "I should have been with you."

"Don't be silly."

"I'm not silly. But I could be wrong about a couple of things." He kissed her and drew back. "I just might be," he said, feeling foolish and happy and young.

She smiled through her tears and reached up a hand to caress his face. "Wouldn't that be nice for a change," she said softly, and it wasn't a question.

"I always thought a family, and love, couldn't withstand scrutiny," he said. "Do you think it can? Are you willing... ?"

"Yes, John," she said firmly, looking into his eyes.

"Will you marry me?" he found himself asking, astonished at the certainty he felt.

"Yes, John."

He gathered her close and drew in the scent of her hair.

"We'll invite the press to the reception," she was saying. "Let the whole world know how much we love each other."

He laughed softly. The sun slipped behind the mountain, and a cool autumn breeze filtered through the golden leaves. Kamisha's hair was soft and fragrant, her body warm against his.

"There's magic here in Aspen," he said. "Everything is possible here."

"Yes, I feel it, too. You've given me the magic of trust, John. You make me feel worthy of love. I want to be with you forever. Wherever you are, as long as we're together."

"New York?" he asked. "The city?"

"If you're there."

"I've been thinking, you know, of having an office here. I can run my business from anywhere," he said.

"And how long have you been thinking that?" she asked, joy bubbling in her voice.

"Oh, about five minutes," he said.

"It's a nice place to raise children," she said shyly.

"A magic place," he repeated.

"Love is the magic, and it's our gift to each other, John."

Harlequin Superromance ®

Family ties...

SEVENTH HEAVEN
In the introduction to the Osborne family trilogy, Kate Osborne finds her destiny with Police Commissioner Donovan Cade.

Available in December

ON CLOUD NINE
Juliet Osborne's old-fashioned values are tested when she meets jazz musician Ross Stafford, the object of her younger sister's affections. Can Juliet only achieve her heart's desire at the cost of her integrity?

Available in January

SWINGING ON A STAR
Meridee is Kate's oldest daughter, but very much her own person. Determined to climb the corporate ladder, she has never had time for love. But her life is turned upside down when Zeb Farrell storms into town determined to eliminate jobs in her company— her sister's among them! Meridee is prepared to do battle, but for once she's met her match.

Coming in February

my VALENTINE 1992

Celebrate the most romantic day of the year with
MY VALENTINE 1992—a sexy new collection of four
romantic stories written by our famous Temptation
authors:

> GINA WILKINS
> KRISTINE ROLOFSON
> JOANN ROSS
> VICKI LEWIS THOMPSON

My Valentine 1992—an exquisite escape into a romantic
and sensuous world.

◆ *Harlequin Books*®

VAL-92-R

HARLEQUIN'S "BIG WIN"
SWEEPSTAKES RULES & REGULATIONS
NO PURCHASE NECESSARY TO ENTER OR RECEIVE A PRIZE

1. Alternate means of entry: Print your name and address on a 3" × 5" piece of plain paper and send to the appropriate address below:

In the U.S.	In Canada
Harlequin's "BIG WIN" Sweepstakes	Harlequin's "BIG WIN" Sweepstakes
P.O. Box 1867	P.O. Box 609
3010 Walden Ave.	Fort Erie, Ontario
Buffalo, NY 14269-1867	L2A 5X3

2. To enter the Sweepstakes and join the Reader Service, scratch off the metallic strips on all of your BIG WIN tickets #1-#6. This will reveal the values for each Sweepstakes entry number, the number of free books you will receive and your free bonus gift as part of our Reader Service. If you do not wish to take advantage of our Reader Service but wish to enter the Sweepstakes only, scratch off the metallic strips on your BIG WIN tickets #1-#4. Return your entire sheet of tickets intact. Incomplete and/or inaccurate entries are ineligible for that section or sections of prizes. Torstar Corp. and its affiliates are not responsible for mutilated or unreadable entries or inadvertent printing errors. Mechanically reproduced entries are null and void.

3. Whether you take advantage of this offer or not, on or about April 30, 1992, at the offices of D. L. Blair, Inc., Blair, NE, your Sweepstakes numbers will be compared against the list of winning numbers generated at random by the computer. However, prizes will only be awarded to individuals who have entered the Sweepstakes. In the event that all prizes are not claimed, a random drawing will be held from all qualified entries received from March 30, 1990 to March 31, 1992, to award all unclaimed prizes. All cash prizes (Grand to Sixth) will be mailed to the winners and are payable by check in U.S. funds. Seventh Prize will be shipped to winners via third-class mail. These prizes are in addition to any free, surprise or mystery gifts that might be offered. Versions of this Sweepstakes with different prizes of approximate equal value may appear at retail outlets or in other mailings by Torstar Corp. and its affiliates.

4. Prizes: (1) ★ Grand Prize $1,000,000.00 Annuity; (1)First Prize $25,000.00; (1)Second Prize $10,000.00; (5)Third Prize $5,000.00; (10)Fourth Prize $1,000.00; (100)Fifth Prize $250.00; (2,500)Sixth Prize $10.00; (6,000) ★ ★ Seventh Prize $12.95 ARV.

   ★ This presentation offers a Grand Prize of a $1,000,000.00 annuity. Winner will receive $33,333.33 a year for 30 years without interest totalling $1,000,000.00.

   ★ ★ Seventh Prize: A fully illustrated hardcover book published by Torstar Corp. Approximate Retail Value of the book is $12.95.

   Entrants may cancel the Reader Service at any time without cost or obligation (see details in Center Insert Card).

5. This Sweepstakes is being conducted under the supervision of D. L. Blair, Inc. By entering this Sweepstakes, each entrant accepts and agrees to be bound by these rules and the decisions of the judges, which shall be final and binding. Odds of winning in the random drawing are dependent upon the number of entries received. Taxes, if any, are the sole responsibility of the winners. Prizes are nontransferable. All entries must be received at the address on the detachable Business Reply Card and must be postmarked no later than 12:00 MIDNIGHT on March 31, 1992. The drawing for all unclaimed Sweepstakes prizes will take place on May 30, 1992, at 12:00 NOON, at the offices of D. L. Blair, Inc., Blair, NE.

6. This offer is open to residents of the U.S., the United Kingdom, France, Germany and Canada, 18 years or older, except employees and immediate family members of Torstar Corp., its affiliates, subsidiaries, and all the other agencies, entities and persons connected with the use, marketing or conduct of this Sweepstakes. All Federal, State, Provincial, Municipal and local laws apply. Void wherever prohibited or restricted by law. Any litigation within the Province of Quebec respecting the conduct and awarding of a prize in this publicity contest must be submitted to the Régie des loteries et courses du Québec.

7. Winners will be notified by mail and may be required to execute an affidavit of eligibility and release, which must be returned within 14 days after notification or an alternate winner will be selected. Canadian winners will be required to correctly answer an arithmetical, skill-testing question administered by mail, which must be returned within a limited time. Winners consent to the use of their name, photograph and/or likeness for advertising and publicity in conjunction with this and similar promotions without additional compensation.

8. For a list of our major prize winners, send a stamped, self-addressed ENVELOPE to: WINNERS LIST, P.O. Box 4510, Blair, NE 68009. Winners Lists will be supplied after the May 30, 1992 drawing date.

Offer limited to one per household.

© 1991 Harlequin Enterprises Limited   Printed in the U.S.A.

BWH192

HARLEQUIN
PROUDLY PRESENTS
A DAZZLING NEW CONCEPT IN ROMANCE FICTION

One small town—twelve terrific love stories

Welcome to Tyler, Wisconsin—a town full of people
you'll enjoy getting to know, memorable friends and
unforgettable lovers, and a long-buried secret that
lurks beneath its serene surface....

JOIN US FOR A YEAR IN THE LIFE OF TYLER

Each book set in Tyler is a self-contained love story;
together, the twelve novels stitch the fabric of a
community.

LOSE YOUR HEART TO TYLER!

The excitement begins in March 1992, with
WHIRLWIND, by Nancy Martin. When lively, brash
Liza Baron arrives home unexpectedly, she moves
into the old family lodge, where the silent and
mysterious Cliff Forrester has been living in seclusion
for years....

WATCH FOR ALL TWELVE BOOKS
OF THE TYLER SERIES
Available wherever Harlequin books are sold

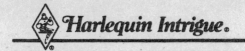 **Harlequin Intrigue**

43 Light St.

It looks like a charming old building near the Baltimore waterfront, but inside 43 Light Street lurks danger . . . and romance.

Labeled a "true master of intrigue" by *Rave Reviews*, bestselling author Rebecca York continues her exciting series with #179 ONLY SKIN DEEP, coming to you next month.

When her sister is found dead, Dr. Kathryn Martin, a 43 Light Street occupant, suddenly finds herself caught up in the glamorous world of a posh Washington, D.C., beauty salon. Not even former love Mac McQuade can believe the schemes Katie uncovers.

Watch for #179 ONLY SKIN DEEP in February, and all the upcoming 43 Light Street titles for top-notch suspense and romance.

LS92